THE WAVE WALKERS

Pirate Curse

ALSO BY KAI MEYER

Dark Reflections, Book One:
The Water Mirror

Margaret K. McElderry Books

THE WAVE WALKERS

Pirate Curse

KAI MEYER

Translated by Elizabeth D. Crawford

Margaret K. McElderry Books

New York London Toronto Sydney

Margaret K. McElderry Books
An imprint of Simon & Schuster Children's Publishing Division
1230 Avenue of the Americas, New York, New York 10020

Originally published in German in 2003 as *Die Wellenläufer* by Loewe Verlag
Published by arrangement with Loewe Verlag

First U.S. edition, 2006

Book design by Paula Russell Szafranski
The text for this book is set in Centaur MT.
Manufactured in the United States of America
10 9 8 7 6 5 4 3 2 1

Library of Congress Cataloging-in-Publication Data
Meyer, Kai.
[Wellenlaufer. English]
Pirate curse / Kai Meyer ; translated by Elizabeth D. Crawford.—1st U.S. ed.
p. cm.—(The wave walkers ; bk. 1)
Summary: In a place similar to the 1706 Caribbean, two fourteen-year-old "polliwogs"—humans who can walk on water—rely on a mysterious figure known as the Ghost Trader and a band of pirates to help them escape from the evil that is chasing them.
ISBN-13: 978-1-4169-2421-0
ISBN-10: 1-4169-2421-3 (hardcover)
[1. Pirates—Fiction. 2. Magic—Fiction. 3. Orphans—Fiction.
4. Caribbean Area—Fiction. 5. Fantasy.] I. Crawford, Elizabeth D. II. Title.
PZ7.M571711l3Pir 2006
[Fic]—dc22
2005035199

THE WAVE WALKERS

Pirate Curse

Contents

The Polliwog

Jolly was racing across the ocean in long strides, her bare feet sinking a finger's breadth below the surface of the water. Beneath her yawned the inky blue abyss of the sea, with perhaps several hundred fathoms to the bottom.

Jolly had been able to walk on the water since she was born. Over the years she'd learned to move easily over the rocking surface—it felt like running through a puddle to her. She leaped nimbly from one wave to the next, avoiding the foamy crowns of the waves, which could sometimes turn into treacherous stumbling traps.

Around her, a sea fight was raging.

Cannonballs whistled past her ears, but one rarely came close enough for her to feel the draft of it. Acrid smoke drifted over the water between the two sailing ships and obscured Jolly's sight. The creaking of the boards and the flapping of the great sails mixed with the thundering of the guns. The smoke from ignited black powder made her eyes burn. She'd never liked that smell, unlike the other pirates. Her friends from the *Skinny Maddy* said nothing smelled as good as the fragrance of fired cannon. And then, if the sides of enemy ships shattered in the distance and their opponents' screams wafted over the sea, it was better than any binge on rum and gin.

Jolly liked rum as little as she did the smoke of the cannons. But no matter how her nose responded, she knew her duty, and she'd carry it out.

It was about fifty yards to the enemy ship, a Spanish three-master with two cannon decks and three times as many guns as the *Skinny Maddy*. The galleon was ornamented with striking carvings all around—faces that now and again peered through the smoke like inquisitive fabulous creatures, some looking so real, even at a distance, that it seemed they might come to life any minute. The Spaniard's dinghies were lashed to the side of the hull. One had been grazed by a ball from the *Maddy*; part of the suspension line was shredded, and now the little boat banged against the mighty hull with each shock, producing a deep, hollow sound.

The current favored Jolly and was carrying her even faster on her run toward the galleon. Jolly need merely place one foot on the water and she could feel the direction of the sea's movement, sometimes even if bad weather was brewing or storms were raging beyond the horizon. Never in her life had she been able to imagine passing a long time on land. She needed the familiarity of the ocean, the feeling of the infinite depths under her feet. The way other people were seized with dizziness at great heights, Jolly was seized with panic if she went too far from the sea and its roaring surf.

Now she ran a little stooped, even if no one on the Spaniard's deck had noticed her yet. Oddly, she saw not a solitary human soul behind the turned posts of the railing. A galleon like this carried at least two hundred men aboard, and all had to expect that the pirates from the *Skinny Maddy* would try to board the Spanish ship. So why wasn't there anyone on deck?

Normally Captain Bannon, the captain of the freebooter and Jolly's best friend, would keep away from a ship like this: too big, too strong, and too heavily armed. Not to mention that there were only seventy pirates on the *Skinny Maddy,* and in a man-to-man fight with the Spaniards, they'd be far outnumbered.

But despite all that, when the ship had appeared on the horizon, some had favored the idea that it could be a rewarding catch. Captain Bannon had personally climbed up to the *Maddy*'s crow's nest and studied the silhouette of the galleon with the telescope for a long time. "She's reefed her sails," he'd called down to his crew. "Looks as if they're in trouble."

The ocean was too deep at this point to anchor. That meant that in spite of good wind conditions, the Spaniard was drifting—which simply made no sense. But Bannon wouldn't have been one of the wiliest pirates in the

Caribbean Sea if he hadn't let his nose and his curiosity lead him in a case like this.

"I have a funny feeling about it," he'd said before he ordered his men to the guns, "but maybe we'll all have more out of this thing than it looks right now." Captain Bannon often said such things, so no one was surprised. His crew trusted him—especially Jolly, for whom Bannon had been something like a father and mother at the same time, ever since he'd bought her as a small child in the slave market of Tortuga and made her a member of his crew.

The thunder of guns, louder than before, made Jolly leap to one side. She felt the drag of the heavy iron cannonball and thought she saw it whistling past her, hardly an arm's length away. When she looked back, her worst fears were confirmed.

The *Skinny Maddy* took the hit.

A cloud of water and splintered wood rose from the stern of the racy xebec, a type of ship not much seen in this region. The *Maddy*'s railing consisted not of decorative spindles, like that of the galleon, but of a smooth, hip-high wooden wall, in which openings had been left for the gun barrels. The ship was painted blood red, and on the prow, Bannon had had white fangs painted along the red edge, so that the bow looked like a predator's open jaws.

Furious shouting came across to Jolly, scraps of voices that drifted through the gray wall of smoke between the two ships.

Jolly half turned and hesitated. From this far away, she

couldn't tell whether the *Muddy* had suffered any serious damage. *Please let nothing happen to her!* Jolly begged in her thoughts.

But then she remembered Bannon's order, her duty to him and the others, and she faced forward again. In a few steps she reached the hull of the Spanish galleon and ran along it until she was standing beneath one of the rear gun ports. The lower gun deck was about nine feet above the surface of the water. Jolly wasn't even five feet tall, but it would be easy for her to toss one of the missiles from her shoulder bag through the opening.

She pulled back the flap of her leather bag and took out one of the bottles, which had clinked together dangerously at every step. They were filled with a bronze-colored fluid, the necks sealed with wax.

Jolly pulled back her arm, took a deep breath—and flung the bottle through the first gun port, just past the mouth of the cannon barrel. Someone cried out an alarm, loud enough for her to hear it outside. Then, out of the port shot a cloud of green smoke, so thick and stinking that Jolly quickly ran to the next opening. There she pulled out a second bottle and threw it. She worked from opening to opening until green vapor was billowing from most of the ports. None of the lower guns was firing anymore. The gunners behind the weapons must have been blinded by the smoke, and from experience Jolly knew that the smell hit even the most hard-boiled sailor in the stomach.

For variety, she tried to throw the next bottle into the second gun deck, which was higher up. Here, too, she made a direct hit into one of the ports. If it kept on like this, her mission would be a complete success. With some luck, she'd disable the crew of the galleon single-handed. Bannon and his pirates would only have to board the ship and meet their coughing, half-blind opponents on deck. They no longer had to expect serious resistance.

But Jolly's next toss to the upper gun deck was less successful. The bottle flew through the port just as the men on the inside were shoving the cannon outside to fire the next ball. The glass shattered on the steel of the gun barrel, and the fluid sprayed against the hull and immediately evaporated into a biting vapor. Jolly dove forward and threw herself flat on the surface of the water to escape the gas. At the same time, the cannon over her fired. A heartbeat later, a second hit resounded from the direction of the pirate ship. Wood shattered, followed by an explosion—the ball had gone through the *Skinny Maddy*'s hull and hit the munitions store.

Tears filled Jolly's eyes as she saw the flames flickering from the gaping opening. She knew what a hit like that meant—she'd experienced it often enough. But it had been the opposing ships who'd suffered such a fate. Now there could be no more doubt. The *Maddy* would sink. Damn it, how could Bannon have made such a mistake! Jolly had lived on three ships in her time as the captain's pupil, but of all of them, the *Maddy* had been her favorite. To see her sink was like losing her home and a good friend at one blow.

There was only a single hope for the pirates: They had to succeed in capturing the Spanish galleon in the little time that was left to them. Otherwise they'd sink to the bottom of the sea along with the *Maddy.*

Desperate determination got Jolly moving again. She pulled out another bottle, and this time she hit her target. The same with the next, and the next. Still no shooters were bending over the railing to place her under fire. But then someone shoved his head out of one of the gun ports, saw Jolly, and bellowed, "They have a polliwog! They have a goddamn polliwog with them!"

A second head appeared. "There aren't any more polliwogs. They're all—" Then he caught sight of Jolly. His soot-rimmed eyes widened. "Oh, goddamn, they actually do have a polliwog!"

Jolly gave the men a grim smile. She took aim and threw a bottle inside the galleon, just missing their faces. Swirling green shot out behind their heads; a moment later they'd vanished.

Jolly ran on. Threw. Ran. And threw again. The thought of her friends drove her forward. She paid no more attention to possible opponents, to her cover, or to the outlines of the sharks that had appeared under the surface of the water a few minutes before. Here and there she saw silver-gray tail fins cutting through the waves like saber blades, but she wasted no thoughts on them. Instead, she flung one bottle after another until her shoulder bag was empty.

She'd now almost reached the bow of the galleon. Poison-green smoke was billowing from all the upper gun ports. No more shots were fired. The Spaniard's deck was befogged with dense fumes that made any more fighting impossible. Even the carved faces around the railing appeared to be grimacing with all the smoke.

Now if Bannon could just bring the *Maddy*—

A creaking made Jolly whirl around. She shouted with relief. Under full sail, the sinking pirate ship was heading toward the stern of the Spanish galleon. It looked as if the painted mouth on the bow of the *Maddy* was opening its jaws to derisively show its fangs one last time. Jolly jumped to safety with a few bounds. Shortly afterward, stern crashed against stern. Grappling hooks and heaving lines flew over to the Spaniard's deck. A wild horde of pirates, with cloths tied over their noses and mouths against the green smoke, climbed up onto the bigger ship. Jolly knew every single one of them, some she'd known all her life, some for just a few months. The pirates wore the clothing of every country in the world: Oriental wide trousers, cotton shirts from the colonies, vests from Italy, and often a patchwork of remains of Spanish uniforms. Some had broad sashes around them, and one even wore a discarded skull-and-crossbones flag as a cape. Like multicolored ants they swarmed up onto the ship, hand over hand on ropes or swinging over from the spars of the *Skinny Maddy* onto their opponent's rigging.

Very shortly Jolly caught a glimpse of Captain Bannon, straw blond and furious as a dervish, who whisked over to the galleon on a rope. Their eyes met in that brief moment and she felt that he was smiling at her, despite the cloth over his face. His eyes could radiate such friendliness that sometimes

Jolly wondered why his victims didn't willingly hand over their ships to him, just on the basis of the warmth in that look, which didn't fit at all with his wild determination and lack of scruples.

Jolly raised her arm triumphantly and gave a jubilant shout; then she also came alongside the bow of the galleon, grabbed a dangling line, and climbed nimbly up it like a cat.

The green smoke on the deck had dispersed quickly. Even as Jolly was climbing the rope, she could hear that the battle was already over before it had really begun. The coughing, spitting Spaniards surrendered with tearing eyes and running noses. Hardly any of them lifted a weapon against the pirates, and if he did, it was only a tired reflex, not a real will to fight.

Jolly swung herself over the railing. Bannon saw her and hurried over to her. "Well done," he said, thumping her shoulder so hard that she almost went to her knees. He turned to his men, who were driving the captured Spaniards to the middle of the deck.

"Cut all lines to the *Maddy* so she doesn't take us down with her," he ordered, pointing to several crewmen. "The rest of you disarm our friends. From now on, this is our new ship!" With a grin in the direction of the girl at his side, he called even more loudly, "I guess the tub needs a new name. From now on she'll be called *Jumping Jolly!*"

Jolly grew dizzy with pride, while all around her the pirates broke into shouts of acclamation.

But at the same time a creaking and groaning sounded from the *Maddy*. The painted predator's mouth clenched its teeth in death.

Ten minutes later the *Skinny Maddy* was still not entirely sunk. She rose slantingly out of the sea like a cliff, a memorial in front of the setting sun. The superstructure on the stern had almost reached the water, but the toothed bow was sticking way up. The figurehead on the prow—a dark Neptune with a trident—was raised toward the deep blue sky, as if it wanted to blare a last, proud cry against the world.

Yet even as the pirates were still gathering the prisoners into a group on the deck, it appeared that something was not right. The captain acted victorious and satisfied, but Jolly saw the uneasiness in his eyes.

There were too few Spaniards.

There were just forty sailors aboard. Not enough men to serve all battle stations, not to mention occupy the necessary positions on a ship like this. Even Bannon, with his crew of seventy, wouldn't have an easy time handling the galleon under sail. But forty Spaniards? Absolutely impossible.

And there was another thing that was strange.

"Those aren't Spaniards at all," said Cristobal, Bannon's steersman. "Most of them speak Spanish, and a few of them even look it, but I'd hazard a guess they were born here in the colonies."

"And so?" Jolly burst out, earning a frown from the steersman before he turned to the captain again.

"Most of them seem to be ordinary cutthroats. Look at the scars. And the boozy faces." He grinned, revealing a blackened incisor. "Basically, they look just like us."

Bannon didn't return the grin. He looked over the deck worriedly, briefly examined the prisoners, and then looked at the empty horizon. "What's going on here?" he whispered tonelessly and so softly that only Jolly and Cristobal heard him.

A shiver ran down Jolly's back. A trap?

"Our people have looked through everything," the steersman said. "No other men aboard, also no explosives or other booby traps. Furthermore, no cargo, either."

"We're getting out of here," Bannon decided. "Fast."

With uncustomary haste he gave his orders to the first mate. Soon afterward the shout came down the deck, "Make ready to set sail!"

"What's going to happen with them?" Jolly asked, pointing to the chained prisoners. Cristobal had walked over to one of them, grabbed him by the neck, and was talking to him.

"We'll set them down on land somewhere," said Bannon thoughtfully, as he walked to the railing. No enemy ships in sight anywhere.

Jolly looked over at the sinking *Maddy*. She still lay slanting out of the water. The current had driven the galleon thirty or forty yards away from the wreck, and the distance was increasing every minute.

Cristobal came back to the captain.

"And?" Bannon asked. "What did he say?"

"That they were prisoners. All sentenced to death. They were promised their freedom if they came aboard this ship and did everything possible to defend it."

"Only forty men? A ship like this? That's laughable."

"Whoever hatched this business must have figured that none of these fellows would survive. They obviously have only one thing in common: They were all cannoneers at some time or other. They weren't chosen to fight hand to hand—they were supposed to polish us off from a distance." The steersman rubbed his stubbly chin. "And there's something else. Obviously another ship towed them here. They were never under full sail—"

A loud flapping drowned out his words as the pirates unfurled the sails in the rigging. The mighty bundles of cloth unrolled within seconds.

"No!" Bannon gasped.

Jolly saw what he meant, and at the same moment she heard it, too.

Out of the sails fell jugs—large, brown jugs, which shattered into thousands of pieces as they hit the deck. There must have been two or three dozen, breaking all over the deck with a hollow popping sound. Some fell into the middle of the screaming group of prisoners; another hit Trevino, the cook, on the head and knocked him out.

The broken jugs held something that at first glance looked like dark wool, a tangle of thick yarn—until the tangle unraveled on its own and divided into hundreds of smaller balls, which swarmed in all directions on scraggly legs.

"Spiders!" someone screeched; then another took up the cry: *"Spiders . . . the jugs are full of spiders!"*

Bannon bellowed orders, but no one heard them in the panic that had broken out on the ship. The prisoners screamed at the top of their lungs as a true eruption of spider bodies shot up among them. The pirates jumped around on deck, some trying to stamp on the creatures, but they quickly gave up when they saw how hopeless a task it was. Ten, then twenty were crawling all over the body of the senseless cook; others sought their way up boots and trousers, along the rigging and the railing. The creatures might be just as panicked and confused as the men aboard, but they were faster and—above all—irritated.

Jolly pulled herself up into the shrouds. Her hands were wet with sweat and her breath was coming in gasps. Everywhere the pirates were bellowing and stamping and shaking themselves. Cristobal knocked several animals off his body at once, but he overlooked an especially fat spider that crouched on his neck. He screamed when she bit him.

At first Bannon struck at the spiders with his saber, then with his bare hands. He was trying to follow Jolly aloft, but then he was bitten too, several times at once, and the pain made him let go of the rope. With a curse he crashed back down onto the deck.

"Those dogs!" he bellowed. His voice faded as the spider venom numbed him. "Jolly . . . the figurehead . . . remember the . . . figure—"

He collapsed. Jolly stared at the lifeless figure beneath her, and her eyes filled with tears.

Damn it—she had to do something, had to help Bannon and the others somehow. Desperately, she looked around for a weapon and knew at once that nothing would help. No one could master the overwhelming odds of the spiders.

Jolly knew exactly what Bannon had intended to say to her.

From her elevated position she had a good view of the wreck of the *Maddy*. The figurehead was sticking up like an outstretched finger, pointing the way.

Jolly brushed off the nearest spiders and jumped over to the railing, where she came to a wavering stand. Spiders were now everywhere, a seething black carpet that covered the deck and all the men aboard. Most men were no longer moving; some had vanished almost completely under the hairy, scrambling bodies. A few still up on the masts were calling for help, but a whole crowd of the eight-legged creatures was already nearing them.

Jolly looked around at Bannon one last time, then she jumped overboard. It was more a fall than a jump. She might just as well have fallen onto a stone floor when she hit the surface of the water without sinking into it. Lucky not to have broken all her bones, she rolled over, was wildly tossed around by a few waves, and finally got onto her feet.

Silvery triangles slid toward her, encircled her. Jolly had had to deal with sharks more than once and knew that they only saw the outlines of the soles of her feet on the surface and didn't recognize them as worthwhile prey. Jolly forced herself not to think of the men who'd leaped overboard in fear of the spiders. They'd certainly not had as much luck as she. Hurriedly she ran over the water toward the *Maddy* in great leaps. This time she was running against the current, her breathing wild, her heart hammering in her chest, but finally she saw the pirate ship in front of her—or rather, what remained of it.

Behind Jolly the Spanish galleon rose against the darkening sky. From afar it looked as if the wood itself had come alive. The dark surface moved, covered with swarming life, which cast shifting shadows.

The water was bubbling around the *Maddy*. Jolly had trouble avoiding the white crests. Sea foam wasn't to be trusted; sometimes the surface beneath it receded a little and sucked at your feet like quicksand, and then you had to be careful to pull them right out again before the water consolidated around you and held you fast.

She was able to grab the edge of the red railing and pull herself up with it. As soon as the superstructure at the stern and the inner spaces of the xebec were filled with water, the *Skinny Maddy* would go under like a stone. Not even a polliwog like Jolly would manage to escape from the deadly vortex in time.

Jolly had to be faster. *Even* faster.

With a gasp she swung herself over the railing onto the deck, lost her footing on the wet incline for a moment, and slipped back a few yards. She felt wildly around her and got hold of a rope, intending to support herself—but the rope gave and fell beside her on the deck. Jolly slipped farther, feetfirst, and now she came dangerously near the bubbling, swirling water. At the last moment she slithered across one of the grating-covered hatches to the hold and hooked her hands and feet into it. From here it was still fifteen feet to the thundering water, but the ship was sinking inexorably farther. In less than a minute, the grating would be under water. By then, Jolly had to be away from here, had to have reached the figurehead, the only place that now offered any safety.

Of course, she could have tried to flee across the open sea. But the walk over the rocking, wavy ocean was ten times as exhausting as the same stretch on land, and Jolly hadn't seen any island on the horizon. At some point she would collapse in the middle of the ocean from exhaustion—and then she would look just as appetizing to the sharks as any swimmer or large fish. And even if the sharks had no appetite, which was unlikely, she'd die of thirst out there anyway.

She *had* to get to the figurehead. It was her only hope.

A powerful shuddering went through the ship; then, with a groan from its very innards, it settled more steeply. With every degree of angle the *Maddy* upended, it became more difficult to climb up the deck.

Now Jolly became aware of something else. At first she saw it only at the edge of her field of vision and then, when she looked more carefully, with merciless certainty.

Among the bubbling and fountains of foam at the foot of the deck, there was a silhouette moving in the water. A form, approaching human, but with long, skinny limbs, skin that shimmered with rainbow colors like oil, and an ugly face that consisted only of a maw and half a dozen razor-sharp rows of teeth. Jolly saw the jaws of the creature snapping open and shut angrily, threatening to bite in the foam and the waves.

A kobalin! A living kobalin! It had been a long time since Jolly had seen one, maybe two or three years, and then it had been a young one, which the pirates had killed in the water with a few well-placed shots.

But this kobalin was fully grown, and he was rampaging down there in expectation of his catch as if he hadn't had anything between his teeth for months. The sounds of the battle must have lured him. Kobalins loved carrion, especially human carrion, and there were stories of shipwrecked crews that had been torn up and eaten within minutes by a handful of kobalins.

Jolly felt as though her entire body were numb. It wasn't enough that she'd lost the captain and all her friends, that she was about to be dragged to the bottom by a shipwreck, that her strength was gradually disappearing—no, of course one of those monsters had to turn up.

She began to climb up again, more carefully this time. First up to the hatch cover, then up to a rope, and then from there—finally!—back to the railing. The sound of the kobalin's jaws snapping at her back overwhelmed even the groaning of the wreck and the booming of the sea. The beast was lurking down there, its teeth bared, hardly able to wait for Jolly to finally lose her grip.

Kobalins were afraid to leave the water. Only the bravest among them sometimes stretched a head or a claw above the surface; most preferred to look for their food underwater. That the one down there was extending his arms toward Jolly—even if he couldn't reach her—was unusual. That he once even raised his torso above the raging waters was extraordinary.

Jolly climbed farther and reached the figurehead. Bannon had explained the mechanism to her more than once, on quiet nights when she and he were the only ones awake. At that time he'd let her in on the best-kept secret on the *Maddy*.

The figurehead with its grim Titan face was hollow and had room for one adult human being. Watertight packets inside it contained provisions for several days. By means of two bolts, the figurehead could be loosened from the hull of the ship and would become a perfect lifeboat for its occupant. Concealed weights ensured that it would always turn face upward; there one could open a hatch to let in fresh air.

The kobalin let out a gruesome cry as one of the masts broke and crashed down on him with its full weight. Out of the corner of her eye, Jolly saw the mast plunge straight into the monster's gaping mouth and ram the creature down into the deep with it.

She snorted grimly, but she had no strength left to exult. With a last effort of will, she opened the hidden hatch cover at the back of the figurehead, laboriously made her way inside hand over hand, and pulled the hatch closed behind her. Leather upholstery covered the crack. For a fraction of a second, she felt as if she'd been enclosed in a coffin alive. Panic cut off her air. She'd rather go down with the *Maddy* than be trapped inside here. But then reason got the upper hand.

The wreck settled steeper and steeper; the final plunge to the bottom of the sea might begin at any moment.

Jolly pulled the two bolts out of their fastenings. They slid out easily, as if Bannon had recently oiled them. There was a shattering noise, and for a long moment Jolly believed that the *Maddy* was breaking up. But no—the figurehead had loosened from the hull. She didn't even notice the free fall into the water, just the landing, which struck the wooden outer shell like a hundred hammer blows. There was a roaring in Jolly's ears, and she was on the verge of fainting. Then the figurehead was seized by the waves. A deafening screeching sounded out of the depths, perhaps the dying kobalin or perhaps the sinking *Maddy*. Jolly could only hope that she was already far enough away from the wreck that the suction of the sinking ship wouldn't take her to the bottom with it.

It was pitch-black inside the figurehead. The air smelled musty. Jolly didn't dare open the little air hatch for fear the boiling sea would enter and fill the cavity with water.

A dull thud sounded as something banged against the figurehead from underneath. Sharks! They took the drifting shape for an especially fat catch. Jolly wasn't sure the wood would withstand the heavy pressure of teeth if one of them really bit into it.

Something stroked her face in the darkness.

She cried out. In the first moment she thought it was a finger. But that was foolishness. The distance between the tip of her nose and the wooden wall of the cavity wasn't more than twelve inches. She was alone, of course.

Or maybe . . . not *entirely* alone.

A spider was enclosed in the figurehead with her! It must have crawled inside Jolly's shoulder bag on board the galleon.

Now it was crawling freely around her body.

Jolly began to kick in the narrow tube, hammering against the wood with her hands and feet, before she got her panic enough under control to be able to form some clear thoughts.

Lie utterly still. Be utterly quiet.

And listen!

Jolly held her breath. Goose bumps spread over her entire body like armor, but that still wasn't any protection from the venomous bite of the spider. She listened to her own heart beating, not faintly, not softly, but so loudly that she thought it must burst her chest at any moment.

Still, there was a sound. Barely audible. Like fingertips drumming gently on a hollow surface.

The spider was scrambling over the wood somewhere underneath her.

Jolly bit her lower lip to keep from making a sound. If she could only see something! A tiny shimmer of light would be enough, perhaps. But she didn't dare lift a hand to open the air vent over her face for fear of really irritating the spider.

Somehow she had to get rid of the thing.

She breathed in and out very slowly, then held her breath again, grew as stiff as if she were a piece of wood herself. She had to lure the spider into a sense of security; she mustn't under any circumstances induce it to attack.

And then, when she knew exactly where the thing was—

Something pinched her on the back of her right hand.

Jolly let out a wild cry and smashed her hand against the inner wall with all her might. The spider's body was harder than she expected, the bristles stabbed like needles, but Jolly struck again, and again, and again. The twitching legs clutched around her hand like fingers; she felt their pressure, then their slackening.

Sickened, she shook her arm until the lifeless spider slid off.

It no longer mattered. Too late.

The spider had bitten her.

Jolly felt her consciousness fading. The blackness inside the drifting figurehead grew in solidity, robbed her of breath, seemed to flow oily and cold into her nose, into her eyes, into her mouth.

I'm going to die, she thought with astonished matter-of-factness.

Once more she raised her hand. Her fingers found the sliding cover above her face and pulled it aside with her last strength.

The blue of the sky over her stabbed her pupils like steel blades. Salty air flowed into the hollow cavity.

Breathe, her mind said.

Now breathe, damn it!

The sky paled, then the light, then the entire world. The spider venom pulsed through her veins and pressed every thought out through her pores.

Jolly's consciousness drifted away like flotsam on a night-dark ocean.

Flotsam

The boy sat on a rock above the bay, which opened out in front of him like a window onto the sea. Whenever his father released him from his duties on the farm, he came up here to dream: of the sea and a life on the great proud ships he saw on the horizon from time to time.

Munk's hand lay on the rusty cannon barrel, in whose mouth a pair of birds had nested the year before. He'd waited until the little ones flew away, then carefully removed the nest. He didn't know how you worked a cannon, but he thought it was a good idea for it to be ready for use at any time. His parents, tobacco farmers and the only settlers on the tiny island, knew nothing of the rusted gun above the bay. The cannon was Munk's secret. Just like this place, this refuge in the rocks with a view over the bay and the turquoise blue Caribbean Sea.

He'd often hoped to see pirates from up here, the proud sloops and brigantines of the freebooters who filled the Caribbean with more fear and horror than any other place in the world's oceans. He wished ardently to discover, just once, one of their black flags on the horizon, with its symbol of the skull and crossed bones or sabers, the gleam of gold shining from their hatches and bathing their sails in the light of an eternal sunrise.

Daydreams, his mother said. Silly nonsense, his father said. And both had warned him several times not to even think of making one of the passing ships aware of the island with smoke or some other signal.

Munk laughed at his parents' worries. As much as he might fantasize about pirates and adventurous privateering expeditions, he'd never go so far as to summon one of the ships. Who was he, anyway? Only a boy with a few odd talents. They'd never take anyone like him aboard. He couldn't duel, only read, couldn't shoot, and had only a few useless magic tricks to make up for it. If pirates ever really were to turn up on the island, he'd certainly be the first one they made walk the plank.

Useless, that was the word he hated so. His father had called him that once when he was angry over one of Munk's mishaps on the farm. And he was certainly right. Munk would never become a proper tobacco farmer, that much was certain. He was lost in his daydreams much too often, thinking about everything else under the sun except the harvest and the care of the young plants. And he had nothing at all to do with the haggling, which his father managed so well when traders came to the island now and then.

Munk sighed and blinked in the afternoon sun. The cannon base was so rotten that he chose not to sit on it anymore for fear the wood might collapse. He'd often wondered who'd placed it here. In his heart he was convinced that thirty or forty years before, in the era of the first buccaneers and the privateering of Henry Morgan, the island had been a secret hideout for pirates. Perhaps they'd waited up here for the Spaniards or, better yet, buried their treasure somewhere in the jungle thickets.

Dreams, Munk thought. *Nothing but dumb dreams.*

This noon he'd thought he heard cannon fire in the distance, and two or three times there'd been bright flashes on the horizon, shadowed by something that might have been smoke. But now the sun would be setting soon, and there were no further signs of a sea battle.

Just another disappointment—a broad, empty hope that sometime, something unusual would disturb the boredom on this island.

He was just about to pull himself together and run back to the farm when he noticed something. Out where the water was deeper and darker, where the sandy yellow-green of the bay turned into the blue of the ocean, he saw something that ought not to have been there.

Curious, Munk leaped to his feet. A narrow chain of reefs

broke through the surface of the sea, a buffer against the breakers, around which lay an ever-present wreath of foam and spray, like a crown of flowers.

Between two of the outermost needles of rock something was floating in the water. It was a little bigger than a man and dark brown. Wet wood, of course. Perhaps part of a wreck. Or, by Morgan's red beard, a chest!

Munk felt the blood coursing faster through his veins. Excitement seized him. He shoved back a strand of his blond hair, peered searchingly down at the thing in the water, and started moving. He stormed down the narrow path leading from the rock summit and through a banana grove to the beach. He paid no attention to the branches and leaves striking him in the face. Sand got into his sandals and ground painfully into the soles of his feet, but it didn't hold him back.

In no time he reached the water, where at last he stopped. He looked cautiously around him—not out to sea but landward, where the white sand disappeared into the shadows of the palms, mahogany trees, and tree ferns, a wall of dark green, from which the cries of the parrots wafted over him.

No one to see him. His parents must actually be back at the farm by this time. His mother probably had supper already waiting. If his father were to see what he was going to do, there'd be a terrible row. They'd forbidden him to, at first with pleas, then with threats, and when he'd asked for the hundredth time why they didn't want him to, they'd only been silent and exchanged dark looks. But how could they expect him to hold to their prohibition—at a moment like this, where great adventure lay no farther than a stone's throw away?

Munk looked back over his shoulder at the jungle one last time, then placed his left foot on the water. The last time he'd done it had been over a year ago, secretly then, too, just to see if he still was able to at all. But his mother had been right when she said he'd never lose this talent. He was the only person in the world, she and his father thought, who had this power: At least they couldn't walk on the water themselves, he was certain of that.

He was a *polliwog,* they'd said. And that there were men who envied him his skill and would harm him if he made it known in public. That was all. No further explanation.

A polliwog, then. The last one in the whole world. Did he believe that? He'd never in his life been off the island, and neither the Ghost Trader nor his parents had ever been able to give him a reassuring answer to his questions.

Munk ran out into the bay. Keeping his balance on the surf was always the most difficult part. There were no waves in the bay—they were breaking outside on the reef—so he made pretty good progress. On the open water he'd probably be knocked down after two or three steps. Perhaps his ability was only good enough to walk on still bays and quiet seas. If it was of any use at all.

The more secure he felt, the faster he went. Not just from high spirits, but because he also wanted to get back onto land as quickly as possible. Heavens, if his father saw him, he'd really be in a lot of trouble.

It didn't take long to reach the reef. In passing, Munk noted how thick with mussels the reef was. Maybe he could still come back sometime later and loosen a few of them. But now he had something more important to do.

The longish wooden thing was half stuck between the rocks, encircled with bubbling froth. It was a ship's figurehead, he realized now, and with a little luck he could grab the trident of the wooden Neptune without setting his feet on the treacherous sea foam. Yes, got it! Without too much effort he dragged the figure toward him. He noticed a small opening in the middle of the sea god's face. Munk suppressed his curiosity. He'd have time enough to examine the thing later, but here in the bay it was too dangerous. He strengthened his grip and dragged the figure landward, until the sand crunched under the wooden back and he had firm ground under his feet again.

Munk fell on his knees and bent over the figure. It was completely clean; nothing had attached to the upper surface. On one side he found a pair of long furrows, which looked like teeth marks. The wood was very light there. The figure couldn't have been floating in the water long. Was it a part of a wreck from the sea battle at midday?

Munk turned to the opening in the face of the figurehead. Meanwhile, the sun had sunk even lower. It hung between the tips of the jungle trees like a glowing fruit. Deep shadow lay on the plate-sized rectangle in the wood. Munk had to roll the figure to one side slightly to see inside.

"By Morgan's red beard!" he murmured.

He said it again, and yet again, until finally he found the opening in the back of the figure and lifted the lifeless girl out onto the beach.

She had long, raven black hair and wore wide, brown cotton trousers and a white man's shirt that she'd pulled in with a belt around her small waist. Four or five gold rings dangled from each ear. On both sides of her nose, precisely between the eyes, were two tiny diamonds, fastened with an invisible pin under her tanned skin.

The girl's eyelids were closed, but the setting sun refracted on the facets of the two jewels, and it seemed to Munk that she was looking up at him out of sparkling insect eyes.

When Jolly awakened, the world was filled with a golden gleam, yellow-red beams of light fanning down through the cracks in a palm-thatched roof. Dust danced in them like tiny fish.

"Good morning," said a voice beside her. "Do you understand me—I mean, do you understand my language?"

Jolly turned her head, astonished at how easily and painlessly she did it. With each breath she also seemed to suck in a piece of her past. Even before her eyes fell on the face of the blond boy, the first fragments of her memory returned.

"Where are the others?" slipped out. "And where am—"

"Safe." The boy's smile wavered; he tried to cover up his uncertainty. "No one here is going to do anything to you."

Jolly's eyes wandered over the room. The furnishings were simple and spare. Her things were lying on a chair beside the open window, neatly folded. Jolly saw her belt uppermost, beside it the dagger.

Too far away to reach it from here. She sat up slowly. If the boy bent any closer toward her, maybe she could grab him by the throat or, better yet, put him out of commission with a blow from the edge of her hand, the way Captain Bannon had taught her.

"You don't trust me, I can feel that." He shrugged. "For the most part, that's all right with me."

Jolly hesitated. There was something in his smile. . . . He didn't look as if he was up to anything. Maybe he was telling the truth.

"Where am I?"

"On one of the outer islands. Eastern Bahamas, in case that means anything to you."

Then she couldn't have been floating in the water for long; at most, a few hours. "I have to get back to my crew."

"There's no boat on the island."

She didn't believe him. No one lived so cut off. But she didn't need a boat. If she had to, she'd take the risk and walk across the sea on foot. Bannon and the other pirates were her family, she had to—

Suddenly she thought of something. "The spider! It bit me!"

With a nod, the boy indicated a small corked bottle beside the bed. "Mother's all-purpose weapon. It helps for foot fungus, head itching, toothache, and most insect venom. Oh, well, sometimes, anyway. My father swears it keeps hair from falling out. Mum brought it from the mainland when we came here. It's very valuable, she says, so she only uses it in emergencies."

Jolly made a face. "It keeps hair from falling out?"

He grinned. "You haven't seen Dad when he finds hairs in his hairbrush." He was laughing now. "He uses it once a week, for luck."

"What's your name?"

"Munk. And yours?"

"Jolly."

"Are you . . . I mean, are you something like a pirate?"

"Yes," she said, with studied casualness, but really she was tremendously proud of it. "I'm Captain Bannon's right hand." That was probably a slight exaggeration, but what would such a farm clod know about these things?

Munk's eyes gleamed. "*The* Captain Bannon? The sea devil of the Antilles? The same Bannon who lured Ossorio's armada into the Gulf of Campeche a few years ago? And who kidnapped the Spanish viceroy's daughter from Maracaibo?"

Jolly wrinkled her nose. "That witch treated me as if I was her damned maid. But I wasn't having any of *that*! I mixed a sleeping potion into her food and then tattooed something on her behind—that shut her up finally."

"'Please enter!' That was you?" Munk's rapture was nearly boundless. "The whole Caribbean was laughing about that . . . at least, that's what the Trader said." He shook his head in disbelief. "That really was you? You must have been only six or seven then, at the most."

"Six. Bannon taught me reading and writing when I was just four." She could tell by looking at him that he still wasn't sure if he should believe her. But she didn't care. She was alive, although she'd been bitten by one of the spiders. Didn't that mean there was still hope for Bannon and the others?

"Listen," she said excitedly. "My crew . . . they were all bitten by the spiders. It was a trap. We have to take this medicine back as quickly as possible and—"

He shook his head, and his smile disappeared. "No."

Her face hardened. "Yes, of course! I don't care whether it suits you or not." She swung her legs over the edge of the bed and at the same time snatched up the little bottle of medicine.

Munk didn't move. "There's no point in it. You were asleep for three days. The poison kills within one day. Even if you found your people out there, it would be much too late."

Jolly grew numb.

"I'm sorry. Really." He stretched out a hand to take the bottle from her, but Jolly was faster. Her left hand shot out, grabbed him by the neck, and flung him backward. With a gasp he tipped backward off his stool, and while he was still trying to grasp what had happened, she was already sitting on him with her knees pressing into his upper arms.

"Stop that," he blurted in a voice filled with pain. "What's all this for?"

Her head was spinning, and she wasn't really sure what she was doing. Bannon was dead? And all the others? Her eyes burned, but she'd rather have collapsed into ashes on the spot than break into tears in front of Munk. If she were honest with herself, her attack only served to distract her, so she'd be doing something. She hated to feel helpless. That was something Bannon had always drilled into her: A pirate never gives up, he always finds a way.

"That hurts!" Munk tried to throw her off, but he couldn't. "What's got into you all of a sudden?"

Jolly took a deep breath, then stood up. After a moment's hesitation, she stretched out a hand to help him up. He struck it away and jumped to his feet on his own.

"That was mean," he said.

"I'm sorry."

"Oh, yeah?" He only shook his head and massaged his upper arms. "What kind of a name is that, anyway—Jolly?"

"I was a little girl when Bannon bought me in the slave market in Tortuga. My parents were no longer alive then, and no one knew what my name was. So Bannon gave me this name. Until twenty or thirty years ago, all the pirates here in the Caribbean had red flags, so the French called them *jolie rouge,* which means "pretty red." And then the English made "Jolly Roger" out of it, and the black pirate flags are still called that today."

"Bannon named you after a pirate flag?" Munk grinned halfheartedly. "That's great. I wish something like that would happen to me."

"That someone would name you Jolly?"

"Adventure on the high seas. Pirates. Sea battles. Treasure

hunts. All of it. Nothing ever happens here on the island."

She looked at his upper arms. "You're going to be black and blue . . . I'm really sorry, honestly."

"It's all right. Now I can tell the Ghost Trader I beat a few wild sea robbers into flight and got seriously wounded."

"What is that, a Ghost Trader?"

He waved her off. "Later. First, I'm going to introduce you to my mother. Dad is on the plantation, but Mum must be outside in the vegetable garden."

Jolly put the little bottle back on the table beside the bed. Her fingers trembled slightly. "Do you really think they're all dead?"

"If none of them got the antidote in time," he said with lowered voice, "they didn't have a chance."

Munk's mother was a rough, good-hearted woman who had no use at all for pirates. Her earlobes were split and she was missing both ring fingers: scars of a freebooter attack to which she and her parents had fallen victim years ago. Captain Tyrone, the leader of the attackers, had been in a hurry to collect all the jewelry, and when the little girl hadn't taken all her rings off fast enough, Tyrone had taken care of it personally with the help of his blade.

Jolly was anything but happy that Munk broadcast the truth about her so freely. Pirates were most unwelcome guests among the simple island farmers, and that wasn't just true for the Spaniards, who'd set themselves up as overlords in this part of the Caribbean and tried to annihilate all pirates.

On the other hand, she had herself to blame. She shouldn't have told Munk anything about Bannon. It would only make it harder for her to get off the island.

For there was no doubt at all in her mind that she must start on the search for Bannon and the others as soon as possible, no matter what Munk said.

Jolly's thoughts were filled with the images of the events on the Spanish galleon as she followed Munk across the fields of the plantation. His mother had suggested he show her the farm, but Jolly heard nothing of his explanations. Bannon had fallen into a malicious trap, which someone had planned way ahead of time. And if she actually was unable to help him anymore, she would stake everything on finding out who was behind the deed. That was the least she owed him.

Munk, who was ahead of Jolly, had fallen silent. He'd probably noticed that she wasn't paying any attention. Silently they pushed through the thickets of the rain forest, under tree ferns that were as tall as five men and from whose fronds water was still dripping, even at midday; past wild orchids and the biggest hibiscus Jolly had ever seen. It must be almost noon, and the air here in the jungle was humid and oppressive, quite different from the open sea. Jolly found it hard to breathe.

Only when they reached the coconut palms on the shore did she feel better. The sight of the ocean calmed her.

Munk turned to her and pulled a shallow wooden box out of a leather pouch fastened to his belt.

"Here," he said, "maybe this is good for something." He opened the box and turned the opening so that Jolly could look inside.

There lay the body of a dead spider, as big as a baby's hand.

"I found it in the figurehead. See the marking on its back? I've never seen one like this here on the island. If you find out where it comes from, you'll probably find out who lured you into the trap."

Jolly looked from the spider to him. "How did you know that I—"

Munk shrugged. "That you were just thinking about it?" He smiled slightly. "I told you I can feel things like that. And—to be honest—it wasn't really hard to figure out, the way you were stomping so angrily through the undergrowth just now."

Jolly had to laugh, in spite of herself. It was clear that Munk was glad to have distracted her, but he quickly grew serious again. "Anyway, it's the best clue you have."

"Not a bad start," said Jolly. "Thanks very much."

She stretched out her hand for the box, but he snapped its lid shut and quickly shoved it into his little pouch again. Jolly frowned.

"Let me go with you," he said. "Otherwise, I'm going to die here of boredom someday."

"It's not that simple." She repressed her anger and tried to be diplomatic. Of course she'd never take him with her. She was a pirate and he was only a farmer's boy. She could walk on the water, he didn't even have a boat.

"I want to get out onto the sea too," he said doggedly. "I want to see pirates and explore other islands. I don't ever want to be a tobacco farmer like my father. I'd rather run away from here." He'd said that so easily, and now he started, though barely noticeably. "Sail away, I mean."

Jolly sighed. "Let's see what happens." She had to find the right time to take the spider away from him. She didn't want to attack him again; that wasn't necessary. Tonight she'd sneak into his room and steal the box.

Munk fastened the pouch to his belt again. "Come on, I'll show you the fields."

She wasn't interested in tobacco farming, but nevertheless she followed him through a strip of jungle, behind whose tangled underbrush a clearing appeared in the sunshine.

"Didn't you say you and your parents live alone on the island?"

"So?"

"Your father can't possibly work the fields without help."

"And he doesn't."

"So aren't there other workers, then?"

Munk grinned broadly. "Oh, well," he said, laughing, "ghosts have to be good for something, don't they?"

Mussel Magic

At first the sun so blinded her that she saw only the silhouettes of the tobacco plants in the foreground and behind them a brown-green confusion, as if a painter had let the colors on his palette run together.

Then she saw something like wisps of fog wafting around between the plants. Wisps of fog that, on closer inspection, had the outlines of human beings.

Wisps of fog with *faces*.

"Oh, good lord!" Jolly stopped, rooted to the spot. "Are they . . . real?" What a dumb question, but it crossed her lips entirely on its own.

"Well, sure."

Carefully she approached the nearest plants. A ghost was hustling along, plucking the sticky-hairy leaves from the bottom up and throwing them into a wagon that he was pulling along the rows. He paid no attention to the two visitors, as if he didn't perceive them at all.

"Can you touch them?"

"You can try it, sure."

She cast a searching look at Munk, then hesitantly stretched out a finger and poked against the gauzy body of the ghost. The white vapors instantly formed a dent around her fingertip and avoided the touch. Jolly pulled back her hand hastily.

"I've never seen anything like this."

Munk acted bored. "We have a lot of them. They're expensive to buy, but they don't eat or sleep, and they aren't lazy at the work. They cost more than slaves, Dad says, but he won't have anything to do with slaves. Anyway, in the long run, it pays."

Real, living ghosts! Jolly had trouble concealing her astonishment.

"The Ghost Trader says they're very popular on some islands. You must have seen them if you've actually been around so much."

She whirled around. "I *have* been around a lot. But this . . ." She fell silent and shook her head.

The ghost kept on with his work without letting himself be distracted. Jolly regarded his face. She could clearly make out eyes, nose, and mouth, and yet the features lacked any particular individuality. It looked as if someone had formed a human being out of fog, without providing him with any trace of personality.

"Will we all become like them someday?" she asked

uncertainly. "I mean . . . so we all look . . . alike?"

Munk shrugged. "No idea. I've never been particularly interested in them. If you have them around you every day . . . well, you know. I just grew up with them."

"And how many do you have?"

"About fifty, I think. Now and then one disappears, simply vanishes into thin air. Then Dad buys a few new ones and they keep for a while again." He looked bored. "It really isn't anything to get excited about, honestly."

Jolly pushed her black hair back over her shoulders with a nervous movement. She'd seen slave plantations before. People from Africa, or China—but ghosts?

For Munk, sailing on the high seas and climbing around in ship's rigging might be a great adventure; for her, on the other hand, this was something completely new and incomprehensible. Not that she'd want to trade with him—God forbid!—but she'd never yet come across anything like this.

One thing was certain, anyway: If this mysterious trader was claiming that ghosts were used as laborers on many Caribbean islands, it was a downright lie.

"Munk!" A voice snatched her from her thoughts. "Ah, and our young guest!"

A man strode up to them through an aisle between the tobacco plants, just walking straight through the ghost. The silent, vapory creature shredded for an instant, then put himself back together and continued working, undisturbed.

"Dad, this is Jolly."

The man stretched out a large, calloused hand and shook

hers so vigorously that her shoulder hurt afterward. Perhaps she was even weaker than she'd thought after the long spell of unconsciousness.

"Good day, sir," she said, regarding him without shyness. Like his son, he had light hair that fell to his broad shoulders. His bare torso was browned by the sun and so muscular that he'd have made a good sailor. The slight beginnings of a belly showed that the tobacco business couldn't be going too badly, not even on such an isolated island. He was unusually big and had a faint accent, which suggested a Scottish origin.

"My Mary has made you well, eh? She knows how to handle herbs and things like that. Munk couldn't wait for you to finally open your eyes. Where did you come from?"

Haiti, she'd been about to say, before she realized that his wife already knew the truth. "From a ship. The *Skinny Maddy*."

His look darkened. "Bannon's ship?"

Jolly cast an uncertain glance at Munk, but he was staring at his father in amazement. "You don't know him, do you?" he asked.

The farmer nodded. "Who hasn't heard of the *Maddy*? I'd already thought you came from the pirates, girl. My wife showed me the tattoo on your back."

Munk's jaw dropped. "You have a *tattoo*?"

Jolly's heart sank, but she straightened her shoulders. "It isn't finished. One of the crew started it before we discovered the Spanish ship . . . the ship with the spiders."

She'd told Munk what had happened, but his father frowned. "You'll have to tell everything at supper," he said.

"I'd like to get back to work now. Munk, you have the afternoon off today." He turned to go, then turned back once more. "And you, girl, don't put any foolish ideas into my son's head, you hear? He daydreams all day long anyway, that boy."

"Don't worry, sir."

After his father was gone, Munk grinned at her. "So," he said, "which foolish ideas do we start with?"

"My parents were cartographers," Munk told her as he led Jolly down to the bay where he'd pulled her out of the water. "They scouted out routes between islands and reefs for one of the big trading companies. My father steered the boat and my mother drew the maps. She can draw really well, you know? She tried to teach me, but I never get it right. I mean, I can draw a bird . . . or a pirate ship." It obviously pleased him that he could make Jolly smile despite the losses she'd suffered. "Oh, well, anyway, my parents passed on everything they found out about the routes between the reefs and sandbars to the company. They got paid for it. Usually it took a while until a route was explored, but the company always wanted, above all, to be up-to-date. My father had warned the traders not to sail anywhere that wasn't completely scouted yet. But one of them didn't listen and took an especially dangerous route before my mother could even inspect the map once and clear up the last inaccuracies. He ran aground, and his entire convoy sank. He and many others were drowned."

"And they blamed your parents for that?"

A bitter expression appeared on Munk's face. "The trader's

brother was Scarab, the pirate emperor of the Caribbean. He put a price on my parents' heads among the pirates. Since then, they've stayed hidden on this island. Their only contact with the outer world is a handful of traders they've known forever and trust."

"But why the caution?" Jolly wanted to know. "Scarab's been dead for years. Kendrick is the emperor of the pirates at New Providence now. People say he killed Scarab to take power himself. He canceled a lot of Scarab's decrees and laws or ignores them. I can't imagine why he or anyone else would still be hunting your parents today."

Munk seemed to weigh her words. But then he shook his head dejectedly. "You know, I don't think my parents are really still afraid of Scarab, or any other pirates. They like it here. They like the isolation and the quiet and—"

"All the things that get on your nerves."

He smiled in embarrassment. "Yes."

"And certainly your father doesn't want you to ever go to sea. Although he himself did it for years. Right?"

Munk nodded. "He says he's seen too many ships sink and too many good men drown. He hates the sea now. He can't understand why I want to go there myself." He was looking really unhappy now. "I never even get the chance to find out if maybe I'll like the sea just as little as he does."

For the first time Jolly felt sympathy. She loved the sea more than anything, and that wasn't only because she was a polliwog. She knew what Munk would be missing if he stayed on this island, and she guessed how he must be feeling.

For a long time they walked silently side by side until they saw the white of the beach gleaming through the thickets. Then Jolly had a thought. "Why did you tell me all this? About your parents and their fear of the pirates? After all, I am one."

Munk smiled in embarrassment and quickly avoided her eyes. "Because I trust you." Then he ran down the incline to the beach and left her standing. "Come on!"

Jolly looked after him in surprise for a moment, then she started moving. Lightly, she ran through the soft sand. All her strength returned in an instant when she saw the sea lying before her. Today the view overwhelmed her more than ever: the green-yellow crescent of the bay, then the teeth of the reef chain, and behind it the endless blue of the ocean. Gulls screamed in the air, and a warm wind carried in the scent of the sea and its spicy, salty taste.

Munk didn't stop until he reached the empty figurehead that had lain just beyond the tide line for three days, unchanged in the damp sand. Jolly examined the wooden Neptune and shuddered when she discovered the traces of the shark's teeth. At the same moment her stomach lurched, and she threw up.

"What's wrong?" Munk asked in concern.

The pictures came again: the faces of Bannon and the others, scenes on board the *Skinny Maddy,* adventures, dangers, but also security at the side of the pirates. The laughter of her friends, the trouble most of them had taken to make a pirate out of the thin little girl that Bannon treated like a daughter. And, of course, the successes to which she'd helped them as a polliwog, the praise, the approval, the cheers.

All that was past now. Only memories that someday would fade more and more.

"No," she whispered to herself, but Munk heard.

"They're dead, Jolly. They have to be."

"You said yourself if someone has the antidote—"

"But no one here does."

"But your mother."

Munk took a deep breath. "It comes from the mainland. That's hundreds of miles from here. Besides, you'd need twenty or thirty bottles of it to save a whole crew. We have only two."

Jolly wouldn't let go. "All the same, somebody or other could still have much more of it, couldn't they?"

"And why would he"—he was about to say *waste* it—"use it to save a whole pirate crew? Especially pirates whom he'd probably just lured into a trap? People like you aren't exactly popular in the islands."

She'd thought of that herself. But it didn't change anything.

"If it had been your parents aboard," she said, "would you have just given up too?"

Munk held her eyes for a few seconds, then shrugged. "No."

Jolly let herself down onto the sand next to the figurehead, the only memento of the *Skinny Maddy* and her friends, and stroked the wood with her fingertips. Then she gave herself a shake and stood up a little unsteadily.

"I'll show you something," said Munk in an attempt to cheer her up. "What do you know about mussel magic?"

"Nothing more than that some say it exists and others say it doesn't." Her thoughts were still trapped in the past; she hardly heard what he was saying, not even what she answered.

Munk wouldn't let himself be distracted. "Then get ready for a big surprise."

She looked at him. "Magic?" she asked, a little perplexed, and the word snatched her from the fog of her grief.

"Magic," he confirmed, and he was beaming.

Munk emptied the contents of his leather pouch onto the sand. Besides the box with the spider in it, it held only mussels, padded with leaves and straw: mussels of all shapes, sizes, and colors. Some were plain shells that you might find on any beach; but there were also some, shimmering in shades and nuances of color, such as Jolly had never seen before.

"Are they all from here on the island?" she asked in amazement.

Munk shook his head. "Only a few, the simplest. The others the merchants brought to me, especially the—"

"The Ghost Trader," she broke in.

"Yes."

"It's time you told me about him."

"You'll soon meet him."

The mussels shimmered as if they'd been polished. Jolly was more curious than she wanted to admit.

Mussel magic was something she knew from stories, like star money that fell from heaven or the giant kraken in the depths of the ocean. But she'd never met anyone who'd seen mussel magic with his own eyes.

Munk began to lay out some of the mussels in a circle on the sand. She didn't understand why he reached for one mussel but left the others lying, and it was an even greater puzzle to her why he moved his lips the entire time, as if he were having a silent dialogue with the mussels. She half expected that some of the shells would snap open and shut to answer him. But the mussels just lay there, apparently any old way, and yet arranged according to a secret, mysterious order.

"So," he said after a while, when he'd laid out a circle of twelve mussels. "Now watch very carefully."

The command hadn't been necessary. She was staring at him anyway, as if he'd lost his mind.

"Not me," he said. "The mussels."

"Sure."

"What do you see?"

"Mussels. Mussels in a circle."

"What else?"

"An idiot who's trying to make himself look important."

He grinned again. "Wait. Now—look!"

Suddenly he moved the palm of his right hand in a circle over the mussels, closing his eyes and again murmuring soundlessly to himself.

The sand in the center of the circle formed a depression. She saw it very clearly, although Munk's hand hadn't touched the ground: a round pit, a little bigger than Jolly's hand and as deep as a wine jug.

In the center of the depression something gleamed. First she thought it was a piece of metal buried in the sand there, perhaps a coin. But then she saw that the light was floating over the sand and radiating from something that hadn't been there a moment before.

In the center of the sand pit floated a pearl, as big as a thumbnail.

"You conjured up a pearl?" She wrinkled her nose. "I've seen better parlor tricks."

"No, I'm not done yet." His voice sounded strained, and he was keeping his eyelids closed. "What shall I do now?"

"If you don't know . . ."

"Request something. Something magic."

"I can't think of anything."

He sighed. Sweat appeared on his forehead. "How would a gust of wind be?"

She raised her eyebrows in surprise and nodded. "Good, a gust of wind, then."

Munk whispered something—and at the same moment Jolly was seized by a gust of wind that would have held its own with any rising storm. With a scream she was swept off the ground, carried two steps backward, and landed on her seat in the sand.

A moment later it was utterly still, no wind at all.

Dumbfounded, she stared at her footprints in the sand, then at the spot where she now sat. "Was that *you?*"

Munk didn't answer. He stretched out his right hand, executed the circular movement again, and pointed his index finger at one of the mussels. The floating pearl went into motion and, in a flash, shot into the open mussel. The shell clapped shut with a noise that sounded like the snapping of bony jaws.

Munk opened his eyes, blinked, looked for Jolly, and found her still sitting in the sand. "Oh," he said as he squatted down next to her. "I didn't mean to do that."

"Are you seriously claiming that was you?"

"Not me. The magic of the mussels. It's only a matter of controlling it and directing it. There's nothing magic about me myself, but about these here . . ." He pointed at the circle of mussels with a gesture that seemed almost tender. "They *are* magic. Do you understand?"

"Not a word." Jolly scrambled to her feet and brushed the sand off her trousers.

"The hard thing isn't setting magic free," he said, "but settling it down again afterward. In the beginning I was careless a few times and didn't get it shut up again. Then the magic stayed free and caused all sorts of catastrophes. Once the roof of the house went up in flames. I was really only trying to heal the broken leg of a goat—but that was quite strong magic, and I didn't know how to get it back in again. Another time, when I didn't get the pearl shut back into the mussel, the next morning the leaves of all the palm trees around the farm were red." He carefully packed the mussels back into the sack. Every single one of them was wrapped and cushioned. "But since I realized that everything you call up you have to make disappear again, there've been no more problems."

"Where did the pearl come from?"

"It's only a kind of embodiment of the real magic. When I will it, the magic flows out of the mussels and forms the pearl in the center. That means that I can use its strength for the magic. As soon as the magic is worked, I have to move the magic back into one of the mussels, and that's it. When I open the mussel the next time, the pearl is gone—it's turned into invisible magic again and can be called up again. The bigger the pearl, the more magic available. Basically, it's very simple—if a person has the talent for it."

"And you aren't pulling my leg?"

"Word of honor."

She grinned. "Not bad."

Munk was clearly flattered. "Oh, well, it's just fooling around. Aside from healing the goat and a few other little things, nothing particularly useful has come out of it. I tried to double the harvest, but that went horribly awry. I'm not strong enough for something like that."

"What happened?"

"Half the tobacco plants died. After that my father forbid me to use mussel magic."

Jolly smiled. "But you just did it anyway."

"Only to cheer you up."

She held out her hand to help him stand up. This time he took it. "That was nice of you," she said.

Munk blushed. "You aren't the moll my father said you were."

"Moll? He said that?"

He nodded. "He meant women who get mixed up with pirates."

She gently loosened her hand from his when she felt that he wasn't going to let go on his own. "Your father probably doesn't know all about everything. And he really doesn't know anything about me yet."

"Just like me."

She nodded silently, avoiding his eyes, and started back to the farm. After a while she finally broke the silence. "I'll tell you something about myself," she said, grinning. "I'm dying of hunger."

The Great Earthquake

Jolly decided not to steal the spider box. As long as there was no trading boat to take her from the island, there was no point in taking possession of the dead spider. Besides, she didn't want to vex her hosts, least of all Munk. He was so completely different from the pirate boys she knew, not a braggart or a loudmouth. He seemed almost embarrassed about his knowledge of mussel magic. He was friendly and nice, and he went to great pains to make her aware of it.

On the third day after she regained consciousness, he led her through the banana jungle up to the rocks over the bay and showed her the old cannon. The rusty gun was waiting up there in seclusion for enemies who would probably never come. Jolly shared Munk's opinion that the island might once have been a pirates' base that nobody remembered anymore. Silently she wondered if perhaps Munk's father were concealing something. Was he actually only the captain of a cartography ship? Or were there other reasons why the then emperor Scarab was hunting him?

Munk confessed to her that he'd often dreamed of firing the cannon. However, he had no idea how to operate a gun like that. Worrying that he might blow himself up, he'd preferred to keep his hands off it. Besides, the explosion of the cannon would certainly not be the only one that occurred on the island if his parents got wind of it—and that could hardly be avoided if it were fired.

Jolly weighed it this way and that; then she decided that she really had nothing to lose. They would just claim that Jolly had stumbled on the cannon in the underbrush and wanted to show Munk how to fire one. She'd take all the blame. The worst that could happen would be that Munk's father would send her away on the next ship, but that was her plan anyway.

"Have you got any gunpowder on the farm?"

"A keg full," Munk said.

She explained to him how much she needed. While he went to get it, she cleaned the gun barrel, wrapped leaves around a branch until she could use it as a ramrod, and discovered in the underbrush beneath the cannon an old copper ladle that came from the former cannoneers.

When Munk came back, breathless and red to the tips of his ears, she used the ladle to fill the breech with gunpowder, enough to equal about a third of the weight of a cannonball.

Then she stuffed leaves in place of the missing wadding, followed by one of the iron balls that were still piled up in a rusty pyramid beside the cannon. Finally, Jolly filled the touchhole with gunpowder and ordered Munk to help her bring the cannon into proper position, and carefully enough so the rotten base didn't collapse. She aimed straight across the water to a tongue of land on the other side of the bay. On its highest point there were three gigantic palms growing out of a thicket of ferns. Jolly told Munk she'd hit the middle one.

With flint and steel she set a branch alight, then ordered Munk two steps back. She used the burning branch tip to light the powder, then put her hands over her ears.

The cannon shot thundered, and it seemed to have torn the blue heavens in two. For a long moment the world consisted only of smoke and splitting wood. The echo of the shot's thunder rolled over the bay, over the entire island. The force of the explosion burst the mounting of the cannon and smashed the pedestal. The gun's barrel leaned at an angle in the debris, only to overbalance a moment later and roll down the hill, mashing several bushes and shrubs before the trunk of a mahogany stopped it; the impact shook a swarm of red insects out of the crown of the tree.

"Phew," said Munk, but his fright was already displaced by an expression of radiant joy. "That was fantastic!"

Jolly coughed and waved the smoke away with her hand. When the clouds had dispersed, she saw that on the other side of the bay there were only two palms still standing instead of three; the left was snapped off like a blade of straw.

"You hit it!" Munk cried excitedly.

Jolly frowned. "I really wanted to hit the one in the middle."

"Oh, so what! As if it made any difference at this distance."

"There *is* a difference between hitting the mainmast or the foresail of a sailing ship."

But Munk paid no more attention to her as he danced in circles with joy. "Crazy! A real cannon shot! Wait till I tell that to the Ghost Trader!"

Jolly walked skeptically around the remains of the cannon. "This could have gone awry. If we'd been standing on the wrong side—"

"But we weren't!" Munk walked over to her and rubbed his neck. "Hm, you think we could rebuild it and try the whole thing over again?"

"Absolutely not!"

At that moment a third voice broke in behind them.

"That was foolish," said Munk's father. "You don't know how terribly foolish that was."

They were sitting on the palm-thatched veranda of the farmhouse. Night was striding in with giant steps, but no stars illuminated the dark blue sky yet. Only the moon had risen and now silvered the tips of the trees with its light. The sounds of the deep jungle could be heard behind the toothed crest of the palisade fence that surrounded the wooden house and the farmyard. It was the hour in which some of its inhabitants lay down to sleep and others awakened to the nightly hunt. A few indignant monkeys were chasing each other wildly through the treetops and shooed up a whole cloud of white butterflies with wings as big as Jolly's hands. A spicy smell arose from the rain forest, the warm air was moist, and every few minutes there was the sound of a slap when Jolly or Munk or one of the two grown-ups slapped at a mosquito.

"Perhaps we should have told you everything earlier," said Munk's father. "But your mother didn't want to."

"Don't let yourself off so easily," said his wife. "We were both of the same mind."

The farmer took a drink from his rum cup, then shrugged. "It began with the destruction of Port Royal in the year 1692, fourteen years ago. At one time, Port Royal was one of the nastiest pirate nests on Jamaica—in fact, in the entire Caribbean. But at the time of the disaster, that was already past, and the pirates had gone looking for better harbors: Tortuga, and later, New Providence. By '92 Port Royal was declining, but it was still a big city, and when the huge earthquake struck, more than two thousand people died in it. The northern section, where most of the docks were, slid into the sea, and a gigantic tidal wave rolled in over the city. It was one of the greatest catastrophes this corner of the world had ever seen, at least since we white men have been knocking around here."

He interrupted his account to light his pipe. Jolly and Munk exchanged uncertain looks. The dressing-down they'd

e know,
ourself.
talking
. . and

a pol-
lready
came
r."
So he
three
. I'm
face.
e in

"I

gs
ke

d, Munk's father had sent them mself had spent the entire after- st point of the island and watch- been certain that the cannon fire d he come back to the house and with them. He didn't threaten, he made it forcefully clear that they'd an they deserved, by God.

uffs on his pipe, he went on with his yone was afraid of more tremors, and relief was enormous. No one could had set something else free, something w could turn out to be worse than the people." Glumly he rubbed the stubble on simple man, I make no secret of it; wiser have explained this to me."

aced her hand over his and sent him a loving e first time, Jolly became aware of how very vo cared for each other.

nyway, somehow magic was set free at that time . . . t, hocus-pocus, whatever you want to call it. And of this magic, there arose what people soon were call- *iwogs.*"

box on the ear couldn't have hit Jolly more unexpectedly. hat did he know about the polliwogs? She was the last one, nnon had said. During her days on the island, she hadn't t foot on the water, and she hadn't even told Munk about ability.

Munk's mother looked at her and smiled. "W
child. You were delirious for two days and talking to
It wasn't hard to put two and two together. You kept
about walking on the water . . . and about two ships
about spiders."

"Besides, word had gotten around that Bannon had
liwog on board," her husband said. "Basically, we
knew before what you are, but then when you said you
from Bannon and the *Skinny Maddy,* the matter was clea

Jolly sent Munk an inquiring look. He only nodded.
knew too and hadn't said a word about it over these last
days. But now he leaned toward her. "I'm one too, Jolly
a polliwog like you." An uncertain smile stole over his
"And up till a few days ago, I thought I was the last o
the whole world."

Jolly swallowed before she found her voice again.
thought that about me, too."

"Let me keep telling," said Munk's father. "The polliw
are children who were born right after the great earthqu
in Port Royal. This magic that came out of the cracks in
earth . . . somehow it got into you children, into the ne
borns. And only in ones who were right in the vicinity. The
were no polliwogs on Haiti or Cuba or here in the Bahama
Only on Jamaica, and only in Port Royal.

"It was two or three years before it became known tha
there were children who could walk on the water, before any
one was sure that for some reason the earthquake was the
cause of it. The Spaniards had the whole business investigated

The English, the Dutch, each got their own groups of missionaries and military and the devil knows who else together to research the whole matter." His mouth twisted in scorn. "The first polliwogs died in their experiments. But it didn't stop there. A curse on them all, those slavers! Soon there were men who hunted for polliwogs and auctioned them off or used them for their own purposes. Some were taken to safety by their parents, at least for a while, and so they were scattered over the islands and the entire Caribbean Sea. Altogether, there must have been maybe twenty or thirty, not more. After five or six years, fewer than half of them were left alive. And now, today . . . I'm afraid you two are the last ones of all."

"Nobody ever hurt a hair of my head," Jolly said hesitantly.

"You were always under Bannon's protection. Hardly anyone would have been crazy enough to take on the sea devil of the Antilles. Until a few days ago, anyway."

"You think . . ." Jolly shook her head, speechless.

Munk's father blew a smoke ring, but it disappeared right away. "I think that this trap was not for Bannon or his crew, Jolly, but for you. Someone is hunting for the last polliwog again, and he is presumably somewhere in the vicinity."

"But I'm . . . I mean, I'm only fourteen years old. I'm not *important.*"

"Perhaps you are. Just like Munk."

The boy's mother spoke again. Her voice was filled with anxiety. "We've always been afraid it would come to this sometime. You can't hide from the entire world forever."

"Then that's why you came here? To protect Munk?"

"That was one of the reasons," said Munk's father. "It's true that Scarab put a price on my head. But the most important reason for our coming here was Munk." He looked his son firmly in the eyes, and now there was so much concern in his expression that Jolly's throat closed almost tight. "Nobody was to know that Munk is a polliwog. That was the most important thing of all."

Jolly cleared her throat, trying to battle the lump that had settled there. "You think I could have led those men here, don't you? That they'll keep looking for me because I wasn't aboard the ship and that they'll follow me to the island."

"There is that danger. And after that nonsense with the cannon today—"

"I'm sorry about that. I had no idea—"

"Of course not," said Munk's mother. "We ought to have spoken with you earlier about it. Right after we realized who we were dealing with."

"That business with the cannon," said Munk. "That was my idea, not Jolly's. I've known for a very long time that the thing was up there and I kept wanting . . . I wanted . . ."

"You wanted to play pirate," said his father, but he wasn't smiling. "What boy doesn't?"

Munk dropped his eyes guiltily.

His mother looked from him to Jolly. "Maybe we'll be lucky. Maybe the whole thing really was a trap the Spaniards set to catch Bannon."

"It was a Spanish ship," said Jolly, remembering the

steersman's words, "but the men weren't real soldiers. They were prisoners forced to go aboard and wait for us with sails reefed."

"That means that someone knew for sure that the *Skinny Maddy* would take this route," said Munk's father thoughtfully.

"We were under way to New Providence."

"That's about two hundred miles from here. How come you were sailing around the Bahamas so far to the east?"

"Bannon wanted to be very certain. He'd received news from the pirate emperor, Kendrick. It's said there's going to be a Spanish attack on New Providence, and Bannon was planning to fight on Kendrick's side. He wanted to do everything to avoid running into the Spanish armada, so that's why he took that course."

The farmer considered that. "Someone must have betrayed you. Did the whole crew know the route?"

"As far as I know, only Bannon, the steersman Cristobal, and perhaps one or two others. But I'm not sure."

He sighed. "This all leads nowhere, I'm afraid. One thing is certain, anyway: If someone has set up such a devilish trap to get hold of you, he won't be content with your disappearance. He knows that you're a polliwog, and perhaps he thinks that you've tried to reach the next island on foot. So sooner or later he's going to turn up here."

Munk's mother covered her chin with the palms of her hands. "We have to leave. Find a new hiding place somewhere."

Her son's eyes widened. "And the farm? You can't just—"

"I'd a thousand times rather lose the farm than you," said his father.

Jolly withdrew ever deeper into herself. "This all makes me so terribly sorry. If I'd known . . . I mean, then . . ."

"Would you have let yourself be caught? That's nonsense. How were you supposed to know that you'd land right here?" The farmer pulled on his pipe as if it helped him think. "Perhaps it's a warning from fate, after all. Possibly God means to show us that we've become careless."

"I thought you didn't believe in God," Munk said, "and certainly not at all in fate."

His father burst into booming laughter. "You're right, my boy. We're entirely dependent on ourselves. What your mother says is right: We have to leave the island."

Jolly turned to Munk. "You said you don't have a boat."

"And we don't."

"We can go aboard one of the traders'," said Munk's mother. "The next one should be arriving in a week."

"The Ghost Trader's coming day after tomorrow!" Munk burst out.

"Who knows who he's in with," said his father grimly. "He's creepy, and I don't trust him across the road. Could be that he'd trade us off to the first pirates who came along."

"He's always been friendly to me."

The farmer took his pipe out of his mouth and gestured in a way that made it unmistakably clear that he would tolerate no argument in this matter. "We're going with the Dutchman, next week. He's always served us well; we can

Ghost Trader

ous visitor appeared on the island two
dicted. He sailed alone in a tiny boat that
it could really cover the wide distances
ds. Jolly just had to take one look at him to
's father had meant: She'd rather have trusted
ortuga than the dark figure who came over
ttle sailboat before dawn and was onshore
irst rays of the sun struck it.

rader wore a wide, hooded cloak of dark,
ch reached to the ground and hid his feet.
l pulled up, despite the Caribbean heat that
eaking day. Underneath the hood's material,
out gaunt features and weather-beaten skin.
band across his forehead and cheek covered
e. He had the stubble of a gray beard and

trust him. Un
watch the sea
"Now it's tim
and I still have
Jolly and M
the house look
In front of J
said, that no o
right. One pers
She felt her
He nodded g

The

The mysteri
days later, as pre
didn't look as i
between the islan
know what Munk
a gutter rat on T
the sea in the li
even before the f
The Ghost T
coarse stuff, wh
He had the hoo
rose with the br
Jolly could make
A diagonal black
his blind left ey

astonishingly white, almost radiant teeth, which didn't fit with his dilapidated appearance.

But the most unusual thing were the two raven black parrots sitting on his shoulders, one with yellow eyes, one with eyes of fiery red.

"Those are Hugh and Moe," Munk whispered to Jolly as they went to meet the Ghost Trader. "He always has them with him and he talks with them."

"Can the two of them speak too?"

"He claims so, yes."

The mysterious man was just coming into hearing distance, but to Jolly it seemed as though he'd been listening to her the entire time, for a knowing smile was playing about his narrow, colorless lips.

"Good day, Munk," he said, and bowed almost imperceptibly—which, remarkably, his parrots imitated. "Greetings to you and all who live on this island." His healthy eye, a brilliant light blue, was directed to Jolly. "You have a visitor, I see."

"This is Jolly. She's a castaway."

"Jolly. Well, well." The Ghost Trader nodded to her as well. "An unusual name for a girl. I thought the pirates only called their flags that."

She could have denied that she had anything to do with the pirates, but she was too proud. It seemed strange to her, though, how suddenly he connected her with freebooters.

"Do you also have a name, sir?" she asked straight out.

The Ghost Trader smiled in amusement. "One or another."

But he didn't give her one, instead turning to Munk again. "I hope your family is well. Your father isn't here?"

"He climbed up to the top of the mountain while it was still dark. But he must have seen that you've landed. He's sure to come right away."

From beneath his closed cape the Trader pulled out a thing that puzzled Jolly even further: a silver metal ring, narrower than her little finger, but with the diameter of a large plate. He let it dangle from his right hand next to his body as he walked together with them over the beach and through the jungle to the house.

"How's the magic going?" he asked Munk when they were halfway there. "Any progress?"

Munk sighed. "Not worth mentioning."

"It will come. Patience is the touchstone of magic."

Jolly made no attempt to hide her distrust. "You know all about mussel magic?"

"I don't like to do it myself, if that's what you mean. But yes, I know a thing or two about it."

"He showed me how to do it," Munk said proudly.

"That isn't quite right," contradicted the Trader. "I've only told you what there is to it—I can show you nothing. I don't have your talent." He sounded very serious when he said that, with no trace of irony.

Munk's mother was waiting for them on the veranda. She'd placed several earthenware cups, a bottle of rum, and a pitcher of water on the table, as well as a wooden board with bread and goat cheese. She greeted the Ghost Trader with reserve, but not in an unfriendly way. The two exchanged a few polite trivialities: how the journey had been, how business was going, whether there was any news from the outside world.

"The indications for a Spanish attack on New Providence are increasing," said the Ghost Trader. "The viceroy has sent an armada, even if no one has seen it yet. At least no one with whom I've spoken."

Munk's father came down from the mountain, and soon they were all sitting around the table and breakfasting together. Despite his ascetic appearance, the Ghost Trader ate twice as much as the others. Now and again he broke off a piece of bread or cheese and handed it to his parrots. Jolly's instinct told her that Hugh and Moe were no ordinary birds, just as the Ghost Trader was certainly no ordinary man. Why ever had Munk put such trust in him that he'd even confided his greatest secret to him?

As if the Ghost Trader detected what was going through her mind, he suddenly reached under his cloak and pulled out three polished mussels, each more unusual than the last. "I almost forgot these," he said with a wink of his one eye as he handed them to Munk. The latter beamed, thanked him, and carefully placed them in the purse at his waist. His father looked on with visible disapproval, but he said nothing.

For the rest of the meal they listened to the Trader's reports, and Jolly had to hand him one thing: He could tell stories like no one else.

He was able to embroider even the most trivial news to

sound like a hero's tale, without his listeners getting the feeling that he was really bending the truth or inventing whatever it was.

"You're still a wonderful tale spinner," Munk's mother said after a while. She'd thawed amazingly during the conversation, in contrast to her husband, who continued to maintain a cool distance.

The Trader shrugged. "Long experience. And perhaps talent. Who knows?"

The men turned to business soon after that, which was on the whole limited to Munk's father's declaration that he was not interested in any more ghosts at this time. He didn't inform the Trader that they intended to leave the island.

"But I have some really outstanding new spirits with me," the Ghost Trader said, marketing his invisible wares. "Princesses from the Far East, heroes from the icy North, and wise men from all directions under the sun. Not to overlook diligent workers from the—"

"Certainly," the farmer interrupted him. "I can easily believe that, but I still have enough here. Only one has gone missing since your last visit. Besides—and I say this every time, my friend—I don't believe a word of your praise. I may be only a simple tobacco farmer"—and with that it seemed to Jolly that his eyes bored with especial persuasive power into the Trader's eye—"but I am not gullible. Spirits of princesses and heroes don't appear to be different from all the others, so your ghosts could just as well be the souls of poor wretches and castaways."

"Princesses also go down with ships," said the Ghost

Trader, giving Jolly an inscrutable side glance. "That has been known to happen."

Munk's father made a gesture of refusal. "You've always been honorable in your business with me, but your talk . . . I heard, for instance, of a spirit rebellion on Grand Caicos, in which an entire plantation was destroyed. What do you have to say about that?"

The Ghost Trader smiled in the shadow of his hood. One of the two parrots, the red-eyed Moe, let out a shrill scream. "Misfortunes happen, I'm afraid. And I assure you, in this case it was the farmer's fault entirely, that jackass. He let some priest talk him into having his ghosts blessed. Good grief, the idiot sprayed them with holy water, which is really no way to handle a spirit. No wonder they all went wild."

"And still, we need no new spirits. Perhaps next time." As if he wanted to encourage the Trader to a faster return, he added, "Yes, I really think next time I'll be able to take two or three of them."

The Trader nodded. "Regrettable, but that's the way business goes sometimes." He turned to Munk. "Tell me, are the ghosts obeying you now? Or are there any who've given you trouble?"

"No trouble. Everything was just the way you said." He looked proudly over at Jolly. "When he was here last time, he told the ghosts that in future they should obey not only my father but also me."

"I asked him to," said his father. "Out here you have to be prepared for everything. I could be sick or have an accident.

Munk is old enough to run the farm alone if necessary."

The Ghost Trader drank a sip of water, then got up. "I won't keep you from your work any longer."

"Aren't you going to stay the night here, the way you usually do?" Munk's mother asked in surprise.

The Trader shook his head. "I must go on as quickly as possible. If the Spaniards really do attack New Providence, it would be especially advantageous to conclude as much business as possible beforehand. Who knows if the plantations will be able to find enough customers for their wares afterward?"

"Not everyone trades with the pirates," said Munk's father disapprovingly.

"I know, I know. You're an upright man." The Ghost Trader made the mysterious silver ring vanish under his robe and bowed toward both grown-ups. Then he said to Munk, "Will you and your friend come with me to the boat?"

"Certainly."

Jolly and Munk joined the Trader as he left the veranda. They turned into the lane through the jungle that led down to the beach.

"Good sailing," the farmer called after them. "And watch out for the weather. It looked earlier as if there could be a storm blowing up. There were clouds on the horizon, and we haven't had a hurricane out here for a long time."

"I'll take care, thank you," replied the Trader.

The farmhouse with its palm frond roof and palisade fence disappeared behind the bushes and trees. Jolly, Munk, and the Trader spoke again only when they reached the beach.

The sailboat rolled in the low water. The only shelter on deck was offered by a canvas awning; there wasn't even a cabin. The thin mast would offer no resistance to a storm.

Jolly found all this more than remarkable. The most puzzling was easily the Ghost Trader himself. Before he picked up his robe and strode through the gentle waves to the boat, he shook hands with them both.

"Be careful, especially in the next few days." He noticed Jolly's raised eyebrows and added with a smile, "The Spaniards are going to make good on their threats, probably very soon. You're very far away from New Providence here, but who knows? Perhaps you'll feel the waves of all these troubles, even out here."

Jolly and Munk watched as the man climbed aboard, set the sail, and maneuvered the boat with astonishing speed between the reefs and out onto the open sea.

Yet there wasn't even a breath of wind on the beach.

"I thought you intended to ask if he'd take you with him," Munk said. He added hopefully, "Or have you reconsidered?"

Jolly shook her head. "I have a better idea."

"Oh, yes?"

"We'll follow him."

Munk stared at her. "We'll do what?"

"Something about him isn't right. Don't tell me you haven't already noticed that. Do you think, in all seriousness, that he travels the entire Caribbean in that nutshell?"

"He doesn't lie to me. Certainly not."

"But perhaps he doesn't tell you the whole truth, either."

"If there's a bigger ship lying out there somewhere, my father would have seen it from the lookout point."

Jolly pressed her lips together and thought about that. "Yes," she said then, "probably so. Nevertheless, let's go after him a little way."

"He'll see us."

"Not if the distance is great enough."

"If he does, he'll be angry."

"I thought he was your friend."

"He won't be anymore if I spy on him."

Jolly sighed. "Then I'll go by myself. You'd probably just hold me up out there anyway."

Anger blazed up in Munk's eyes. "I'm just as much a polliwog as you!"

"But you have no experience walking on the open sea. The waves will throw you down."

"They will not!"

Out of the corner of her eye, she kept the Ghost Trader's boat in sight; now it was only a white spot on the endless blue. "Then you have a chance to prove it now."

And with that she jumped away over the breaking surf, landed between two waves, and ran off.

She'd been right to have misgivings: Munk did in fact hold her up. But she didn't let it bother her. Anyway, she couldn't run too fast or she would come too close to the boat and risk being discovered.

Munk had trouble keeping his balance on the swaying

surface under his feet. A number of times he stumbled or made the mistake of walking on the crest of a wave against the current, which almost snatched him back. However, he was trying as hard as he could, that was clear, and Jolly only had to support him once when he threatened to topple; the other times he caught himself on his own. With time he grew a little more secure, and soon Jolly was paying more attention to the boat far ahead of them and not just to him.

"My father has certainly seen us," said Munk, casting a look back at the lonely mountain that towered above the roof of the jungle on the small island. Somewhere up there, the farmer was keeping a lookout for strange ships—and instead, he was having to look on while his son and the pirate girl disobeyed one of his oft-repeated injunctions.

You've really had a bad influence on this boy, Jolly said to herself in amusement.

Nevertheless, she couldn't reign in her curiosity. She had a bad feeling about this Ghost Trader. He was concealing something from them. Was she afraid of him? He made her uneasy, certainly, but she was a polliwog, after all, and if necessary she could always run away from him across the waves.

And what if he set his ghosts on her?

"Hey," Munk said suddenly, after they'd been under way for almost an hour, "look at that."

"Yes, I see it."

On the horizon a broad, wavering bank of fog had appeared, and was quickly coming closer. White, vapory arms wafted at its edges, as if they were feeling for the gulls in the sky. The Caribbean sunshine made it radiate with blinding brightness. The Ghost Trader's boat was heading straight for it.

"Are those the clouds your father spoke of?" Jolly had experienced more than one hurricane, but none of them had announced themselves with fog.

"Well, hardly."

"I knew it!" Jolly hastened her steps triumphantly. "Something's not right about that fellow."

"And that from a pirate, of all people!"

"Did he ever tell you anything about this fog?"

"Perhaps he didn't know anything about it beforehand." Munk's defense sounded halfhearted.

"And therefore he sails right toward it? Every halfway sensible seaman in a boat like that would make a gigantic detour around this fog bank."

Munk said nothing more. It wasn't in him to distrust his friend, but what he saw in front of him appeared to please him still less. Jolly wasn't sure if he shared her distrust; but very clearly, he was wondering.

The Ghost Trader's boat kept heading straight toward the fog. Very soon white vapory fingers reached for sail and hull. The Ghost Trader could be made out as a tiny figure standing straight as a candle in the stern.

Munk was having trouble keeping up with Jolly. "Don't you want to go back now?"

"How else are we going to find out the truth?"

"Maybe there is no truth. Maybe that's just normal fog up there."

The boat had almost disappeared now; only a dark spot vaguely indicated its position.

Jolly swore. "We're going to lose him in there if we don't hurry."

Munk couldn't go any faster, she knew that—he'd had too little experience with this water walking; the waves were going to throw him back and forth like a plaything. "You go on," he said. "I'll be along for sure."

"We stay together," she countered. "Anything else is too dangerous."

Munk tried once more to increase his speed, but the result was that he stumbled. At the last moment he caught himself with both hands, leaped up again, cursing, and ran on.

Finally the fog had completely swallowed the boat. Jolly hoped the Ghost Trader had maintained his course. That way she could stay on his trail if she just ran straight ahead.

The wall of mist lay like a wavering mass on the sea, forty or fifty yards wide and as high as the mast of a warship. Its foremost billows wafted toward Jolly and Munk. After the searing sun of the past hours, the cloud felt pleasantly cool on the skin.

Instinctively, Jolly held her breath when she pushed into the interior of the fog. An unnatural stillness extended on all sides of them. She felt strangely oppressed by the white walls enclosing and towering over them. Munk was running along beside her as a gray silhouette, but she didn't dare speak to him for fear the Ghost Trader could be nearby and hear them.

They hadn't gone fifteen yards through the fog when the view abruptly cleared. Soon they could see the reason: The wall of fog was not a compact mass but a ring, which was hiding something in its center.

Jolly's heart missed a beat.

Before them rose a galleon.

The ship lay, its rigging creaking, in the middle of a clearing in the fog. The galleon's hull was made of dark wood. A ridge of algae and mussels had collected above the waterline. The sails on the three tall masts were gray and tattered. Not even the most neglectful captain would have overlooked something like that. But anyway, Jolly doubted that there was a captain on board this ship, any more than there was a crew.

"Is that what I think it is?" Munk's voice wavered.

"Yes," she said. "Your Ghost Trader has just the tub that fits him."

"And I thought there were no ghost ships."

She looked at him mistrustfully. "I thought there were no ghosts."

Reluctantly they moved forward, finally leaving the fog and walking into the light of the blue sky. But not even that was able to lift their dark mood. The ghost ship drew all their attention.

"There are kobalins in the water!" the Ghost Trader's voice called suddenly, even before Jolly had seen him. Munk looked up at the stern of the galleon. The Trader had both hands on the railing and was looking down at them with his robe billowing out. Beneath the open cape Jolly could see the silver ring at his belt. His dark-clad body was sturdier than she'd expected from seeing his gaunt face. A black shirt stretched across his broad chest.

It was a moment before she really took in his words. "Kobalins?" she repeated in alarm.

Munk stood there as if rooted.

"I'd keep moving," said the Ghost Trader. "If you stand still, it may encourage them to attack. Come aboard. You're safe here."

"He's right," said Jolly grimly, grabbing Munk by the hand and pulling him forward.

"Did you see any?" he whispered tonelessly. "Kobalins, I mean."

Her eyes skimmed over the water, but she couldn't see anything suspicious. "No."

"Me neither. Do you think he just wants to scare us?"

"Would he have needed tales of kobalins to do that?"

Silently they crossed the last distance. A ghost who looked just like the flickering workers on the plantation threw them the end of a rope ladder. Jolly climbed up first; Munk agilely followed her.

"Welcome aboard." The Trader came toward them, while the ghost pulled up the ladder. "It was clear to me that you wouldn't come with me if I asked you to."

Munk grew even paler. "Come with you? Where?"

"Away from the island." Regret lay in the man's voice. "And your parents, I'm afraid."

"Never in your life!"

"But that was what you always wanted," said the Trader, and Jolly confessed that she'd had the same idea.

"I'm certainly not just going to go away." Munk turned around and walked back to the railing. Jolly could see the feelings battling in his face, disappointment and also rage. "The ladder!" he cried imperiously to the ghost, but the ghost didn't move. Other ghosts were now wafting over the ship, some from below deck, others from the rigging, where they'd been indistinguishable from shreds of fog.

"All right," said Munk, "then don't."

He made a move toward the railing, but Jolly ran forward and held him back. "Wait. Let's hear what he has to say first."

The Ghost Trader nodded to her and came forward. "Please, Munk, I mean you no harm, and I do not intend to abduct you against your will."

Munk hesitated, cast a quick glance at Jolly, and then pulled his leg back on deck. "What do you want, then?"

"And what kind of a ship is this?" Jolly asked.

"A former slave ship," said the Trader. "The crew let most of the men and women they'd crowded belowdecks starve to death. The ones who stayed alive decided to revolt. So the crew and the slaves mutually annihilated each other, until finally there was no one left alive at all. The ship ran aground just off a small island, where I found it twenty or thirty years later."

Jolly examined him disdainfully. "What you do with the

ghosts is no different from what the slave traders do with their prisoners."

"But I haven't called them up. I only gather in those who wander around restlessly anyway. Basically, they're happy if someone cares about them and gives them occupation." He smiled, but there was concern in the smile and a hint of sorrow. "But it's not about the ghosts now, it's about you. You are both in great danger." His eyes skimmed over Jolly. "Had I known that you're a polliwog . . . it appears I've made a mistake. I've always looked only at the farmer and not at you pirates." After a shake of the head, he continued, "I'll help you. But if you remain on the island, they'll find you. And I fear it won't be long now. The signs are increasing. The winds bring disquiet with them, and there's something in the air that I don't like."

"Who'll find us?" Munk asked.

Jolly took a step toward the Ghost Trader. "The same men who set the trap for the *Maddy*?"

"Worse than them, although they're on the same side," said the one-eyed man. "The Maelstrom is turning again. And he hunts for servants who carry out his will with every fiber of their bodies."

Jolly and Munk exchanged a look. Maelstrom? Servants? What was he talking about?

"You'll soon understand some of this if I can persuade you to come away from here with—"

A smack interrupted him.

All three whirled around. At first Jolly didn't see what had made the noise. But then her eye fell on something lying on the deck, only a few feet away.

A dead fish.

"Where did that—"

Again the same noise. And again. Jolly saw a fish body drop from above, crash through a ghost, and shred it to fog before the body reassembled itself just as quickly.

"Damn it!" swore the Ghost Trader.

"What is it?" Jolly poked her toe against the fish that lay closest to her.

Now other dead fish were hailing down onto the deck. One grazed her shoulder; she avoided another just before it could hit her in the face.

As if from nowhere, a regular rain of dead fish poured from the cloudless sky.

"The breath of the Maelstrom," murmured the Ghost Trader, staring tensely into the wall of fog. "There's something here."

From a distance there came the sound of a primitive shriek.

The Trader's eyes narrowed. "The Acherus. They've sent out the Acherus!"

Munk was jumping with agitation. "Where did that come from?"

Jolly bent over the railing as if she could better gauge the direction that way. But the shriek echoed and was not repeated a second time.

"Did that come from the island?" Munk's shrill voice was

almost out of control. "Is it . . . is it *on the island*?"

Jolly looked back at the Ghost Trader. She was frightened when she saw how pale he'd become; he looked like one of the beings he dealt in.

"It's at my parents', isn't it?" Munk stared at the Trader, wide-eyed. The man didn't need to reply. His expression was answer enough.

"Munk!" cried Jolly. "Wait!"

But it was too late. With a bound, he leaped over the railing.

Messenger from the Maelstrom

Jolly heard a smothered oath as Munk hit the water. He was lucky he hadn't broken both legs. But as she looked down, she saw him running over the water straight at the fog wall.

"Munk!"

"Jolly," cried the Ghost Trader warningly, "don't do it! The Acherus is no—"

She didn't hear the rest as she swung herself over the railing on one hand and jumped down to the water. She landed on her feet and one hand, cursed loudly and much more distinctly than Munk over the pain in her limbs, and at the same time rushed away.

"Munk, wait! I'm coming with you."

She saw him ahead of her in the fog but caught up with him only when they'd just broken out of the fog again and were running over the open sea toward the distant island as fast as they could.

Several times she grabbed Munk when, in his panic and anxiety, he lost his balance on the rolling waves. But he ran silently on, not looking to the side, only running obdurately toward the island, the gray cone of the mountain over the dark green of the jungle.

Once Jolly looked back over her shoulder and had the impression that the fog was following them. But she didn't worry about it. She thought she knew what Munk was feeling—she'd had similar feelings when she'd had to leave Bannon and the others behind aboard the galleon. It seemed wrong to be unharmed while the people you cared about were in danger of their lives. Just as Munk was unwilling to give up now, she was also unready to accept Bannon's death.

They were now close enough to the shore to see the colorful swarms of birds fluttering over the forest trees. Hundreds, thousands of birds of all species, as if all the feathered creatures on the island had taken flight at once, to now circle around the island with indignant screeching.

Below Jolly's feet something flitted along under the waves, looking blurry and splintered under the shimmering water.

Kobalins!

But they were cowardly, weak ones, who didn't dare grab for their feet—most of them avoided the air and the sunshine. Only the biggest of them were brave enough to stick their claws out of the water. The kobalin in the wreck of the

Maddy must have been a chieftain, one of the leaders of the deep-sea tribes.

Nobody knew much about them. They hadn't been around for that long. But for them to attack men on land was as improbable as an eagle's hunting underwater. And although they could screech and bellow like berserkers, that shriek before was something different: a hundred times louder than any kobalin shriek Jolly had ever heard before now, and a thousand times angrier.

She was gradually running out of breath, while Munk kept racing along with a determination born of fear for his parents. She was also worried, but they would both soon lose their strength if they kept up this pace.

"Munk . . . there's no point if we're . . . completely done in by the time we get to the island . . . that won't help anyone." Whatever had uttered the shriek would easily take on two completely exhausted fourteen-year-olds.

But Munk didn't listen to her.

"Munk, damn it all!" She grabbed him by the shoulder as they ran.

He turned furiously, so angry that she shrank back before him. This wasn't the Munk she'd gotten to know in the past few days. Anger and fear distorted his face, and in his eyes was a determination that sent a shudder down Jolly's back. "It's my parents, Jolly! I'll do what *I* think is right!" His voice showed his exhaustion, but he had himself amazingly well under control.

She wanted to say something, but he was already running

on again, just leaving her standing. Jolly cursed softly and bent over with a stitch in her side, but then she gritted her teeth and followed him. Soon they were running even faster.

The shriek came a second time, and this time the bird swarm exploded over the island in all directions, like a shimmering fountain. Shots sounded, one after the other, then, after a pause, a third.

Jolly looked over at Munk, but his face was frozen. Sweat beaded his forehead and cheeks, his neck glistened, but he ran onward like a ship under full sail that nothing and no one could stop.

They rounded the reefs, crossed the shallow semicircle of the bay, and finally stumbled onto land. When Munk's feet touched the ground, he stood still for a moment. All over the beach lay dead fish, strewn around like seed that a giant had thrown on the island in passing. The corpses had already begun to decay in the sun, and their stench hung over the island like a bell jar.

The stink of death. In spite of the heat and her exhaustion, Jolly began to shiver. Her arms were covered with sweat and with gooseflesh at the same time.

Munk closed his eyes for a couple of seconds.

"You can't help them . . . if you . . . kill yourself," Jolly gasped. "We have to find out *what* it is, first. . . ."

"Yes," he said grimly. "By looking at it."

And he ran again, up to the edge of the jungle and soon through the muggy shade of the trees. Jolly's breath rattled when she inhaled. She had drawn her narrow dagger, which she'd worn since the attack on the alleged Spanish ship; now it looked ridiculous against whatever it was that she pictured from the sound of that shriek.

They stumbled through the dense underbrush—and suddenly were standing in a narrow, extended clearing.

A strangled sound escaped Munk.

Something had mowed down the jungle around them. House-high mahogany trunks were broken in two or uprooted, giant ferns and hibiscus bushes completely ground up. And over all lay a carpet of dead fish.

In the sky the birds were screaming so loudly that it hurt Jolly's ears.

"They're all still in the air," she said softly.

Munk looked at her. "What do you mean?"

"They aren't coming back down. Not even to eat the fish. And they're screaming with excitement. That means that—"

Munk's lips were bloodless. "That it's still here."

They ran together now, following the path of the destruction. Soon it was clear even to Jolly where it was leading.

Something had broken through the palisade fence as easily as through a straw wall. Sharpened tree trunks lay strewn in all directions. Some had been slung with such force that they'd bored into the ground like oversized arrows and now stood upright like heathen totems of some island tribe.

"Mum! Dad!" Munk leaped over the debris and ran up to the destroyed house.

The roof over the veranda had been torn away in one piece and was lying a few yards away in the brown grass. The

table and the chairs on which they'd sat that morning were mashed as if by a giant fist.

The door of the farmhouse was gone. And with it a piece of the front wall.

"Mum!"

Jolly tore through the ruin and saw Munk fall on his knees beside his mother's lifeless body. Tears streamed down his face. Jolly stood helplessly beside him and considered what she should do, how she could help. Finally she let herself down on the other side of the woman, took her hand, and with trembling fingers felt for a pulse.

"She's alive!" she burst out a moment later. "Munk, your mother's alive!"

He looked at her through a veil of tears, then back into his mother's face, stroked her cheeks, and blotted her scratches and cuts with his sleeve.

"I have to find Dad!" Reluctantly he detached himself from his mother and jumped up. "You stay with her."

"Munk, it's too dangerous out there!"

"I have to look for him."

"Then let me come too."

He shook his head and ran off. A moment later he'd disappeared. She heard wood snapping as he leaped over tree trunks and broken boards; then the only noise was the screaming of the birds that would not end.

Shattered and at a loss, she knelt there, holding the unconscious woman's hand, trying to sort out her thoughts, to somehow find a meaning in all this. She found none. Instead,

she stood up, selected one of the still-whole jugs, and hurriedly got water from the kitchen. She sponged Munk's mother's face with it and, as well as she could, washed the crusted blood from her face and neck and then opened her torn dress.

The wound beneath the dress was horrible. For reasons Jolly didn't understand, it had hardly bled—neither Munk nor Jolly had noticed it before. And yet one look was enough to tell her that no one could survive with such an injury.

Munk's mother would die. No matter what Jolly did and how she tried to treat the wound, it was hopeless.

Now she began to cry uncontrollably, torn by the wish to stay with the dying woman and the urge to follow Munk and stand by him. She hated herself for her helplessness. Very gradually, she realized that none of this would have happened if she hadn't been washed onto the shore of this island; if she'd remained with Bannon and the others; if she hadn't led the destruction that was pursuing the polliwogs here.

The shriek sounded a third time, and this time it was so loud that the ruins of the farmhouse vibrated; single boards broke out of the upright supports and clattered to the floor.

"Munk!"

Gently she laid the woman's head on the ground, gave her a last sorrowful look, then ran.

Behind the house a broad track of destruction led into the jungle, a chaos of burst palisades and split trees. Jolly leaped and stumbled over the torn-up bush and for the first time

forgot her exhaustion and the pain that was tormenting every part of her body.

The path led through the rain forest to one of the tobacco fields, in a clearing a hundred yards behind the house.

There she saw Munk again. Saw the motionless body of his father on the ground. And became witness to a struggle that she could not have painted even in her nightmares.

Like biting dogs, the plantation's ghosts were hanging onto something that was too huge and too horrible for Jolly to be able to take in with one look. Munk was standing beside his dead father with arms widespread, as from his core flowed a power that compelled the ghosts to obey his commands—and into a hopeless battle with the Acherus.

Jolly was still about twenty steps away when the creature again uttered a long, drawn-out shriek, shredded the ghosts with a slash of its claws, and howled again when the vaporous beings reassembled themselves and renewed their attack. But it was becoming clear that the ghosts' efforts were merely delaying the monstrous figure without really weakening him.

The Acherus might possibly have been human once. At least he was humanlike, even though his body was assembled from the detritus of the ocean: black slime, mats of rotten algae, and moldy nets of seaweed, through which protruded hundreds of brighter needle points, the skeletons of sea animals. Mournful rotted fish eyes stared out of the stinking body all over, but it was impossible to say if the Acherus could see with them. He reeked of death, and as he turned around in his battle against the ghosts, Jolly saw the rib cage of a decomposed shipwreck victim curving out of his back like pale fingers. The Acherus had sucked them all up or been created out of their remains; perhaps he hadn't been *one* human but many, assembled from corpses and the cadavers of fish, kraken, and man-eating sharks.

"Munk, back!"

Jolly stormed up to him when she realized that he didn't see the creature's attack coming—in his concentration, he was keeping his eyes closed. She stepped over the body of his father and tried not to look at it. But even out of the corner of her eye she knew that the man must be dead: The wounds the Acherus had inflicted on him were too gruesome.

She just succeeded in pulling Munk back by the shoulder as the claws of the corpse creature shot forward to grab him. A claw as long as a saber and just as sharp stabbed into emptiness, then fastened on a ghost, which was cut in two but immediately put itself back together.

"Out of here!" Jolly bellowed, but Munk turned in her grip and tried to go back to engage the beast. That was no longer courage, it was madness! Jolly screamed at him, shook him, and finally brought him to his senses.

Together they ran. As they ran, Jolly snatched up the double-barreled pistol from Munk's father. One hammer was snapped shut but the other was still loaded.

They ran along the lane and heard the Acherus thundering behind them. Jolly looked over her shoulder: The creature, as tall as the trees and nimble as a panther, had taken up the chase on two disproportionate legs. The ghosts were hanging all over the Acherus's body, and he was pulling them along behind him like a trail of fog. The ground trembled under his every step, the birds screamed in the air, and all around them the leaves rustled from the trees, shaken loose by the powerful thumping on the earth. Again they rushed away with daredevil leaps over vines and roots.

"Not down there!" screamed Munk suddenly. "Otherwise we'll lead him back to Mum."

At his side, Jolly turned to the left through the undestroyed undergrowth of the jungle. They were smaller than the creature and could move better than he could through the tangled undergrowth; on the other hand, the Acherus had demonstrated that he could easily mow down the forest. Nevertheless, Jolly hoped that at least his ferocious speed would be braked.

"Where?" she gasped out.

Munk didn't answer.

"To the water, then," she decided without hesitation.

"But he comes from there! You saw that!"

"*Out* of the water," she cried. "But we run *on* the water." She was as little convinced by her plan as he was, but it was the only way out that occurred to her.

"I need time," Munk panted, as they broke through a wall of fern and fleshy leaves. "Then maybe I can make the ghosts stronger."

"Stronger?"

"I just sicced them on him. But they couldn't fight if

someone didn't tell them how. Before, they only had to pick leaves. If I had time to give them orders—"

Behind them came an ear-shattering din as the Acherus left the track and followed them through the jungle with brute force. The breaking of the tree trunks reminded Jolly of the bursting of hulls of sinking ships. During a sea battle once, she'd seen two out-of-control galleons ram into each other; it was the same power, there'd been the same murderous noise, just as final and just as hopeless.

Munk panted in anguish. "If we can get across enough water, maybe that'll give me enough time."

Jolly had a dark recollection of the kobalins in the waves, but she nodded hurriedly. After all, they'd made it to the island without any of the kobalins attacking last time. But if not . . . well, it didn't matter if they fell into the clutches of the deep-sea tribe or the Acherus.

Something fluttered past her face—two black, winged silhouettes against the sunbeams that fanned down through the jungle ceiling,

"Hugh!" exclaimed Munk. "And Moe!"

Jolly also recognized the Ghost Trader's parrots. Was he following them and already right nearby?

"There—they're showing us the way!" Munk turned around the dead root of a forest giant, which might possibly be wide enough to halt the Acherus.

What way? Jolly would have loved to ask, but she had no chance to.

The Acherus broke through the trees immediately behind

them. Several trunks shattered and tipped in their direction, catching others with them and causing such chaos around the beast that he was invisible for another moment.

Jolly shouted a warning and tried to run faster, although it was as good as impossible. It was hard enough to avoid the vines and roots, to keep from stumbling over bushes or stepping into hidden holes in the ground under fern fronds.

She was at the end of her strength and hardly able to get her breath, compounded with fear that any moment she would feel one of the saber claws boring into her back.

Hugh and Moe had fluttered up at the appearance of the Acherus and now made a loop and flew toward the cadaverous beast. What the birds intended to accomplish was a mystery to Jolly—but she had no time to worry about the two of them, for now the undergrowth was thinning ahead of her and Munk, the ground became sandier, and soon they were running as hard as they could through a thin palm grove. On the other side of it, within sight now, lay a beach. The broad strip of sand glittered golden in the afternoon heat.

Jolly cast a glance over her shoulder. The parrots were flying on both sides of the Acherus, at the height of his deformed head, which God knew what power had created out of mud, algae, and human bones. The birds were screaming and chattering angrily, and it seemed to Jolly that something they were doing was slowing the Acherus. He didn't stop, was still incredibly fast, but his body had lost its deadly momentum; now he even avoided palms instead of uprooting them.

Jolly whirled around and raised the pistol. She aimed at the beast's head, pressed the trigger—and hit him. But the shot had no effect. The bullet was swallowed into the dark mass without halting the Acherus. With an oath, Jolly flung the useless weapon away.

Munk coughed with exhaustion and gasped for air. "Not much farther."

They left the striped shade of the palm grove and stumbled out onto the beach. The soft sand slowed their run, but somehow they succeeded in reaching the water. Jolly kept an eye out for kobalins—and instead she saw the cloud bank, which was just pushing against one of the rocks in front of the island. So the Ghost Trader wasn't onshore yet.

The water was much deeper here than in the shallow bay. They'd left the rain forest a long way farther east, a good five minutes' walk back to the bay on foot. On a rise in the distance Jolly recognized two tall palms: She'd shot off the third a few days before with her cannon shot.

They hastened over the waves with wide, staggering steps. Soon they had around fifty yards between them and the beach.

Jolly stopped. If they couldn't escape the Acherus now, they'd never manage to at all.

Munk stopped beside her. He pressed both hands into his sides, panting so loudly that he drowned out the crashing of the beast, which just then broke out between the outer palms, not halted but markedly slowed by the spells of the two parrots. The ghosts were still sticking to the creature's deformed body like misty burrs.

The weariness in Munk's face changed to determination. "Now, we'll just see who's stronger," he whispered. He was obviously having trouble staying on his feet, and if Jolly's own weak knees were any gauge of his exhaustion, he wouldn't be able to stand much longer.

But he was still holding on.

The Acherus had stopped on the beach and was staring over at them from hundreds of blind fish eyes, a grim figure, as tall as four men, with knotty limbs and too many joints. He looked as if someone had piled him up there out of muck and refuse, a repugnant caricature of human life.

He seemed to be considering. He no longer paid any attention to the ghosts, which were still clinging to him. The parrots left him and flew over the water to Jolly and Munk.

"Bastard!" Munk murmured, and then he concentrated.

Again he closed his eyes, spread his arms, and whispered his orders to the ghosts with quivering lips, without a sound coming from his throat. Jolly wondered whether anyone could have done that or whether it required the Ghost Trader's special magic to transfer the power of command over the ghosts to other people.

The Acherus put one foot into the water.

"He's coming!" Helplessly, Jolly clenched her fists and bounced up and down on the waves. "You've got to hurry." It was probably a mistake to press him, but her panic was rising again and overshadowed any reason.

Not allowing himself to be distracted, Munk continued

to give his silent orders. His eyelids twitched, his hair stuck to his sweaty forehead. Jolly's felt no better.

Now the Acherus had waded up to his knees in the sea. Anyway, he couldn't walk on top of the water like the two polliwogs. Would he swim to them? Or push up at them from the bottom of the sea?

The Acherus kept on coming. And now there was movement in the seething mass of ghosts on his shoulders, on his chest, and on his back. Jolly was too far away to be able to make out the details, but she thought she saw the misty beings drilling their arms into the rotten body like blades. No longer were they content with dragging on it—now they went on the offensive. Munk's orders were taking effect.

The Acherus's scream pierced Jolly to the quick. Even the waves rose higher. They made Jolly and Munk almost lose their balance.

Munk's eyes snapped open. "Spirits can determine when and where they become solid to pick something up or carry it. . . . I ordered them to go inside the Acherus and then become solid bodies."

What happened to the creature next was not a pretty sight. The ghosts vanished inside his massive interior, which swelled more and more as more of them took on solidity. They were now no longer wisps of mist but bodies of . . . yes, what? Flesh and blood?

It was only a matter of seconds before the mass burst the limits of his body.

Jolly averted her eyes as the screams of the beast died

away. When she looked back at the shore, the ghosts were scattering. A viscous carpet of black muck and algae was floating on the waves. A horrific smell wafted across the water and made Jolly gag.

The parrots flew away over their heads, farther out over the sea. Jolly reeled as though she'd been stunned.

Arms of fog reached for her, but they couldn't stop Jolly from falling forward, landing feebly on all fours, and vomiting with exhaustion. Out of the corner of her eye she saw Munk crouching; he was even more done in than she was.

Hugh and Moe uttered shrill screams as they plunged into the fog.

Then there was only milky white around Jolly, too, as if the air had frozen to ice in an instant.

"She will die." The Ghost Trader sat on the edge of the bed on which they'd laid Munk's mother. "She has already forgotten that she's still alive."

Munk didn't break down. He didn't even cry. His face was as hard as glass. "There must still be something that could be done."

The Trader shook his head under his hood.

Munk was silent. Jolly put her hand over his. His fingers were ice-cold. She had infinite sympathy for him. She felt the tears rush to her eyes and wasn't ashamed when they rolled down her cheeks.

"There is one thing I can do for her," said the Trader.

Munk's expression became colder, and his voice could have

cut steel. "Do you want to make her into one of your ghosts?"

"I am speaking of something better. Something good." He paused a moment, then added, "Something she deserves."

"What do you mean?" asked Jolly. She didn't care if she sounded rude. After all they'd gone through, politeness had become meaningless.

"I can give her another kind of life. One that never ends." The Ghost Trader lowered his voice to a piercing whisper. "A life as *story*."

"And what does that mean?" Jolly remained mistrustful, while Munk only continued to look silently at his mother.

"She will live on, not as human, not in a body, but as something that people continue to recount, from one generation to the next." He leaned forward and smoothed a strand of hair away from the dying woman's face. "I can make her into a legend, a most beautiful fairy tale, or a new myth."

Shaking her head, Jolly looked at the floor, but out of consideration for Munk, she kept quiet.

"Munk?" The Ghost Trader touched him on the arm. "I will only do it if you agree."

The boy gazed at his mother's face as he held her bloodless hands. They'd bound up her wounds, but as they did so, it was clear to them that it wouldn't save her. She was already in deep unconsciousness, and her breathing paused more and more often.

"Munk," said the Trader urgently, "I can do it only as long as there is still life in her."

Jolly pressed her lips together. She didn't know what advice she could give Munk, and if he'd want it anyway. She didn't trust the Ghost Trader, despite the help of his two birds. However, she couldn't rule out the possibility that he was speaking the truth.

"Do what you can," Munk whispered, without raising his eyes from his mother. Now his eyes filled with tears, but his tone was so hard and determined that it gave Jolly gooseflesh.

The Ghost Trader nodded. "You can hold her hand if you like."

Munk bent over, embraced his mother one last time, and whispered something into her ear. When he sat up again, her cheeks were wet with his tears.

Something in the Ghost Trader's face melted, as if from beneath his face another suddenly came into view. The many lines that radiated from around his eyes and the corners of his mouth smoothed, but it didn't make him look younger—only more unblemished, more superhuman. His one eye gleamed, as if it had turned into polished marble. He whole face radiated power.

"I make you into a story," he said softly to the dying woman, as if she could understand each of his words. "You will be a story in which young girls meet powerful magicians and poor wretches meet brave princesses. In which fate turns sometimes in one direction, sometimes another, and thereby the progress of a world is decided. In which doors are in places where no one looked for them, and windows everywhere. And in which the old gods wander over the earth, just as they still occasionally do today."

Munk's mother took her last breath. Then the air escaped from her in a gentle sigh, and it came to Jolly in a flash that they had all become part of that story the Ghost Trader had just conjured up: As if they were also legendary heroes, of whom people would be telling in centuries to come; as if there were also in her own life a goal of which she had never dreamed but that unavoidably awaited her just over the horizon.

"She will live on from mouth to mouth," said the Ghost Trader, "and one day someone may even write about her, so that she will never be forgotten."

He stroked the dead woman's hair one last time. "Fare well and give solace and happiness and sorrow. Fare well and truly forever."

With these words, he got up and left the house.

Jolly looked from the dead woman to Munk. He folded his mother's hands on her breast.

"We'll bury them together," he said in a cracked voice. "Both in one grave. They wanted it that way."

Sea of Darkness

The very same night, the Ghost Trader summoned Jolly and Munk to him. They'd returned to the ghost ship several hours before and put out to sea immediately after their arrival. Now the fog and ship were gliding through the darkness.

Jolly was burning with a multitude of questions, but she sensed that the Ghost Trader wouldn't let himself be hurried. For the time being, it was enough that he'd agreed to take her back to her own world, to New Providence, where she could forget her experiences on the island and begin her investigation into Bannon's fate. New Providence had also been Bannon's original goal. In addition, it was the headquarters of the pirate emperor, Kendrick, and if anyone were to know something about betrayal of the *Maddy,* it would be the leader of the freebooters and corsairs.

The Ghost Trader was sitting on one of the steps leading

up to the bridge, just beside one of the swaying oil lanterns. At each movement of the ship, the lantern swung toward his face, then away again, momentarily bathing his angular features in glowing firelight. The eyes of the parrots on his shoulder gleamed like semiprecious stones.

On both sides of the railing there was impenetrable darkness. The fog ring around the ship made the night even darker, swathing them in deep, saturated black. Only high over the masts, in a round cutout of the night sky, did the stars show themselves. Even they seemed farther away than usual.

Except for the creaking of the timbers and the moaning of the rickety rigging, there was utter quiet, with even the splashing of the wake silenced. The fog seemed to bear the ship through the night on a cloud; they hardly felt that it was moving forward.

Munk had said scarcely a word since they'd left the island. His tears had dried, but he was only externally contained. His eyes were staring into the dark night, and even when the Ghost Trader began to speak, Munk didn't turn toward him.

"The Acherus," said the one-eyed man, "is a creature of the Mare Tenebrosum. Few have ever seen one like him, and if they have, it was a long, long time ago, when the powers of the Maelstrom tried to take over the world once before."

"What's that—Mare Tenebrosum?" Jolly asked.

"Sea of Darkness. Sometimes it shows up in places where no one expects it. Then there's foul weather where none should be, ships are wrecked, although there are no reefs or sandbars, and always men are killed then, swallowed by something that is infinitely deeper than the craters of burned-out volcanoes on the bottom of the sea and blacker than all the places to which no light reaches. The Mare Tenebrosum is a sea that knows no borders, in which there is no land, and whose creatures cannot be compared with any that show themselves here among us."

Jolly and Munk exchanged a mystified look. "Here among us?" Jolly asked. "So is this sea you're talking about somewhere else?"

The Ghost Trader nodded. "In a place that, normally, none of us can reach, in a world that lies directly below ours. It's separated from us by boundaries that neither ordinary mortals nor even the gods can cross. At least, not the gods of *this* world."

"And what about the gods from that one?" Munk asked coldly.

To Jolly, who believed neither in one god nor several, this question seemed strange. But perhaps Munk was only trying to distract himself from his grief. She thought that was very brave. When she thought of Bannon and the others, she was pierced by a powerful stab of grief, followed by a moment of deep despair. Nevertheless, she still had the hope of finding the men sometime. Or at least the traitor who'd lured them into the treacherous trap. When the loss hurt too much, she could cling to this hope. Munk, on the other hand, had buried his parents with his own hands. He would never see them again.

"I don't know if it's gods or mortals who come over from

the Mare Tenebrosum," said the Ghost Trader. "Breaches in the wall between the worlds have occurred in times past, though only very rarely. Then a bit of the Mare Tenebrosum sloshes over to us, like spillage from an overfilled kettle. Those are the unexplained disasters on the high seas you sometimes hear of and that I mentioned: the vanished ships, the terrible hurricanes and floods, the black fogs on the water from which no one returns. Usually, these breaches close so quickly that nothing living can get through them to us."

"But the Acherus is something living. Or at least something comparable," said Jolly.

The Ghost Trader nodded sadly. "You're right. The powers of the Mare Tenebrosum don't intend to be content with the water any longer. They now want to conquer land as well—land that does not exist in their world. They've created a doorway into our world: a powerful maelstrom, larger than anything you can imagine, several miles wide at its broadest place and as deep as the bottom of the sea. A maelstrom with a sharp, dark intelligence."

He paused to allow the picture evoked by his words to sink in. "When it opens—and I pray that it hasn't gotten so far yet—it will mercilessly suck everything in its path into the abyss, into the darkness of its world. Yet, at the moment, it has changed direction and spewed harbingers out of the deep to us in the daylight, sometimes fish and monsters and sometimes creatures—"

"Like the Acherus," said Jolly dully.

"Indeed."

"Why did he . . . ," Munk began, groaned, and was silent for a moment. Finally he got his feelings under control. "Why did he kill my parents?"

"He wasn't after them," said the Ghost Trader, and then he spoke Jolly's fear, "but after you."

"But why?"

"Can't you guess?"

"Because we're polliwogs," Jolly blurted without stopping to think about it.

The Ghost Trader nodded.

Munk's eyes narrowed with anger. "But what does he want from us? Why did he want to kill us?"

For a while no one said anything. The oil lantern swayed back and forth and with each movement illuminated the Ghost Trader's features before they disappeared into darkness again. Light, dark. Light, dark.

"I'm not sure if he really wanted to kill you," he said finally.

"What else?" Jolly asked. "Abduct us?"

"Possibly."

She wasn't satisfied with this answer, just as she viewed most of the Ghost Trader's explanations with skepticism. Perhaps he was telling the truth. But was that really all he knew? She didn't believe that for a moment. And did he really only intend to protect them from this maelstrom? Or was there more behind it? His airs of mystery made her angry, and she grew even angrier because he made it so clear that he thought they were dumb children who could be put off with a few hints.

She looked at Munk and realized he was thinking the same thing.

"That isn't everything," she said, turning to the Trader. "We have a right to—"

"To the truth?" the man interrupted her. "The Mare Tenebrosum is the truth. Just like the Maelstrom and the Acherus."

Munk's eyes narrowed. "Who are you, really?"

"Only one who sells the souls of others." That sounded so ambiguous that Jolly would have liked to take him by the shoulders and shake him. Selling ghosts was one thing; the souls of the living, another. Had they lost their own souls long since, just because they'd gotten mixed up with him?

"Tell us everything," she demanded. "Everything you know."

The Ghost Trader turned his eye away and looked straight into the glow of the swaying lantern. As if at a silent command, the parrots' eyes also followed this movement.

Munk's voice broke the silence like a thunderbolt, although his words were very softly spoken, almost whispered. "My parents are dead. What price did *you* pay for your knowledge, Trader?"

Jolly's stomach contracted. It wasn't long ago that Munk had called the Ghost Trader his friend. But now he appeared to be blaming him entirely for what had happened. The excited, exuberant boy Jolly had come to know had changed. He was more serious, more withdrawn, almost a little weird.

"This knowledge is dangerous," said the Trader, "and anyone

who possesses it has paid dearly for it. One through loss, another through responsibility, and some even through the guilt they must take upon themselves. It is always painful to cross a threshold. New experiences rarely come as gifts."

"New experiences?" Jolly's voice had the crack of a slap on the face. "It strikes me that a heap of experiences in the last few hours are ones I'd have preferred to avoid."

Munk didn't move.

"I would only bring you into greater danger if I initiated you into everything." The Ghost Trader stood up. "There will come a time when you will understand everything. But not here, not tonight. The Mare Tenebrosum is closer than we all guessed. The Maelstrom is turning. It isn't good to speak too long about these things without knowing how far his senses reach." The Ghost Trader passed between them as he left, his black robe grazing Jolly's cheek like an icy wind. "Go to your berths. Rest as long as you can."

Munk's eyes shot sparks, but he continued to sit there. Jolly, on the other hand, couldn't contain her anger. She jumped up and grabbed the Ghost Trader by the arm. She withdrew her hand immediately, but nevertheless, one of the parrots struck at her furiously with its wings. The other uttered a shrill scream that hurt her ears.

"Shhh," the Ghost Trader said soothingly to the birds. He stopped, but he didn't turn around to Jolly and Munk. His back rose in front of them like the tower of a dark cathedral.

"I'm sorry," he said, "and that's the truth. I'm not the cause of what has happened, but I ought to have foreseen it."

Now he did turn around, but his voice grew fainter, as if it were lost in the shadows of his hood. "Things have occurred that we might perhaps have been able to prevent. The Maelstrom is awake. And the polliwogs have gained importance much earlier than we all hoped."

Hugh emitted a sharp hiss in Jolly's direction, but the Trader soothed him by stroking his black plumage.

"Loss, responsibility, and guilt," he said once more. "Each pays in his own way, believe me."

Then he left them there and went below.

Jolly stared after him as if she could draw him back outside with her gaze alone. When, still angry, she turned to Munk, he surprised her with his astonishingly calm eyes.

"You don't know him," he said. "He's always like that."

"Do *you* know him, then?"

He hesitated. "Anyhow, I've heard him speak that way before. He's just like that."

She snorted angrily, then let herself down opposite Munk, sitting cross-legged on the deck. "I wonder why he agreed."

"To what?"

"To take me . . . us to New Providence. Certainly not just to do me a favor. He doesn't care anything about Bannon."

"Perhaps there's something there he's interested in himself?"

"He keeps saying he doesn't want to bring us into danger—and then he simply agrees to head for an island that could be attacked by the Spanish armada any day? And what's all this talk about gods and guilt and responsibility and all that stuff supposed to mean?"

Munk shrugged, then stretched out his arm and took her hand. "Whatever happens—let's stay together, okay?"

It sounded like a request, but wasn't there also a trace of demand in his tone?

"I want to go back to the pirates," she said firmly. "And I'm going to find Bannon and the others, that I swear. All this nonsense about the Mare Tenebrosum and some sort of maelstrom . . . that's no concern of mine."

"Jolly! If that brute that killed my parents—if he really was sent by this Maelstrom, then I have to know more about it. Then I have to know *everything* about it." His eyes blazed.

Jolly laid her other hand on his. They'd both suffered a loss, and they were alone in their grief. Perhaps it would actually be simpler if they acted together. But did she really want to be part of his revenge? And besides, how realistic was it for a fourteen-year-old boy to take on powers like the Mare Tenebrosum?

God, how realistic was it to go find Bannon and the others again?

Deciding quickly, she increased the pressure of her hand. "If I manage to find out something—about Captain Bannon, I mean—then I'll help you afterward."

Munk looked at her and nodded.

Silently they made a pact whose consequences neither could evaluate. But it seemed the right thing to do.

They remained on deck and curled up together on the planking to sleep. Neither one had any desire to become familiar with the interior of the former slave ship. Even out here, the atmosphere was oppressive and creepy; below deck the closeness and darkness would certainly rob them of breath.

At some point Jolly fell asleep, although in the morning it seemed to her that she'd had hardly any rest that night. She was weary, as if nightmares had snatched her from sleep, even if she couldn't remember any of them. Nevertheless, the feeling remained: During the night, she'd been visited by things she didn't want to know about.

Almost the same as the reality. She hadn't asked to be snatched from her familiar surroundings into this nightmare.

"The polliwogs have gained importance" she heard the Ghost Trader's voice saying again and again. And each time, the phrase seemed more ominous to her.

Gradually, the morning light penetrated the fog ring around the ghost ship. The shadows lost their depth only when the blue Caribbean sky was already dazzling in the opening high above them. Like the stars the night before, the sun also now seemed farther away than usual. The outside world seemed to have receded into the infinite distance, which was either the nature of the ghost ship or a consequence of their experiences.

Sorrow lay over the ship like a fog of its own, and Jolly felt in no position to do anything about it.

After she got up, she left Munk sleeping and considered whether she should explore the ship on her own, but she decided against it. Instead, she clambered forward onto the bowsprit, letting herself down onto it like a rider on a horse and remembering sadly how often she had done the e thing aboard the *Skinny Maddy,* which was now lying ewhere on the bottom in the depths of the sea.

'ccasionally she looked over her shoulder and saw Munk distance away, kneeling on the deck and frowning. He'd d all his mussels out in front of him and was forming a tude of patterns with them. Sometimes he made a ng pearl rise over the empty shells, but it would imme- y close itself inside one of the mussels again. Whatever s trying to do—perhaps strengthen the wind for a sail, ps something that took away his grief—he seemed not having any success with it.

Ghost Trader didn't appear again until early after- . He placed a hand on the mainmast and closed his eyes. r a while, Jolly realized that he was having a dialogue h the ghost in the crow's nest in this fashion.

He moved his lips, just as a cool gust of wind carried the words to Jolly's ears.

"We're there," he said. "The island ahead of us is New Providence."

She strained to see ahead, but she saw nothing but muffling fog. Sometimes it seemed to her that the billows formed into fuzzy forms, into faces, into entire scenes.

New Providence, she thought with relief.

A place almost like a home.

The Pirate City

The pirate emperor declined to receive Jolly.

The inn where he held court was scarcely worthy of the name. Taverns and taprooms lined the narrow streets, but only two or three gave reason to hope that the food might be enjoyable, the rum not watered, and the beds free of vermin.

The Fat Hen lay in the center of what grandiosely called itself a city, although the civilized sound of the word was deceptive for a place like this. Nowhere could one meet so many scoundrels, murderers, cardsharps, and grandiose posturers as on New Providence. And here in Port Nassau, the only developed harbor on the island, was the heart of this pirate kingdom, the pit in which so much scum met each other that white gloves turned black soon after coming in contact with it.

Jolly felt snug and cozy.

She'd grown up on the high seas, but it was places like this where she'd been on land with Bannon now and again. Civilization, for her, was the sight of stinking, narrow lanes, overflowing taverns, and the occasional spectacle of a fist-fight, a stabbing, or even a throat-cutting in the half light of burned-down lanterns.

She knew nothing else. The notion of perfumed palaces, powdered wigs, and uniformed lackeys produced in her the same disgust that would probably have overwhelmed so many Spaniards, Englishmen, or Dutch at the sight of this murderous cesspit.

Port Nassau was her capital and Kendrick was her emperor.

That's what she told the guard standing at the entrance to the Fat Hen and barring her way. The man, a particularly dirty and unattractive individual, was picking his teeth with a knife; he didn't even take the blade out to shake his head. Only when it became clear to him that Jolly wouldn't be shaken off did he stick the knife back into his belt and lean forward.

"I know you, girl." His breath smelled of stale beer and remains of food. "You're the little one from the *Skinny Maddy*. You're a loudmouth and a show-off and a pain in the neck, and you could only get away with it because the great Bannon held his hand over you." His grin exposed teeth the color of curdled milk. "But the *Maddy* has gone down and Bannon's gone to the dogs. As far as I'm concerned, you're only a cheeky brat who deserved a whack on the seat of your pants a long time ago. That's what I think, y'know? Hey, in a few years, if you're still alive, you could turn out to be a pretty good-looking female. Then you can come back and say hello. But until then—be off with you!"

With a self-satisfied smile, he stood up again and yawned loudly; as he did so, he shut his eyes for a moment.

When he opened them again, his dagger lay in Jolly's hand and was pointing at a place a hand's breadth below his belt buckle.

"Kendrick," she said grimly. "Right now!"

"Jolly, quit it," whispered Munk, who was standing directly behind her. "You're going to set the whole pack on our necks."

"Did you want to see pirates or not?"

"Not so *many*."

"You should have considered that before."

Munk sent Jolly a pleading look. They'd come here together.

The Ghost Trader had let them go off alone—right after they'd left the ship—without saying much. But it hadn't been a farewell, and Jolly felt certain that the Trader didn't intend to let them out of his sight except for a short time.

The pirate stared at Jolly's knifepoint, which was poking into his fly. A nervous grin fluttered over his scarred face.

"You're not serious, girl. You aren't as crazy as everyone says, are you?"

"And you're not as dumb, are you?"

He blinked at her as if he still couldn't grasp what had just happened to him: A girl of just fourteen had tricked him and was threatening him with his own knife. Jolly saw how hard his mind was working. If anyone saw it, this embarrassment would be the talk of all Port Nassau in no time.

"What shall I do?" he asked reluctantly. "I can, of course, go in and ask if Kendrick will come out to you."

Jolly tried to ignore Munk, who was hopping nervously from one foot to the other. "Is Kendrick staying here in the inn?"

"Of course. Taken all the rooms, bought all the beer and rum, and paid all the girls. It's sort of like his palace, the Fat Hen."

"And you're sort of like his bodyguard?"

The pirate grinned proudly. "Sure. Me and a few others. One at each door, front and back. But it's clear who's the most important, isn't it?" He gave a mean little laugh. "The one at the entrance, naturally."

Heavens, how could Kendrick rely on such a fool? He seemed to feel very secure here in Port Nassau. No wonder—after all, he'd killed all those who'd supported his murdered predecessor, Scarab, or driven them from the island.

"Good," said Jolly, putting a little pressure on the blade. "If I let you go inside there to tell Kendrick I want to speak with him, will you give me your word that you won't try any rotten tricks? You come out again and without any pistol or saber or anything like that?"

"Word of honor, for sure!" The pirate nodded and noticeably repressed a grin. "It's a good idea, just as you say. A very good idea. You're a clever child. You can rely on me, for sure."

Munk's voice quavered. "You still trust this fellow?"

Jolly paid no attention to him. "Then vanish and do what you promised," she said to the pirate. She threw the dagger into the air, grabbed it adeptly by the point, and flung it purposefully across the street. Vibrating, it stuck in the middle of a window cross. Munk's eyes grew even larger.

Wordlessly the pirate disappeared inside the bar. Noise and stench billowed out as he opened the door and closed it behind him again.

"Are you completely—" Munk was beginning, but he was interrupted as Jolly grabbed his arm and pulled him away with her.

"Out of here! Fast!" she cried, and then together they ran down the street between dirty men and scantily clad women, through several gateways and lanes, which sometimes were knee-deep in garbage. The stink that lay over the entire settlement was horrible, and yet Jolly took hardly any notice of it.

After some minutes, she halted. Munk came to a breathless stop beside her.

"What was that all about?" he asked angrily. His breathing was fast and jerky. "That whole performance could have cost us our necks."

"Quite possibly—if Kendrick catches us. But he won't. He'll certainly have a lot of fun when that moron tells him what happened. And in case the guard and his flea-bitten friends look for us . . . well, we're gone, right?"

"And why do all that?"

"I found out what I wanted to know. Kendrick is hardly guarded. He feels very secure in the Fat Hen." Her grin grew wider. "Bad for him. Good for me."

"You can't be . . . no, you're not that crazy."

Jolly laughed. "I'm going to pay His Majesty a visit tonight. And then I'll find out if he knows anything about the trap for the *Maddy*."

"You're mad!" Munk hit his forehead with his hand and turned in a circle in place. "Completely out of your mind!"

She waved him off. "I grew up among this mob. Kendrick is a bastard and a murderer, but if he knows something, he'll tell me—provided I bring the right arguments with me."

"Not knife-sharp arguments, by chance?"

"Could be."

Munk's suntanned face turned as white as chalk. "You really have lost your mind! That was all too much for you. The shipwreck, the ghosts, the Acherus . . ."

Jolly beamed. "I haven't felt so good for a long time."

"That's what I was afraid of."

"You wanted to have adventures, didn't you?" She gave him an ebullient kiss on the cheek. "Well, now you're right in the middle of them."

Whereas the nameless island on which Munk had lived with his parents lay on the eastern edge of the Bahamas, a last outpost before the gigantic, empty Atlantic, New Providence was in the center of the island group. It was a small island, oval and extending from west to east, with only one harbor on its coast. New Providence was officially an English colony, to be sure, but the officials of the British kingdom earned themselves sumptuous dividends by permitting the pirates and fences there. It was said that the English governor on the island took in—instead of the meager thirty pounds a year his government paid him—a total of forty thousand pounds when he did business with the freebooters and collected part of their take.

So the old fortress of the British colonial masters was enthroned high over Port Nassau and visible from a great distance, but it had been a long time since it had impressed anyone. Kendrick was the true ruler of the island, not the English governor, who seldom showed himself outside the fortress walls and passed his days with high living, with wine and women supplied to him by the pirates.

Port Nassau offered all the pleasures the freebooters could wish. The harbor was deep enough for their sloops and brigantines, but too shallow for the heavy warships of the navy. From the surrounding mountains there was a wide view of the sea, and attackers couldn't approach unseen. In the island's thick forests there was an abundant supply of wood for building new ships, tropical fruit, and wild pigs; not to mention the delicacies to be taken from the ocean in this region, the tasty fish, crabs, and sea turtles.

The place itself was a closely packed collection of shacks and wooden houses, mostly thatched with palm leaves, some only covered with oilskins. Everywhere there were miserable shanties and sheds in which the pirates lodged during their

shore leaves. The traders who booty had settled in an extensive Nassau. The supply of games of chan of pleasure was enormous—they were, booty, the only source of income for the island.

From time to time, danger threatened fr that now and then swept over the Caribbean Se places like Port Nassau within a few hours. But the pirates in their warm nest didn't give up—the everything was built up again in a hurry, the dea buried, and soon everyone was having a good time a enjoying the advantages of pirate life and denying themse nothing at all.

Jolly told Munk all she knew about the island as they sat in the harbor and waited for sundown. Munk had tried several times to talk her out of her plan, but she was determined. When he offered to go with her, she vehemently refused. Not even the prospect of a little helpful mussel magic was able to change her mind.

The Ghost Trader hadn't shown his face since the morning. He hadn't found it necessary to let them in on whom he had to see in Port Nassau, either. He'd merely gotten them to promise to look after each other—whoever had set the trap for Bannon on the high seas might also have spies and henchmen in New Providence.

Although the ghost in the crow's nest had already reported the island on the afternoon of the previous day, the Trader

eferred to spend the night aboard and just out of view e island's mountains. It was only in the first gray of ning that the three had climbed into the small sailboat ed by the ghost ship and thus transferred to the island.

The boat now lay docked in the harbor of Port Nassau, nong a multitude of rowboats and dinghies the freebooters sed to go from their anchored sloops to land—and to one or another captured galleon.

Jolly and Munk were sitting on a couple of empty kegs and boxes not far from the water's edge.

This wasn't an extensively developed harbor like the big cities on Haiti or Jamaica but only a paved beach, along whose edge stood a row of taverns and shacks, interspersed with the tents of the traders. The steady wind from the sea wafted food vapors and stale beer smells inland; in fact, the shore was one of the few places in all of Port Nassau where the smells of the pirate hideaway didn't hit you in the stomach.

Munk's face was gradually getting its color back. Despite the prospect of Jolly's nighttime expedition and his grief over his parents, a smile stole over his face occasionally, and sometimes even a look of outright fascination. Even if the majority of the pirates staggering around drunkenly in front of the taverns were degenerate individuals without worth or standing, there were still some among them who exactly fit Munk's dream image of the noble corsair: men in expensive clothes, with knee-high boots, glittering swords, and feathers waving on their hats.

"Show me your tattoo?" he asked Jolly abruptly, after she'd

been silent for a long time, observing the drunken goings-on by the taverns.

She laughed, and it made her earrings bump each other, jingling. "You want me to undress? Here?"

Munk turned dark red. "I didn't mean it that way. I just thought . . ." He fell silent. "'Scuse me, I'm sorry."

"Oh, never mind." With a wave of her hand, Jolly turned her back to him, still sitting. "Push the shirt and vest up. Then you can see it."

"I should—"

"Don't stand there stuttering, just do what I say."

She felt him put both hands on her waist. Was she deceiving herself, or was he trembling? For heaven's sake, she'd grown up among pirates, a crew of seventy men. Never had there been any personal remarks or suggestive looks—everyone had known he'd have to deal with Bannon personally.

Hesitantly Munk pushed up her linen shirt and vest. She held it in front with both arms crossed, but her back was soon bare.

"What is it?"

"That's supposed to become a coral. Trevino, our cook, had just begun it when the lookout reported the Spanish galleon. It's still not more than a few curlicues and lines, I'm afraid."

"Are you going to leave it that way?"

"Maybe sometime I'll find someone who has enough talent to finish it." She turned around. He quickly pulled his hand back, and shirt and vest slid down again. "But at the moment, to be honest, I don't think about it at all."

"Of course." He was still red, which for the first time since his experiences on the island made him look completely healthy again. A little excitement was much better for him than his dark brooding and meditating aboard the ghost ship. She must get him to think about other things, and now was the best opportunity: no Ghost Trader anywhere around to spread gloom with his doom-filled stories.

"Come," she said, standing up. "We'll go get something to drink."

"You mean . . . alcohol?"

Jolly gave him her most winning grin. "You want to become a pirate."

"Not a *drunken* pirate."

"Well, that's part of it too. You'd better get it behind you early." She herself didn't like rum, and beer was too bitter, but she had now and again had a cup of wine with the pirates. She didn't know if Munk had any experience with it—but if not, it was high time. Lord, this was the Caribbean. Nowhere else were so many rules violated.

Munk's astonishment turned to doubt. "You just want to keep me quiet so I'll let you go tonight."

"You'll do that anyway, Great Magician." She took his hand and pulled him across the beach to the first tavern.

"I don't know if this is a good idea," said Munk.

"Now, don't be a coward."

Jolly was heading for the nearest bar, when its door flew off its hinges with a loud crash, and a tangle of bodies sailed out in a high arc onto the sand. Moaning and groaning came from the bunch of pirates, a curse over a twisted ankle.

Munk would have preferred to turn back, but Jolly stopped enthusiastically. "A fight!"

"Couldn't you watch from a distance just as well?"

Jolly sighed as if he'd said something inconceivably childish. "But then you can't see anything at all!"

"Especially if anything knocks you out—like fists, or heavy objects."

"You are *so* chickenhearted!"

He said nothing more and stayed there beside her while the knot of men untangled itself. Just as the cursing men were about to stand up, another figure sailed through the open door, landed on top of them, and knocked them all to the ground again.

There were more outcries, and then from inside the tavern came the clatter of furniture falling, and a chair followed the last figure out the door—one of the heavy objects of which Munk had spoken. The chair missed the crowd on the ground and landed a yard ahead of Jolly with its back stuck in the sand.

"Had enough?" Munk turned away, ready to leave.

Jolly stayed where she was. Her eyes huge, she was staring at the boy who'd been the last to fly through the door. "*Griffin?* Devil take me—that's Griffin!"

Munk grimaced. "Who?"

Jolly kicked the chair aside and approached the men, who were hurriedly struggling to their feet. The first sought safety in flight as a powerful man walked out of the tavern door into the sunlight. He was bigger than all the others and so broad-shouldered that he had to turn his torso so as not to get stuck in the door frame. He wore black knee breeches and boots, but instead of a waistcoat, he'd put over his shirt a corselet of metal, such as were sometimes found in surrendered Spanish forts. But the most astonishing thing was the iron helmet that covered his entire head. The visor was closed, concealing his face. Knights in the old world had worn helmets like this. Jolly knew that from stories: men like St. George or Lancelot. But a pirate, and furthermore, in the humid Caribbean? That was more than unusual.

Meanwhile, the bunch on the ground had dispersed, leaving only two figures cowering on the sand: the man with the injured ankle and the boy Jolly had recognized.

"Griffin, good Lord . . ."

Munk crossed his arms. "Are you going to tell me who that is?"

"Griffin," she said again. "Just about our age. He grew up on several pirate ships—and was thrown off just as many. He claims he was already a better card player at six or seven than all the pirates together." She smiled. "He's an awful loudmouth. I can't stand him."

Munk regarded her searchingly. "It doesn't look like that to me. At all."

Her smile grew broader. "Looks can be deceiving."

Munk uttered a scornful snort, but now he watched what was going on with newly awakened interest.

The giant in the knight's helmet stomped forward silently. He swept the injured man aside with a single thrust; the man landed a few steps farther down the beach, painfully worked himself to his feet, and limped away, protesting.

Griffin was holding his head dazedly. He was blond, like Munk, but he wove his shoulder-length hair in a dozen small braids, which twirled around his head like snakes when he moved. Slaves from Africa wore their hair this way, but Jolly knew no whites except Griffin who did. His clothing was the usual gaudy outfit of the pirate: knee breeches, boots, shirt, and instead of the waistcoat a blue frock coat of silk, which was mended in several places.

"He has a knife," whispered Munk. "Why doesn't he defend himself with it?"

"This is a fight between honorable men."

"Oh, of course."

"Griffin probably tried to cheat the other one at cards. In fact, I'm sure of it."

"And for that he's going to let himself get killed now?"

Jolly had begun to have the same fear. The giant in the helmet didn't appear to be open to a friendly agreement. His fists were as big as buckets, the backs of his hands covered with dark, bristly hairs.

Griffin was gradually getting his wits together. He hadn't seen Jolly; his eyes were fixedly focused on the giant, who was standing astride him.

"Ehm, Buenaventure . . . really, that was an oversight. A little mischance. You understand, don't you?" A broad grin appeared on Griffin's deeply tanned face. His blue eyes sparkled like the ocean in sunshine. "Come on, you wouldn't do anything to your old pal Griffin? We're friends. It was a fair game, wasn't it? All except for that tiny thing at the end, maybe, but a person can forget something like that pretty quickly, don't you think?"

Buenaventure said nothing, just looked down at the boy through the slit in his helmet.

Griffin shrugged. "Then have it your own way." Immediately he shot his right leg up and kicked as hard as he could at the giant's lower abdomen.

Sympathetic *oohs* and *aahs* went through the crowd of onlookers; some hands involuntarily twitched toward their breeches' laces.

But Buenaventure didn't move. No sound came from beneath the helmet. His fists remained clenched.

Griffin came scratching and scrambling to his feet. He was about to turn and run, when a powerful paw grabbed him by the shoulder. A second closed around his throat.

Jolly gasped. Munk stared spellbound at what was playing out in front of him. He uttered not a sound.

A noise came from under the helmet that didn't sound like words. Buenaventure growled like a fighting dog.

Jolly considered whether there was a chance of helping Griffin. Against Buenaventure he had no chance on his own, that was clear. But Jolly wasn't sure she wanted to take the risk. What she'd said was entirely true: She didn't like Griffin particularly. Sometimes, at least. Now and then.

But next the giant's paws felt into both pockets of Griffin's frock coat, tore them out of their stitching, and seized the gold pieces that were in there. Then he let the boy drop, turned around, and walked away. A lane in the crowd immediately opened to let him through. Moments later, the giant had vanished into a gap between the huts.

Griffin jumped up, grinned at the crowd in embarrassment, murmured something like, "Everything's all right! Nothing happened! I got rid of him!" and hurried away as fast as he could—just in time. For now the other men who'd sailed through the door with him took up the chase, also wanting back the winnings he'd fleeced them of. Amid the shouting and growling of the loitering pirates, Griffin ran, braids flying, along the beach and turned into a narrow street. The others chased after him. Soon the mob vanished from the onlookers' sight. After a while, the angry cries of the pursuers died away too. The crowd dissolved.

Jolly shook her head. "He'll never learn."

Munk eyed her skeptically. "You like him."

"No!"

"Yes, I can see it."

"Poppycock."

"How long have you known each other?"

She sighed. "Half an eternity. He was cook's boy on one of Bannon's ships once—but then the steersman threw him overboard for cheating at cards."

"Just like that? On the high seas?"

Jolly grinned. "Griffin's a good swimmer—by necessity."

She wiped away the memory with a shake of her head. "Come on, we'll go have something to drink."

Resigned to his fate, Munk heaved a sigh, then followed her over the broken door and into the interior of the tavern.

Princess Soledad

Nights on New Providence were brightly lit with lanterns and open campfires. There were shadows only in the narrowest streets, the most secluded corners—and in the rear courtyard of the Fat Hen.

Jolly was balanced over one of the few tile roofs in Port Nassau. The block of houses around the inn lay below the English governor's stronghold and, in contrast to the other parts of the city, consisted of stone buildings, some with two and three stories. The stone district rose out of the sea of palm-thatched roofs and one-storied huts like a fortress, higher and more massive than the rest of the city. In case of attack, passages and gates could be closed, turning the district itself into a small fortress in which Kendrick and his men could entrench themselves.

The tavern's courtyard lay some eighteen feet below Jolly,

a black rectangle from which a back door must lead into the interior of the Fat Hen. But it was too dark down there: Jolly could see neither the door nor the guard who was said to be posted there.

She tried listening, in vain. The only noise came from inside the tavern: the bawling and singing of the revelers, now and again a clatter or a shout, mixed with the screams of the barmaids.

She had no choice but to keep her eyes on the shadows and move hand over hand to one of the windows in the second story. Anyway, the pirate at the entrance seemed to have told the truth. There was only one man down there—any more and they'd have been talking, so she'd have heard whispers at least.

Nevertheless, she didn't like the idea of climbing across the open, steep roof where she might be seen from below by invisible eyes. How long would the guard wait before he sounded the alarm? Until she was in the middle of the roof and utterly unprotected?

Just do it. Go. Now!

She inched forward, seeking for finger- and toeholds between the fragile roof tiles and doing her best to make no sound. The black chasm pulled at her, whispered to her to let go. *You can't do it,* it whispered in her ear, *you haven't a chance!*

She already had half the distance behind her when one of the tiles under her right foot cracked. Jolly froze. Hesitantly she looked down and saw that the clay tile had broken in two.

The lower half had loosened and threatened to slide off the roof as soon as Jolly lifted her foot.

What now? She was stuck if she didn't want to risk alarming the guard in the courtyard with the falling piece of tile.

If there was even a guard there.

But above all, she couldn't wait here until they saw her. She had to go on, one way or the other.

She was just about to move when there was a creaking down in the courtyard. A band of light fell through the darkness; the noise from the inn suddenly became louder.

Someone had opened the back door. Jolly could now see for the first time that she was on the right wall of the house as she was looking at it. A man walked outside, swaying slightly as he walked and holding a beer pitcher in his hand. He stopped, lifted the pitcher, cursed in Italian when he found there was no more beer in it, and swung back to fling it against the wall.

"Hey!" bellowed a voice from the shadows before the man could throw the jug. "Kendrick wants that door to stay closed. I wouldn't be spending the night sitting here otherwise. Go inside, will you! No one has any business out here!"

The pirate in the door uttered another oath, raged at the invisible watcher in the courtyard—and smashed the empty jug angrily against the opposite wall.

Jolly lifted her foot. The half of the roof tile slipped, slid scraping over the edge, and fell. She heard it break on the ground a few heartbeats later than the shattering of the clay jug. She clenched her teeth, squeezing her eyes shut. Held her breath.

In the courtyard below, the door slammed behind the drunken pirate.

The second man, who'd been standing over in the darkness the entire time, was quiet again—in fact, it was hard to tell whether he was still there. He must have heard the crash of the tile but obviously connected the sound with the broken jug—just as Jolly planned. Her heart raced with relief.

Half the roof still lay ahead of her. Anyway, now she knew for sure that someone was in fact in the courtyard. She hadn't been able to see him in the band of light that came through the opened door; he must therefore be on her side of the courtyard, directly beneath her. At least then she was also outside his field of vision.

She shivered. She was lucky the tile hadn't fallen on his head.

Onward!

Even more carefully than before, her hands and feet sought holds on the fragile incline. Somewhere in the distance, in the tangle of streets east of the stone quarter, she could hear the sound of saber blades, wild cries, then a scream. There were peals of laughter, joined by others. Welcome to Port Nassau!

Jolly reached the other end of the slope. Here the roof of the annex met the wall of a building with more floors. It was the upper story of the main house. Somewhere in this part, she guessed, was Kendrick's room.

A last look into the black chasm, then she pressed firmly

Jolly could clearly see the rose-colored remains of the ear pinna.

"You have great trust in your men," said the young woman, and she stretched. "Aren't you worried they can be bribed by the Spaniards?"

"My people are men of honor." Kendrick removed his frock coat and slung it over a trunk. "I can depend on every single one of them . . . like a brother."

For the first time Jolly noticed that Kendrick's voice wavered. He was drunk, although it was said that he hardly touched alcohol—unusual for a pirate. His movements were erratic, his step uncertain.

"Don't you feel well?" purred the girl, baring her knees as if casually.

Good Lord, not that, too, Jolly thought. *Do I really have to watch? That's really revolting.*

Kendrick approached the bed with a crooked grin. "Only a little . . . dizzy. I wonder why. I didn't drink any rum." He stopped for a minute before he planted himself straddle-legged in front of the girl. "If I didn't know better, I'd bet someone had mixed something into my food."

The young woman raised her eyebrows. "Who would dare do something like that?"

The pirate emperor laughed maliciously. "Hah, not one single one! Their hearts all drop to their boots if I so much as look at them crosswise, those cowards."

"No wonder, with such big, strong muscles."

Jolly rolled her eyes.

against a window. It was bolted from the inside. She pulled her dagger, slipped it into the crack, and effortlessly lifted the latch. Silently the window swung inward.

Jolly slipped inside. When her eyes had adjusted to the pale moonlight coming from the opened window, she found herself in a small sleeping chamber. The bed was dirty and tousled; pieces of clothing lay on the floor everywhere. A small, iron-bound chest stood next to the spotty washstand; the chest was secured by a chain to one of the roof beams. Two padlocks were supposed to keep someone from tampering with the pirates' hoard. Jolly surmised that this room belonged to one of Kendrick's close confidants.

The only door had no lock and could be opened easily. Through a crack Jolly looked out into a narrow passageway. There was no one to be seen.

She whisked out, pulled the door closed behind her, and listened. Down below there were steps on the staircase and the voices of a man and a woman. They were both coming nearer.

Jolly gasped, ran to the end of the passageway, and tried another door. She looked into a large room dominated by a four-poster bed with a silk canopy, decorated with a coat of arms in gold and silver. It probably came from the ship of a Spanish or English nobleman. Countless trunks, caskets, and chests stood all around the room, whose floor was covered with several layers of Oriental carpets. There were half a dozen candelabra, besides some wardrobes, some so full of expensive stuffs and articles of clothing that their doors would no longer shut.

Kendrick grinned. "Come, pull off my boots."

He set one foot on the edge of the bed beside the girl. She looked at it for a moment as if hesitating, then grabbed the boot and tried to pull it off.

Kendrick kept laughing, but then he suddenly lost his balance and promptly clattered onto his backside. Dazed, he remained sitting on the floor.

Now! thought Jolly.

She pushed open the wardrobe door, sprang at Kendrick from behind, and pressed her dagger blade against his throat.

"Be quiet!" She sent a threatening look toward the young woman on the bed. "Not a peep and nothing will happen to you."

She was aware how crazy this situation was: a fourteen-year-old girl threatening the emperor of the Caribbean pirates and at the same time trying to hold a grown woman in check.

Kendrick tried to spring up, but Jolly brought the knife blade ever tighter against his throat until his resistance flagged.

"Who are you?" asked the pirate. "Do I know you?"

"Jolly," she said. "We've met a few times. I belong to Bannon's crew."

"Jolly . . . of course. The little polliwog. Damn it, girl, stop this nonsense or I'll throw you to my dogs."

"To the ones with four legs or two?"

"What do you want?"

"Only for you to take the wax out of your ears . . . oh,

well, the one ear, anyway." That slipped out before she could stop it. She hadn't come to make fun of Kendrick.

The young woman sat on the edge of the bed and didn't move. She didn't act the least bit frightened, more astonished.

"I'd let you go," Jolly said to her, "if I were sure you wouldn't alarm the entire pigpen downstairs right away."

A smile stole across the woman's face. She really was stunningly beautiful, in spite of the small scar that ran down her left cheek. But then her expression suddenly turned serious, almost angry. Still she kept silent, listened, and watched.

"Take the damned knife away!" said Kendrick. "I'll have you strung up on the highest gallows in the city. I'll single-handedly skin you and feed you to the animals. Your innards will—"

"Yes, yes, yes," said Jolly, but secretly she shuddered. "Let's get down to business."

"What business?"

"I need your help."

"And are you sure this is the best way to get it?" He sounded clearer now, as if the shock had diminished his stupefaction.

"Your life for your help, Kendrick. That's the deal. I want your word." She wasn't sure if Kendrick's word of honor was worth a tinker's damn, but she had to begin somehow. "Do you know what happened to Bannon?"

"The *Maddy* sank," he said. "Everyone's talking about it. The Spanish killed him and his crew or took them prisoner, no one knows precisely. Why weren't you with him?"

"Those weren't any Spaniards," said Jolly, without answering his question. "You're powerful enough to find out the truth. You have ships you can send to look for Bannon."

He laughed grimly. "You're asking that of me? That I have Bannon searched for?"

"That's why I'm here."

"You could have spared yourself the trouble, girl. No one found any wreckage or bodies."

Jolly remembered the poison spiders, but she threw the thought away again immediately. She mustn't weaken now. After all, Kendrick himself had said it—no one had found the bodies.

"Then look for proof."

"I'll be damned if I will."

The blade bit into his skin. A drop of blood beaded on the steel. But Kendrick tried once again to shake Jolly off—in vain.

"Good God," sighed the young woman suddenly. "Shall I show you how to do that right?" She balled her right hand into a fist, looked at the white knuckles for a moment—then sprang like lightning and hit Kendrick in the face with all her might.

She grinned when Kendrick collapsed with a groan. "*That's* how it's done!" Blood poured out of his broken nose. She twisted her face and imitated Jolly's voice: "Let's get down to business. . . . I need your help. . . ." She laughed scornfully. "God in heaven! *That's* what this toad understands!" And with that, she hauled off and kicked the pirate emperor between the legs. Kendrick gasped, blanched, and almost lost consciousness.

Jolly looked at the young woman, dumbfounded. "You're no ordinary whore, are you?"

"Hmm, apparently my disguise wasn't as perfect as I thought." Full of loathing, she looked down at Kendrick. "In any case, it was good enough for this scum. I guess you can put your knife away now. He won't defend himself so quickly anymore."

"Hey, this is my affair! I decide what happens."

"It was *mine* until you turned up."

"And what do you want from him?"

The woman waved her away. "Certainly not his help." She was about to hit him again, but Jolly cried, "Wait! If he's unconscious he's of no use to me."

"What do I care? I want to see the swine die for what he did to my father. If you hadn't gotten in the way—" She broke off, looked around, and grabbed a saber out of an open trunk. "It would be best if you disappeared now. This isn't for children."

Jolly clenched her fist around the dagger. "How about *you* disappearing? Without Kendrick I can't . . . wait a minute . . . your father, did you say?"

"Scarab. The true emperor of the pirates—who this bastard here murdered."

"You're Scarab's daughter?" Jolly considered briefly, then remembered her name: "Soledad?"

The young woman nodded, but she didn't for a moment take her hate-filled gaze from the semiconscious Kendrick. "I planned this for months. It wasn't any child's game to get through to him. The innkeeper down there is devilishly choosy when it comes to the girls he hires on."

Jolly wrinkled her nose. "I climbed through a window—that works too."

Soledad stared at her angrily. "Not through one of the windows on the courtyard?"

"Why not?"

"Nice going! How long have you been in here?" Soledad leaped over Kendrick, tore open the door to the passageway, and listened outside. "Well done! Absolutely magnificent! They're already on the way!"

In fact, there was now the sound of many boots on the stairs, a noisy swirl of thundering steps, calls, and clinking steel.

Soledad slammed the door and shoved a trunk in front of it. "All the windows are secured with strings. If one is opened, it rings a bell in the kitchen. Kendrick's idea. If someone breaks in, he only knows he's been detected when he's already surrounded. You're lucky they're all drunk and stupid or they'd have had you long ago."

Jolly felt the blood rush into her face. "I couldn't know that."

"Do you think I put this rubbish on for fun?" Soledad indicated the wanton dress. "I spent weeks hanging around here *in order* to know such things. It's not as simple as you think to dupe Kendrick."

"Right," groaned the pirate emperor, who was gradually regaining consciousness. Jolly's dagger was immediately back at his throat. "You're done for," he said, "both of you."

Soledad grinned mockingly at him. "What do you suggest? That we give up?"

"No," he said, unmoved. "You'll die one way or the other."

The pirate princess snorted scornfully, then began reinforcing the barricade in front of the door. With strength that Jolly wouldn't have expected from her slender body, she put a second trunk on top of the first. Then she started to shift a commode.

Suddenly Kendrick's fist shot upward. The blow was aimed at Jolly's chin, despite the knife blade—perhaps he thought she wouldn't stab him anyway. But Jolly wasn't so easy to outwit. She ducked swiftly, and the blow missed by a hairsbreadth. Instinctively, her own hand shot forward, curled into Kendrick's hair, and snatched his head back. He cried out. His throat now lay bared before her. She could have used the dagger as any other pirate would have, but she hesitated.

Kendrick was her only chance. If anyone could find out something about the trap that had been set for Bannon, it would be the pirate emperor.

"You owe me something. I just saved your life," she whispered.

"Pah!" was all he said.

"You heard her just now." Jolly pointed to Soledad. "She was going to kill you tonight, if I hadn't gotten in the way."

Soledad's eyes blazed. "Don't count on it, little one. I'm not finished with him yet."

Jolly paid no attention to her. Her gaze bored into

Kendrick's brown eyes. "I *did* save you from her, didn't I?"

"No," he said coolly. "My men are going to do that now."

Something cracked loudly against the door. Outside in the passageway there was high excitement. Numerous voices bellowed back and forth, boots thumped on the attic floor. Then a shot cracked and the barrier trembled. The bullet must have remained stuck in one of the trunks or in the commode.

"How long do you think you can hold them off?" Kendrick grinned triumphantly. "You're already dead."

Soledad raised her saber and leaped toward her father's murderer. "You first!"

Once more Jolly leaped in. Sparks showered when she parried Soledad's saber blow with the dagger, only a few inches away from Kendrick's chest.

The man froze, as a silent battle of strength blazed over him. Jolly held as well as she could, but gradually Soledad succeeded in pressing the knife lower and lower with her saber.

"Stop it!" Jolly got out with difficulty. "He's of no use to us if he's dead."

"He's useful to me that way or not at all." The pressure of her blade did not slacken. Soledad's eyes spit poison. "I want to see him die."

Jolly's left foot shot forward and kicked the pirate princess in the knee with all her might. Soledad screamed in surprise, then fell to her knees.

"You dumb little weasel!"

"We have to get out of here! And I know how, too."

"Oh, yes?"

"But it will only work if he stays alive."

"Funny—I don't think."

Jolly sighed. "You have to help me."

Soledad held her painful knee. "First him, now me—can't you do anything on your own?" She didn't wait for an answer but stood up again and glanced toward the door, which was now trembling under rhythmic blows. The pirates outside were ramming something against it. It was only because of the narrowness of the corridor that they hadn't already overcome the barrier: More than two men couldn't get at the door at once.

Jolly aimed the dagger at Kendrick. He was still white in the face, but he tried to get up. "You lie there!" she ordered him. "Soledad, we have to tie him up. But he has to remain conscious."

An impatient pirate fired at the door again. This time the ball went through the back wall of the commode, whistled past Soledad, and smashed a carafe beside Kendrick's four-poster bed.

The princess didn't let it distract her. Together with Jolly she tied the pirate emperor with a golden cord that they tore off the canopy of the bed. He swore the whole time, but he no longer tried to defend himself. Possibly he'd realized that he'd stay alive as long as the younger girl was in command.

"And now," said Jolly, "onto the trunks with him."

Soledad's eyebrows came together in a frown. "Humpf!"

she said when she grasped what Jolly had in mind. Then she murmured, "Could work," and grabbed Kendrick's shoulders, while Jolly took his feet.

He protested, but they didn't listen to him. Seconds later they'd heaved him onto the trunks. He lay straight across the barricade, stretched lengthwise toward the door, with hands and feet tied.

An ax plunged through the wood less than six inches away from Kendrick's head.

"You idiots!" His voice broke. "Stop it, you mindless monkeys! I'm right behind the door! You miserable riffraff—stop, I say!"

Jolly smiled with satisfaction. "That might buy us a moment's time." She hurried over to the window and opened it. Light fell through the open back door onto the deserted courtyard. The guard must have run upstairs with the others.

Soledad stood indecisively in the middle of the room. On the one hand, she wanted to run; on the other, she still burned with the desire to exact revenge on Kendrick.

He, meanwhile, was screaming to his people not to touch the door or shoot through it.

"But Captain," said a dull voice through the wood, "how else can we get to you?"

Kendrick would doubtless have pulled his hair if his hands had not been tied behind his back.

"Come on!" cried Jolly, and climbed onto the windowsill.

Soledad saw that Kendrick was a help to them only as long

as he bellowed at his people and kept them from breaking down the door. With a regretful shrug, she turned away from him and ran over to the window.

Jolly had already shoved off from a crouch and jackknifed over to the nearby slanting roof. She landed on the tiles with a clatter, grabbed on, and whisked quickly up to the ridge of the roof.

Soledad was a head taller than Jolly and had much more difficulty pushing herself out the small window in a bent position. But she came through safely and sought frantically with her hands and feet for a hold. She was threatening to slide down when Jolly quickly grabbed her by the arm.

Moments later they were running, crouched, over the ridge of the roof.

Kendrick's cries followed them outside. "They're through the window, you stinking sea snails! Run down and grab them! . . . Lord God, am I surrounded by soft-boiled jellyfish brains?"

Immediately there was the sound of the clattering on the staircase again—at least a party of his men were on the way down. Already, shadows interrupted the light stripe in the courtyard.

"Along here!" Jolly pointed to the tavern's rear building, which connected the side wings. "The rope I climbed up to the roof with is hanging on the back side."

They reached it just at the moment that a great outcry arose in the courtyard below. One of Kendrick's men had seen them on the ridge just before they slid down the back slope. Pistols were cocked, then the first balls whistled through the night.

"Quick!" Jolly's hands burned like fire as she slid down the coarse hemp rope.

Swearing, she landed on the ground and leaped to one side to get out of Soledad's way.

They took off side by side. Soon the pirate princess took the lead, since she knew the streets and corners of the stone quarter better than Jolly. They ran through gates and under makeshift bridges connecting some houses, then crossed small squares on which, even after midnight, the confusion of the Oriental bazaar reigned; they pushed through alleyways that were almost too narrow for their slender shoulders and clambered over mountains of garbage, once even over a heap of grumbling drunks an innkeeper had thrown out of his tavern.

Then, after endless minutes, Soledad stopped.

"They've lost our trail," she said, panting. "Otherwise they'd have caught us by this time."

Jolly pressed both hands against her sides. Her throat burned with exhaustion. "How far is it from here to the harbor?"

The princess pulled her thin dress straight, without much success, then she pointed to the left. "Run in that direction, then it's just a cat spring. But stay away from all the open squares."

Jolly thought for a moment. "You can come along. I have friends in the harbor and a boat, perhaps you can—"

"No." Soledad's tone was final. "I don't need anyone to get what I want."

"Kendrick's head?" Jolly smiled thinly. "Looks rather as if neither one of us got what we wanted."

"Because you kept me from it."

"And you me."

They looked at each other silently for a moment, then Soledad shrugged. With a hasty motion she pushed a strand of red hair out of her face. "Another time. Kendrick won't get away from me." She hesitated, then added, "You saved my life up there on the roof. Thanks."

Jolly smiled. "What're you going to do now? He'll have a search out for us."

"First I have to get out of these horrible rags." And again she tugged in vain at the tangled straps and ribbons of her dress. "Then I'll see what's next."

"You're still planning to avenge your father?"

"Of course."

Jolly sighed; finally she nodded. "Then good luck with it."

"If you want some advice: Get out of New Providence right away if you can."

"I'm not afraid of Kendrick."

Soledad smiled, and for the first time it looked almost friendly. "No, well, hardly . . . nevertheless, the Spaniards are going to attack, perhaps even tonight."

"Tonight? But Kendrick—"

"He's a fool. Another reason he doesn't deserve to be leader of the pirates. He actually believes his men are so afraid of him they'd refuse the bribe money of the Spanish spies. Yet it's swarming with traitors here."

Jolly remembered what Soledad had said in the inn. "You mean the lookouts in the mountains are bought? By the Spaniards?"

"Definitely. If Kendrick paid more attention to what was going on around him, he'd have seen that long ago. Everyone in the Caribbean—except Kendrick and his pals—is saying that the attack of the armada is about to happen. In the past few days, more ships have put out to sea than in the last four weeks. Those that are still here are just as blind as Kendrick—children who close their eyes and think no one can see them. But the Spanish are somewhere out there at this moment, not very far away. I intended to use the last night to kill Kendrick—now it's too late."

"What will you do?"

"Retreat inland. There are a few ships anchored on the other side of the island whose captains were loyal to my father—one of them will take me aboard."

"Why don't you come with me?"

"Kendrick knows who I am now. If he survives the Spanish attack, he'll chase me with everything he's got. There are still many who despise him and would rather see Scarab's daughter on the throne than him. He has every reason to fear me, not only because of tonight. I'd be no help to you if half the pirate fleet were chasing after you."

Jolly saw that Soledad wouldn't be convinced. The princess shook her hand in farewell.

"One more thing," said Soledad. "About Captain Bannon . . ."

"Yes?"

"You should think about whether Kendrick might not have had something to do with the affair."

Jolly frowned. She wanted to hold Soledad back, but her red mane had already melted into the shadows of an underpass. Her steps resounded in the darkness.

Gideon's Grave

One of the two parrots was waiting for her on the little sailboat in the harbor. It was Hugh, she saw by his poison yellow eyes. He was sitting on a piece of paper that was covered with fine, looping handwriting.

It's too dangerous to spend the night outside, it said. *I've rented a room in an inn called Gideon's Grave. Munk and I are waiting for you there. Follow Hugh. He'll lead you to us.*

The message was signed with the initials GT, which Jolly thought was a little silly. Underneath there was a postscript: *What the devil did you pour down Munk? He turned poor Moe crimson!*

Jolly giggled to herself. Munk had drunk two large beakers of wine and suddenly become so befuddled that she had trouble getting him back to the boat. There she'd laid him under the tarpaulin in the stern so that he could sleep off his drunk and she could carry out her plan unhindered.

Now she pictured the Ghost Trader's face when he returned to the harbor and found his protégé in that condition. She had to laugh, despite the fear still lurking in her bones after her flight.

Yet the thought of Soledad's words turned her abruptly serious. Not only did she have the pirate emperor and his entire pack on her heels, but the impending Spanish attack gave her even more concern. She must find Munk and the Ghost Trader and convince them to leave without delay! Perhaps they'd manage to get aboard the ghost ship before the armada reached New Providence.

Hugh rose into the air with a flutter and flew ahead. Jolly crumpled the Ghost Trader's note as she ran. She hoped it wasn't too far to the tavern where the two were waiting for her. Heavens, who would lodge in a hole named Gideon's Grave?

The inn was on the outer edge of the harbor, a two-storied wooden house from whose downstairs windows came the noise and the dubious smells of an overfilled taproom. The upper windows were dark.

"Jolly! There you are at last!" The voice rang out from one of the pitch-black rectangles above. It was only at a second look that she saw the outline of the one who was up there watching for her, almost invisible, as if he possessed no more substance than the shadows.

She waved to the Ghost Trader.

"Wait," he called. "I'll come down and get you."

She shook her head. "Not necessary." And with that, she walked through the door to the interior of the tavern and slipped quickly through the crowd of men before anyone could catch more than a fleeting look at her. It was good of the Trader to be concerned about her, but she'd been in worse cutthroats' dens than this one, with Bannon. She knew how to avoid the drunks and to defend herself if necessary.

Not even the landlady or any of the barmaids paid any attention to her. Rum, gin, and beer were flowing in streams. Moist heat filled the room, and the fumes of countless pipes limited the view to a few feet.

Jolly found the stairs that led up to the guest chambers. She ran quickly up them. The triangular silhouette of the dark hooded cape rose abruptly above the end of the stairs. The Ghost Trader indicated an open door.

"In there."

Munk lay on one of the room's three beds, snoring to wake the dead. The Ghost Trader pressed the door closed behind him and shoved the back of a chair under the handle. There was no lock.

Hugh landed next to Moe on the windowsill. The Ghost Trader hadn't exaggerated: The red-eyed parrot's plumage shimmered flaming crimson in the candlelight. Munk's mussels lay spread out on a small table.

"It will fade," said the Ghost Trader. "In a few hours, his feathers will be black again."

"The Spaniards are attacking!" Jolly burst out. "Tonight!"

His left eyebrow moved up hardly perceptibly. "Who says that?"

"Princess Soledad. Scarab's daughter!"

The eyebrow slid higher, until it almost disappeared under the edge of the hood. "*Princess* Soledad? Since when do pirates have titles of nobility?"

"I believe she spoke the truth."

"Before we rush into anything, you should tell me everything first."

"But we have to get away from here!"

"Later . . . perhaps. First I'd like to hear your story."

She uttered an impatient sigh, glanced at the sleeping Munk with a touch of guilt, and began to tell everything. The Ghost Trader listened attentively without sitting down. He stood there, kneading his chin between thumb and forefinger and looking piercingly at Jolly, as if he could read things in her eyes that went beyond what she was saying.

"Hmm," the Trader said finally, and after a pause, he said it again: "Hmm, hmm."

"What's that supposed to mean?" You could have pumped out the hull of a leaking ship with Jolly's racing heart.

"Scarab's daughter is a shrewd girl. She certainly wouldn't speak such warnings carelessly."

"Then what are we waiting for?"

"Well, to be honest, for a ship. And its captain."

Jolly was hopping from one foot to the other. What sort of nonsense was he talking? They already had a ship! It might not be the most inviting in the Caribbean, but who cared about that at the moment?

The Ghost Trader looked at her and answered her question without her having to ask it.

"We must give up the ghost ship. We need a nimble, fast ship. And an experienced captain."

"I can sail a ship, if I have to."

The Trader smiled indulgently. "I don't doubt it. But what we need now is an old hand. Someone who knows all the tricks of the trade—and whom one can nevertheless trust."

She frowned skeptically. "And you've found someone like that? Here?"

"Captain Walker. He's sitting in the tavern downstairs and playing. As soon as the party is over, he'll need money. And then he'll talk with me."

"Walker?" Jolly put her hands over her face and uttered a groan of despair. "*The* Walker? The same one who personally cheated Scarab out of a whole shipload of Jamaican rum? And who in a fight between Spaniards and English goes from one side to the other faster than the cannonballs?"

The Trader nodded. "He commands the fastest ship on the Caribbean Sea. And he's a cutthroat with a certain sense of honor. We won't find anything better than he is here, I'm afraid."

"Honor!" she cried disparagingly. "May be that he's so keen on honor that he hands me over to Kendrick." She dropped, exhausted, on the edge of Munk's bed. Suddenly a thought came to her. She stared at the Trader suspiciously. "Why do you really want to get away from the island so fast? Up until a few minutes ago, you didn't even know the Spanish were going to attack."

The Trader's face darkened. "If we can't put an end to the

moving of the Maelstrom, there will be neither Spaniards nor pirates here. Believe me, the Acherus was only a shallow specter compared to what the Maelstrom will spew out if his power becomes greater. And it is *becoming* greater, with every day, with every hour."

Jolly only understood half of what he was saying, but at these words she began to shiver.

"What are you planning?"

The Ghost Trader didn't answer. Restless, he paced to the window and looked out. Then he turned to her again. "Much remains in darkness, and everything is going much faster than we feared."

Jolly thought of what had happened on the island and said nothing.

Suddenly Munk stretched in his sleep and laid a hand on Jolly's thigh.

"My lord!" She angrily pushed his fingers away and leaped up. "Any field mouse can drink more than this . . . this . . ." She trailed off. Munk looked very peaceful as he lay there, as if he'd finally been able to throw off his grief for his parents for a few hours.

"Don't blame him," said the Ghost Trader. "He can help what is to happen just as little as you can."

She looked at the floor. "I led the Acherus to his island," she said sadly. "I can never make amends for that."

"Yes, you can. In fact, sooner than you imagine."

"But what do I have to do?"

The Trader came over to her and, smiling, took her hand. "In time you will understand everything, little polliwog."

Jolly sat on her bed with her knees drawn up and stared out into the night through the open window. She couldn't sleep, although the Ghost Trader had advised her to. The starry sky of the Caribbean seemed to her too bright tonight, the roaring of the surf too loud. Many thoughts were buzzing through her head. She felt a vague, indefinable responsibility on her shoulders, an obligation she'd been given against her will. What did the Ghost Trader really intend for the polliwogs? And what would become of her search for Bannon? She wouldn't give up her investigations, no matter what, with or without support. Kendrick, the Ghost Trader, this Maelstrom—they could all go to hell, as far as she was concerned!

She gave a start as a bone-shaking racket sounded through the floorboards. In the taproom below, something was flung against the ceiling with great force. Something—or someone!

She put her feet on the floor—and pulled them right back up again when the shaking was repeated, this time even harder. Then came the sound of breaking window glass, and voices outside the tavern grew loud. Obviously, a terrible fight was in progress down there.

The door flew open. The Ghost Trader, who'd just gone downstairs a few minutes ago, stood in the doorway, legs apart, his robe pulled back on one side. His left hand rested on the silver ring at his belt.

"Come, it's starting!"

"Walker actually intends to help us?"

"Not yet. But when he has a clear head again, he'll agree that there's no other choice open to him. We'll just pick him up in front of the window—at least he was lying there a minute ago."

Jolly stared at him. "Something tells me you had your hand in the game."

"Who knows?"

"But you're no magician, you said. Only a ghost conjurer."

The Trader laughed suddenly, a sound that made Jolly recoil. Even Munk made a face in his sleep.

"No conjurer, only a trader. I collect the ghosts of the dead, I don't conjure them up. But I can't expect you to understand the difference . . . not yet. And as concerns the good Captain Walker: In this tavern there are more ghosts of men who've drunk themselves to death or been killed in fights than in any other—for no other reason is it called Gideon's Grave. I've only directed a few of the poor souls to interfere a little with the captain at his card game."

"That's a dirty trick," said Jolly, but the Ghost Trader had already whirled around and run down the stairs. "Bring the pack along with you!" he called back over his shoulder.

Jolly sent an ill-humored look after him. "Yes, Master. Gladly, Master. At your service, Master."

With an oath, she stood up, packed Munk's mussels into his leather pouch, fastened them to her own belt, and started trying to awaken the boy on the bed. He moaned and groaned, but he got up, swaying.

A little later the two of them were pushing their way along the wall of the taproom, avoiding flying jugs and staggering men, ducking as an empty keg crashed against the wall over them, and doing their best to escape the blows, kicks, and fists of the fighting pirates.

In the middle of the melee of bodies, a gigantic man was raging like a berserker. Jolly recognized him by his mighty knight's helmet—Buenaventure, the giant from the tavern that afternoon. He crushed chairs and tables—not with his fists but with the bodies he swung around him like weapons—and thus struck wide clearings in the crowd of fighters. Because everyone was paying attention to him and not to Jolly and Munk, the two quickly left the battlefield behind them.

The Ghost Trader was standing outside beside a man who sat dazedly on the sand, holding his head.

Walker hadn't changed since Jolly had last met him at Bannon's side—except for the bloody laceration on his forehead. He was medium-tall and slim. He wore his dark hair shoulder length; at the moment it wasn't a particularly attractive sight, since it was stuck across his face in dark strands, as if the shadows of all the bars he'd ever sat behind were burned into his features.

Bannon had liked Walker, in contrast to Jolly. Walker had always treated her like a little child at their rare meetings. For that alone, she couldn't forgive him.

Walker was struggling to his feet just as Jolly and Munk hurried up.

He looked up and saw her for the first time. "If it isn't the little toad."

"Polliwog," the Ghost Trader corrected him.

"Toad or polliwog or frog . . . all one and the same."

Munk, who now had some of his wits back, looked dubiously at Walker. "Who's that wreck?"

"The best captain in the Caribbean," said the Trader. "At least he was until he almost got his skull smashed just now."

"Let's get out of here before Buenaventure follows us."

"Buenaventure?" Walker laughed, which in view of the laceration looked rather painful. "Puh, he's the one who just kept those weasels away from me."

Jolly pursed her lips. "He's your friend?"

"My steersman," Walker declared. "And the best there is." He turned to the Ghost Trader. "Is the toad going to be aboard too?"

Jolly sent him a disparaging look. "I can't wait to see the *Carfax* again."

"You always were a terrible child. Forward and a know-it-all and—"

"We can talk about that once we're aboard," the Ghost

Trader broke in, as he pushed himself in between the two fighting cocks. "It may not be much longer, and the—"

He fell silent.

Everyone fell silent.

From one moment to the next, there was silence over Port Nassau as if an incomprehensible power had sucked up all sound. Behind them, in Gideon's Grave, a last crash sounded, and then it was quiet even in there. Buenaventure walked out the door and stopped, staring like all the others, motionless, out at the night-dark sea.

The unreal moment lasted hardly the length of a breath, but to Jolly it seemed like an eternity.

Then, on the other side of the bay, a blaze of light flamed up. A second and a third and a fourth followed, until there were so many that they couldn't be counted anymore. They illuminated slanting silhouettes out on the sea, as if someone had erected an entire city on the waves. An earsplitting succession of thunderous crashes resounded, as broadside after broadside was fired at Port Nassau.

Screams sounded. Roofs shattered. Instantly, fire flickered out of the labyrinth of shacks and houses.

Jolly and the others had dropped flat on the sand.

Gideon's Grave exploded, blasted into millions of wooden fragments, which brushed over their heads like malicious swarms of mosquitoes.

Something heavy hit the ground beside Jolly—at first she thought it was a cannonball, but when the dust settled, she saw Buenaventure. He was already scrambling up again; his massive body filled her entire field of vision.

In front of her lay his helmet on the sand.

In the midst of the inferno of hits and conflagration she looked up and saw his face.

Buenaventure was no ordinary man.

He had the head of a pit bull.

Firestorm

"Run!" roared the Ghost Trader. "Run for your lives!"

For an instant, Jolly thought the warning was because of the pit bull man. Buenaventure bent over her and grabbed her by the arms. While she was still screaming in protest, he'd already set her on her feet, growled something like "Run!" and turned to Munk to help him up the same way.

And then they did run, storming along the beach in a group, Walker and Buenaventure leading, followed by Jolly, Munk, and the Ghost Trader. The two parrots fluttered above them, screeching.

The front line of Port Nassau's houses was in flames. What was happening behind them couldn't be seen through the fire and smoke. Everywhere, cursing men were breaking through the fire and billows of black smoke. The Spanish armada's cannonballs shredded the palm-leaf roofs and wooden walls, and where candles, torches, or lanterns had been burning inside, the fire spread quickly. Fire was also now blazing from muzzles on the battlements of the governor's palace and the stone quarter to the west of the harbor, but the defenders had nothing to place against the superiority of an entire fleet.

"Where's the *Carfax* lying?" cried the Ghost Trader.

Jolly saw Walker look over his shoulder, illuminated in the flickering glow of the fires. "There might be an additional little problem," he said.

"What sort of a problem?"

"The *Carfax* doesn't belong to me anymore."

"What?" roared Jolly, Munk, and the Ghost Trader in chorus.

Three cannonballs struck close by in quick succession. Clouds of sand wafted over the beach. Cries were coming from all directions. More and more men were breaking through the ruins and walls of flame to the harbor.

"I lost her," yelled Walker, without slowing down. "Two days ago, at dice with a trader."

For the first time, Jolly saw the one-eyed man really angry. At the death of Munk's parents he had been sad, disappointed, and depressed, but now a rage flickered over his features that was scarcely any different from the firelight of the burning city. "You must have forgotten to mention that in our conversation, Captain."

Walker grinned, which appeared doubly inappropriate in view of the circumstances. "Then there's another situation."

"Does that mean you also no longer have a crew?"

ows of smoke. She was anchored a little to one side with a other ships, and none of the other boats had tried to reach r. Walker frowned. "Better we should take one of the ships ith enough men on her to make us ready to run out."

The Ghost Trader shook his head. "No, it has to be the *Carfax*. You'll have your crew, Captain. Don't worry about that."

In fact, most of the fugitives were trying to climb onto two of the ships lying next to her, a brigantine and a run-down galleon.

"How could *I* worry?" Walker's voice was full of mockery. "We will simply set all sails, the six of us, lift the anchor, and—"

"A crew will be waiting for us aboard the *Carfax*, Captain. Trust me."

The pirate was about to speak again when a cannon shot hit the mainmast of the galleon. It collapsed with a grinding sound, burying a dozen fleeing pirates beneath it, and smashed full length across the deck of the second ship.

"Agreed," Walker growled.

They brought the rowboat alongside the hull of the *Carfax*. The ship could have used painting, but she was otherwise in fine condition. She resembled the *Skinny Maddy* in size and construction, with an unadorned railing and an unpretentious stern cabin. The sails on all three masts were reefed, the long, narrow deck deserted.

The Ghost Trader was the first to board the ship. He immediately took a few steps to one side, released the silver

"Well, yes. Regrettably."

Jolly looked from Walker to Buenaventure. The giant with the dog's head looked grim: His teeth were bared. He held his ears sharply erect. The destruction of Port Nassau was reflected in his round brown eyes as an orange, scorching hell.

The Ghost Trader pointed to the bay where most of the pirate ships lay at anchor. Some had lost their masts, two or three were already sunk. But most were astonishingly unharmed—obviously the Spaniards were concentrating their attack on the city first and on the men before they demolished the fleet, too.

Angrily, Jolly pictured the pirates at the lookout points over the city counting the gold they'd received for their treachery—gold that gleamed and shone in the glow of the distant fires, blood money.

The companions were among the first to reach the rowboats.

"Where now?" asked Jolly, as Buenaventure rushed like a dervish into a group of pirates who tried to fight them for one of the escape boats. Men flew through the air left and right, their cries fading into the thundering cannon fire.

"Where's the *Carfax*?" asked the Ghost Trader urgently.

Walker pointed out at the crowd of ships. "In the front row. As far as I know, she was going to run out tomorrow with a new cargo."

"Good," said the Trader. "Then kindly do what you know best—steal her!"

Walker grinned. "Think of my good reputation. . . . In the long run, I'll have financial losses from it."

"We'll be responsible for those," retorted the Trader grimly.

Munk clenched his fists. "I can't understand this fellow dickering over a few ducats while the world is collapsing."

Jolly was going to reply when her eye fell on a single figure approaching them with a fluttering hooded cape.

"Soledad?"

The pirate princess's hood slipped back. Buenaventure was about to block her way with an angry growl, but Jolly kicked him in the leg from behind. "Leave her alone! She belongs to me."

Munk stared at her. "Oh, yes?"

Buenaventure sent Jolly a dark look from his dog eyes, but he allowed Soledad to join them. She was completely out of breath, her cape singed. She smelled as if she'd just rolled in soot.

"Is your invitation still open?" she panted in Jolly's direction, paying no attention to the others.

Jolly nodded and was about to say something when Walker shoved her aside, assumed a beaming smile, and bowed gallantly before the princess. "The invitation to accompany us, lovely lady? But most assuredly."

Buenaventure growled and rolled his eyes, which looked so curiously human in his dog's face that it made his utterly strange appearance still more incredible.

Soledad made a wry face, as if someone had just shown her a disgusting insect. Shaking her head, she pushed Walker to one side and looked again at Jolly. "Charming friends you have."

Jolly snorted angrily. "That's no—"

"A good friend." Walker grinned even best, so to speak."

The Ghost Trader stepped between the about a hundred men over there coming straig who most certainly want to save their lives with t should postpone this matter."

While Buenaventure stationed himself protect front of them, Walker, Munk, and the Trader pushe boat down to the water. Jolly and Soledad leaped int together. The pit bull man came last. Soledad looked at h suspiciously but said nothing.

The four grown-ups seized the oars, while Jolly looked keenly about her. She and Munk could have run across the water, but the waves were so churned up with the hits of the cannon shots that she doubted that Munk could have managed, with his limited experience.

A large group of pirates, some women among them, had just reached the place where the rowboat had lain. Too late. All the boats were already on the water and approaching the anchored ships with all possible speed. Cannonballs hissed over their heads. The Spaniards had the city under unceasing fire. Explosion after explosion sounded, intermixed with the ghastly sound of countless death screams. Suddenly one of the first rowboats received a hit, a shot that catapulted bodies in all directions; seconds later the boat had vanished, only a few boards and a boot floating on the water.

"That's the *Carfax* up ahead!" Walker pointed into the darkness, where a slender sloop lay in the water in the middle of the

ring from his belt, and slowly moved his finger along it.

"So!" cried Walker, who couldn't decide between triumph and despair. "Now, where's the—" His eyes suddenly grew large and his tone uncertain. "Where's . . . ," he repeated; then he snapped his mouth shut.

Everywhere aboard the *Carfax* foggy shapes rose from between the planks, ghosts who were obeying the Trader's call. Immediately, a large number of them floated up into the rigging and began to unfurl the sails. Others manned the guns.

"Jolly!" called the Ghost Trader. "Come here to me."

She obeyed, while the rest of them stared at the apparitions. Only Munk was unimpressed. His worries were for the cannon fire of the Spaniards, which was more and more falling on the area of the anchored ships.

"Place your fingertips on the ring," the Trader commanded.

A strange tingling went through her hand when she touched the silver ring. Nevertheless, she did not withdraw her fingers.

The Ghost Trader murmured incomprehensible syllables and words.

Jolly felt a quick, pricking pain in the ends of her fingers. Then the Trader said, "It is well; you can let go now." More loudly, so that everyone, but especially Walker, could understand him, he added, "From now on the ghosts aboard this ship are under the command of this girl. They will obey you, Captain Walker, so long as it is a matter of nautical orders. However, should you try to undertake something against your passengers, Jolly will bring them down on you and your pit bull friend, and then nothing and no one will be able to save you."

Walker grimaced, brushed back his long hair, and looked darkly over at Buenaventure. "This is all your fault! You talked me into taking on this lousy commission!"

The pit bull man shook his head, grumbling, and rejected this reproach with a wave of his huge hand.

"Don't worry," said the Ghost Trader. "You'll both be sufficiently paid for this trip. Take Munk and Jolly to Tortuga. There you will all learn more."

Tortuga? thought Jolly in astonishment. *Why there in particular?*

Soledad touched her on the shoulder. "If you'd just told me what interesting people you know, I'd have considered your offer sooner."

Munk cleared his throat. "Don't you think it's time we put to sea?"

"I don't like this. I don't like it at all." Visibly uneasy, Walker turned to the ghost crew. "Men!" he shouted, "raise the anchor! Set the sails! We're running out!" His surprise couldn't have been greater when the vapory beings swarmed over the ship in a flash and followed his orders.

"I have to leave you for a while," said the Ghost Trader. Several cannonballs landed in the churning water behind them.

"Leave us?" Jolly stammered in confusion: "But why—how—"

"We'll meet again on Tortuga. If I should be late, you can use the time for your search for Bannon."

"But how?"

"Munk," said the Trader. "Do you still have Jolly's spider?"

Munk's hand went to his belt, where ordinarily his leather pouch had hung. Behind him the gray sheets of the sails were unfurled and mercifully hid the sight of the destruction of Port Nassau.

"Here, I have them," said Jolly, releasing the pouch from her own belt and handing it to Munk. The boy opened it, burrowed in it briefly, and pulled out the little wooden box. He let the lid snap open. Inside lay the corpse of the poisonous spider that had hidden in the figurehead in Jolly's flight from the *Skinny Maddy*.

"Good," said the Ghost Trader, satisfied. "On Tortuga, there's an old flag maker by the name of Silverhand. Show him the spider. Perhaps he can tell you where it comes from. Possibly that will be a clue to whoever lured Bannon into the trap." He added softly, "But don't forget that there's much more at stake at the moment."

"The Maelstrom?"

Smiling, the Ghost Trader clapped Jolly on the shoulder. "It's good there are two of you. Our chances have thus been doubled." He turned to Munk, who slipped the spider and box into his pouch again. "And you, Munk, must promise me to improve your magic art further. You possess a great talent. Sometime, perhaps, you'll save us all."

Munk's eyes glowed with pride, in spite of the destruction around them, in spite of his fear. But then worry shadowed his face. "Can't you stay with us? New Providence is being wiped out!"

"The pirates, perhaps, but not the island. Nothing will happen to me." And with that he wrapped the robe across his body, material fluttered, and a gust of wind hit them all in the face and made them close their eyes for an instant. When they opened them again, the Ghost Trader was gone. Jolly saw him appear briefly on another ship, fifty yards away. But there, too, he disappeared later in a dark swirl of fabric, to turn up again on a ship farther away, and to vanish into thin air yet again.

With a creaking and groaning, the *Carfax* began to move. When Jolly looked up, she saw the pit bull man at the wheel, while Walker stood straddle-legged on the bridge and bellowed orders to his undead crew.

The cannon thunder grew louder as the three-master glided toward the bay's exit with increasing speed—headed directly for the wall of Spanish warships.

The armada had taken up position in a semicircle around Port Nassau. Unremitting, the cannon fire thundered out across the bay and cut deep lanes into the city's tangle of streets.

Only a handful of Spanish ships on the starboard side of the *Carfax* had been ordered to fire on the anchored pirate fleet rather than the houses. The bulk of the armada was concentrated against the city and the fortress of the governor. The English artillery on the battlements was able to land a few shots, in spite of the massive inferiority of their cannon; three Spanish ships were so badly damaged that their crews had to transfer to neighboring galleons in lifeboats.

Walker made two decisions. First, at the exit from the bay, he had the *Carfax* turn to larboard, away from those ships that were aiming at the pirate fleet. Second, he ordered Buenaventure to take a direct course toward the Spaniards in the lifeboats. As long as the *Carfax* was in the midst of the castaways, he hoped none of the captains would place the sloop under full fire.

"Anyway, he knows what he's doing," murmured Munk, pulling his head down as a few shots from individual muskets whistled over the deck.

Jolly hissed with scorn. "Even a revolting person like that has *one* good characteristic."

"He's a good captain," Soledad agreed; she was crouching beside them between barrels and boxes, part of the cargo with which the new owner of the *Carfax* had intended to put to sea the next morning. Now they gave good cover against musket fire and crossfire.

"You can marry him," Jolly retorted snippily.

"Who knows?"

Jolly stared at her wide-eyed.

Soledad laughed. "Don't worry." She looked up at the

bridge where Walker stood giving orders, unmoving in the midst of the crossfire of muskets, while Buenaventure maneuvered the ship with remarkable skill between lifeboats and warships. Jolly calmed herself with the thought that Soledad surely admired only that cutthroat's nautical skill, not his questionable human qualities.

The Spaniards had fanned their fleet out wide to place as many corners of the pirate nest under fire as possible. That was tactically skillful, as long as not too many freebooters' ships succeeded in leaving the harbor. The lookouts' treachery had given the attackers the advantage of surprise—they were trying to shoot down their opponents in their shacks and tents. Leaving the English governor's fortress in debris and ashes was, of course, entirely incidental.

For decades, Spaniards and Englishmen had been fighting each other in the waters of the Caribbean. Each country hoped to develop its colonies overseas, to conquer new and fruitful islands, and to bring the gold mines and spice plantations of the mainland under its control. From the outside, the attack on Port Nassau might look like the Spanish Crown's reprisal for the pirates' numerous trespasses against their trading ships. But in truth, behind it there was also the desire to send the administrators of the British Empire home in a huff.

The loose formation of the warships made it possible for Walker to break through the siege ring without much difficulty. The ghosts at the cannons of the *Carfax* did not fire a single shot; the flight succeeded without returning fire.

In the protection of the lifeboats, which were frantically avoiding them, they succeeded in getting behind the Spanish fleet and were soon on the open sea. One Spanish captain sent a broadside after them, daring it only, however, when they'd left the castaways far behind them—but by then it was too late. Not a single ball hit its target.

"Why aren't they following us?" asked Munk in amazement, as he looked back over the railing toward the inferno in front of the island's coast. Powder smoke floated in a yellow veil of fog over the sea. As long as the muzzles weren't pointing in their direction, the deep thumping of the cannons seemed strangely unreal—like a thunderstorm taking place at a great distance.

"It isn't worth it to them to bring down a single ship," said Soledad. "Port Nassau, as the pirates' capital, is a thorn in their eye. First they cleaned the freebooters out of Tortuga—at least most of them—now New Providence. However, I'm not sure they'll really manage it unless they station a garrison there permanently."

"Which again they wouldn't dare to," added Jolly, nodding, "because New Providence is in English colonial territory and the Spanish could start a war with an open takeover of the island."

Munk shook his head in incomprehension. "But they're attacking the island. There's nothing much more than that to a conquest."

Soledad yawned and smiled indulgently. "They'll put it out that the attack is a punitive expedition against the pirates, not an attack against England. If the English contradict them, they'll accuse them of supporting piracy, which certainly doesn't lie in their interest."

"That means," said Munk, "the Spaniards will shoot Port Nassau into the ground, then turn around and disappear again."

"Exactly."

Jolly looked intently over at the narrow ring of smoke and fire illuminating the night horizon under the starry sky. By now there must be a scant ten miles between the ship and the island, but the stink of fire and powder still hung in the air; the *Carfax* was pulling it along behind it like a tow. "The English will send a new governor," she said, "who'll build the fortress up again from the rubble, and in six months it will all be just the same as it was before."

Soledad made a grim face. "I hope that at least Kendrick escaped it."

"We aren't the only ship that broke through the Spaniards' ring," Munk said. "I saw two others. One was right behind us, but then it turned."

"If the bastard was aboard, I'll find him."

Jolly looked up at the mast, where the ghosts had hoisted the English flag at Walker's command. As on any pirate ship, there was on this one a choice of flags of all nations, in particular that one for which Jolly was named, the Jolly Roger, the black skull-and-crossbones emblem of the freebooters. Usually the pirate flag was run up shortly before an attack, when the opponent no longer had a chance of fleeing.

Soledad leaned her back against a chest, pulled up her knees, and closed her eyes for a moment. Under her cape she no longer wore the dress in which Jolly had met her in the Fat Hen, but trousers, a shirt, and a wide weapons belt, into which were stuck a half a dozen throwing knives. She hadn't a saber with her, but Jolly had seen enough to wager that she could handle any sort of blade superbly. If only half of what people said about Scarab's daughter was true, she was a better fighter than most male pirates, in addition to being blessed with calculation and beauty. It by no means escaped Jolly that not only Walker but also Munk kept stealing glances at her every now and then.

Soledad yawned again, bored a finger into her nose, rolled a hardened piece of snot between her fingers, and flipped it into the shadows.

Jolly giggled as she watched Munk's face twist.

The pirate princess wadded up her cape and shoved it under her behind as a cushion. "Wake me up if something important happens." Within a few moments she was asleep.

Jolly motioned to Munk to follow her. She led him to the railing, out of Soledad's hearing. They held onto the railing and gazed absently into the night. Jolly told him what had happened in the Fat Hen and listened patiently to his reproaches because she'd put him out of commission so underhandedly. After he'd given vent to his anger, they both fell into a brooding silence.

After a while, Jolly asked, "Why didn't he come with us?"

"The Ghost Trader? No idea."

"What could be so important that he had to go back for it?"

"Did he tell you about the sea eagle he sent out?"

Jolly shook her head. She felt a sudden prick of jealousy. Why had the Ghost Trader confided in Munk and not her?

"He looked up an old acquaintance in New Providence, the only man in the Caribbean who knows how to tame sea eagles."

Jolly had never heard that anyone had been able to train one of those proud creatures, but she waited curiously, without interrupting Munk.

"They sent out one of those eagles to spread the message about the awakening of the Maelstrom."

"So that's why he agreed to bring us to Port Nassau."

Munk nodded briefly. "Probably." After a short pause, he added, "Maybe he's staying on the island to wait for an answer."

"And that's worth dying for?"

"This business seems to be very serious with him. The Maelstrom, the Mare Tenebrosum, all those things." He was silent for a moment, as the shadow of a dark memory brushed over him. Jolly put her hand on the railing over his. She knew there was nothing that could provide comfort for Munk, and yet she longed to be able to say something that would pull him out of his grief.

"Hey," said a voice behind them suddenly, "I'm sorry to disturb your intimate get-together. But I have to talk to you."

Jolly turned around with a sigh. "What do you want, Walker?"

"Your gloomy friend with the poultry made me a lot of promises, certainly, but aside from a few coins, I haven't seen much of all the riches that are supposedly coming to me."

She held his piercing eyes easily. She'd learned years ago not to let herself be intimidated by any pirate in the world. Nose high, eyes straight, and an expressionless face—she'd mastered a thousand moments like this already. "That's not our problem."

"Oh, yes, I'm afraid it is. You're passengers who haven't paid for your passage yet."

"Have you forgotten what he said about the ghosts?" She tried to give her voice a dangerous undertone.

He looked her over. "Now, who's talking about such . . . well, inconveniences? Buenaventure up there is a veteran of the fighting pits of Antigua. There's very little he couldn't handle. But am I threatening you with him on that account? Such a thing never crossed my mind."

"You are so noble and good, Walker."

He grinned and showed his white teeth. "What it's about for me is just business. No argument, no idiotic back-and-forth about who's the stronger one here. Only . . . purchasing power. You understand?"

Munk stared at him wordlessly, but his dark look spoke volumes.

Jolly thought for a moment, then she took a deep breath. "So, you want a guarantee that you'll really get your gold, right?"

"That would be a fine gesture."

"Agreed." She paid no attention to the questioning side

glance Munk sent her. "I'm on the search for Bannon. You've probably heard what happened."

"The *Maddy* went down, the entire crew vanished without a trace. It's said they're dead." He examined her searchingly. "How did you actually get out of that business safe and sound?"

"That's no concern of yours. You only need to know that I want to find Bannon—or at least a clue to what happened to him."

Walker nodded. "It's clear so far."

"If we succeed in finding Bannon again, dead or alive, there's a gigantic reward waiting for the one who helps me."

"Nice words," said Walker, unimpressed.

Jolly sighed, then turned her back to him and lifted her shirt. "See the tattoo?"

"Ugly. What's that supposed to be?"

She let the shirt drop again and turned around to face him. "It's half of a map. The way to Bannon's treasure. The other half is on his back. If we find Bannon, the treasure belongs to you."

Walker mulled that over. "That wouldn't be all right with him."

"You have my word."

"Oh, well, you know how it is in business. . . ."

"I can't offer you any proof. Only my word of honor. If we find Bannon, I'll personally see to it that you have a chance to copy the half of the map on his back—and the other half from mine."

ade the descent, although the broad backs of re visible from above. "An especially fat and d," he said. "The French were the first to breed Haiti, so someone dubbed them Jean-Paul. der I lost the *Carfax* to must have intended to em."

left the ladder and joined Munk while Walker ed down below, cursing and moaning. But after a few ites he came back.

Disgusting. On my ship! It'll take months to air it out wn there."

"Will their weight hold us back very much?"

Walker shrugged. "We'd be somewhat faster without them, anyway." He considered it for a moment. "We could drive them overboard."

Jolly was shocked. "Absolutely not!"

Walker rubbed his chin. "Better them than us, I'd say."

Munk came to Jolly's aid. "We aren't even being followed. They aren't holding us up."

"Not yet," said Walker.

The idea that the pirate could drive the defenseless animals into the water horrified Jolly to the core. Furthermore, he thus confirmed all her prejudices. "The animals stay aboard!" she said firmly.

Walker scratched the back of his head. "Well, that makes them passengers, right?"

Jolly took a deep breath. She felt she was going to burst, right then and there.

Walker thought it over. He took his time. Perhaps he was weighing the little "for" and the overwhelming "against."

"Agreed," he said finally. "Your word of honor?"

"My word of honor." She held out her hand. He took it and shook it hard.

"Good girl," he said before he turned around and went back up the steps to the bridge. "Bannon can be really proud of you."

Munk inched closer to her. "You said that thing on your back was going to be a coral someday."

"It's supposed to be."

"But—"

"I lied to him."

"Oh, marvelous."

She glared angrily at him. "Did you perhaps have a better idea?"

Walker's voice made her fall silent in alarm. "Jolly!"

With thumping heart, she turned up to the bridge. "Yes?"

"Your ghosts might be a fine thing," he called down to her, "but for my taste they're a little tight-lipped."

"What do you mean?"

"I need someone to go below deck and report to me how it looks down there. The *Carfax* is lying deeper in the water than usual. See if everything's in order. I don't want any unpleasant surprises."

"I can do that," cried Munk.

Jolly shook her head. "I'll go."

She left the railing and ran to the cargo hatch. With both

hands, she flipped it back and clambered down a steep ladder into the hold.

Munk watched her disappear, then looked over at the sleeping pirate princess, slowly shook his head, and resumed staring out at the quiet sea. The light of countless stars twinkled over the waves, silvery, almost white, like the shards of millions of broken mirrors.

"Uh, Walker?" Jolly was clambering out of the belly of the sloop again and standing on the top step of the ladder.

The captain broke off his conversation with Buenaventure. "What's the matter?"

"Bad news."

"How bad?"

"We have stowaways aboard."

Walker slammed his fist on the railing. "I'll come right down. Stowaways? Several?"

A pained smile spread across Jolly's face. "At least fifty, I estimate."

"Fifty?" Walker leaped down the steps to the main deck in one bound.

Jolly nodded. "And they smell . . . well, not good, I'm afraid. Not good at all."

The G

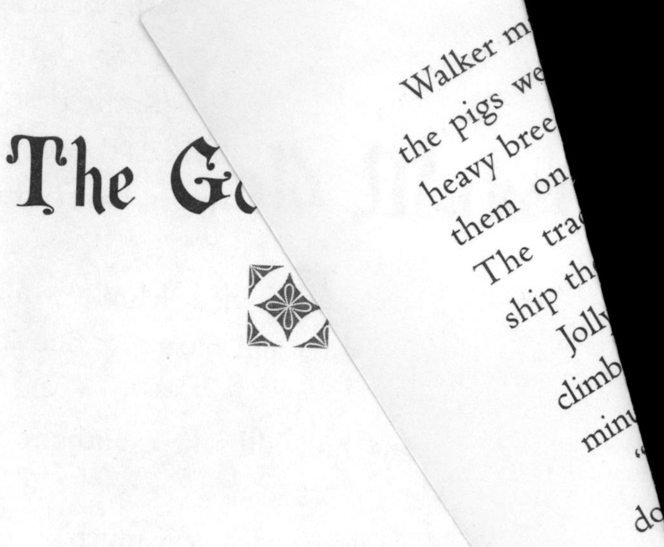

Walker and Munk hurried over to whe standing. Walker looked down through the cargo ha

"Well, I'll be damned!" escaped the captain.

"Uh," said Munk, and he turned away. "That sn like—"

"Jean-Pauls," said Walker.

Jolly's eyes widened. "Jean who?"

Munk held his nose. "You mean French people smell like that?"

"Those aren't French," said Walker impatiently. "They're only called that."

"Pigs," said Jolly. "The entire hold is full of pigs."

The grunting and snuffling of the animals was clearly audible on the ladder, even drowning out the sound of the ocean and of the wind in the rattling sails.

"If you insist that they remain," Walker continued, "then you must pay for their passage too, whether you like it or not, not just for your own."

"You can't be serious!" Jolly had to keep herself from going for his throat.

"Fiddlesticks! There are rules on board. One is that the transport of passengers must be paid for. And if you want these swine to make the voyage with us, you have to pay the price for them."

"I've promised you an entire *treasure!*"

He thought about it. "It must be a really *large* treasure."

"It is, damn it all!"

"How big?"

"It's . . . it's . . ." Jolly could hardly get out a coherent sentence, she was so furious.

At that moment Soledad came to her rescue. "Walker!"

The pirate turned to her.

"You know who I am, don't you?"

He nodded. "Your father was a good . . . business friend."

"You swindled him."

"Oh, *that* . . . only a slight misunderstanding."

"A whole shipload of rum. He swore to have your head for it."

"God bless him. He was an upright man, in spite of everything."

"You owed him something. And now, since he's dead, you owe me. How many ducats were all those barrels of rum worth, Walker? A hundred? Five hundred?"

He gave a deep sigh. "I see it already . . . the pigs can stay. But with that, we're quits."

Soledad did something that Jolly found utterly and completely horrible, but the effect was enormous: She walked up, kissed Walker lightly on the cheek, winked at him, and whispered, "There's still some honor, even among us pirates, isn't there?"

Walker beamed from one ear to the other, scratched his neck in embarrassment, cleared his throat, murmured "No hard feelings" to Jolly, and stomped back up onto the bridge.

Jolly blew her stack. "What a repulsive, shabby, underhanded—"

"Do you think he'd be a good kisser?" Soledad was looking after Walker.

"What?"

Soledad laughed, and this time Munk joined in. Jolly stared darkly from one to the other. "Can it be that no one takes me seriously around here?"

Soledad and Munk laughed even louder.

Next morning they had a meeting in the captain's cabin.

Walker had taken a chair behind a wide desk. The morning sun was streaming in through the bull's-eye window at his back. Soledad had claimed the only other chair. Jolly and Munk leaned against the wall, arms crossed.

"We need about four days to Tortuga," said Walker. "That is, if we have good winds and no Spaniards or anyone else crosses us. We'll sail around the Bahamas on a northeasterly course. The weather on the open Atlantic will be a little rougher, but perhaps it'll help us move ahead faster. Then we go through the Caicos Passage south, straight to Tortuga."

Several sea charts, yellowed and cracked from many years of intensive use, lay open or half unrolled on the wide desk. Some were weighted at the corners with various objects: a pistol, delicately beautiful nautical instruments, a handful of tin figures, a shrunken head, a golden statue of the Virgin with a third eye in the forehead, a rotten, dark brown banana, and a pipe with artful carving. The room smelled pleasantly aromatic, of good tobacco and polished wood; both were hard to fit into the picture that Jolly had made for herself of Walker as the wild, dissolute pirate.

"Does anyone have any objections?" the captain asked the circle.

The two polliwogs shook their heads, but Soledad frowned. "Isn't it quite daring to trust to the Atlantic winds in our situation?"

"No more daring than breaking through the Spanish armada. Besides, these ghosts your friend left us are quite passable seamen. Do you think I can keep them when this is all over? As a friendly gesture, because I've declared myself so disinterestedly ready to help you out of a jam."

Munk smiled, savoring his answer. "These are the ghosts of all the men who've died aboard this ship. It's very possible that they have nothing good to say about you, Walker."

"Oh?" The pirate gulped. "Well, maybe not such a good idea." He turned quickly to Soledad. "As for the storms, this time of year they usually go a different way. I think we'll have no problems."

The princess shrugged. "Your decision, Walker. You're the captain. What does Buenaventure say about it?"

The pit bull man was the only one who'd remained on deck. Since they'd weighed anchor, he'd stood at the wheel as if nailed there and taken no breaks. Jolly wondered how much dog there actually was in him. All the dogs she knew snored all day long, curled up in some corner or other of the ship.

"He's in agreement," Walker said, as he smoothed the topmost chart with the flat of his hand. "To be honest, it's not the weather that concerns me. Recently there've been reports—or, let's say, rumors. . . . In any case, people say that the man in the whale has been seen in these waters."

Jolly and Soledad exchanged a quick look.

"The man in the whale?" asked Munk. "Who's that?"

"Someone sea people in this region tell about," Jolly explained. "A gigantic whale who has a man living in his belly. He surfaces out of nowhere, rams ships, and carries them under. Those who survive the sinking are swallowed by the beast."

Munk smiled. "How can a man live in a whale? That has to be a sailors' yarn."

He looked from Jolly to Soledad to Walker. Not one of

the three returned his smile. "Isn't it?" he asked uncertainly.

"The man in the whale is one of the great scourges of a sea voyage," said Walker portentously. "Worse than the deep-sea tribes, worse still than the giant kraken."

"Have you seen him?" Munk asked.

"I wouldn't be standing here before you if I had, boy. No one who sees the man in the whale with his own eyes survives the encounter."

Jolly and Soledad nodded in agreement.

Munk said nothing more. Possibly he was imagining the horizon of the Caribbean Sea breaking apart from one moment to the next and something gigantic rising up from the deep, a humpbacked body, in his open mouth a human figure pointing to the *Carfax* and goading on the rage of the monster with wild cries.

"Munk?"

He jumped. "Yes?"

"Everything all right?" asked Jolly.

"Sure, of course. Why?"

Walker's grin was almost tender. "You were just mighty pale around the tip of the nose, boy."

Munk merely shook his head silently. Instead, Jolly spoke as she glared angrily at the pirate. "Munk lost his parents just a few days ago. Satisfied now, *Captain* Walker?"

The pirate stared at her, surprised at her burst of anger. Then he gave Munk a look that might even have been sympathetic.

"Leave it," said Munk to Jolly. "That's my business."

She inspected him closely, sad because he was closing her out along with the others.

Walker turned to Soledad. "Can you steer a ship? Buenaventure has to have a few hours' rest. This seems to be a good time for it. The sea is quiet, everything is going as planned."

"Of course," she said.

"What about us?" Jolly asked. "Can we do something?"

Walker got up from his chair and nodded. "Take care of your friends in the cargo hold. They're going to be hungry in time. There are a lot of sacks standing around down there. I just hope there's feed in them."

"Aye, aye," said Jolly. "Are you coming with me?" she asked Munk.

"Of course."

The galley and the weapons store adjoined the narrow passage in front of the captain's cabin. A few steps at the end led up to the deck. Outside, Jolly breathed deeply. The Caribbean Sea lay brilliantly blue under a cloudless sky. The wind blew warm over the waves and caught in the sails. The air smelled of salt. From one of the masts came the screeching of a bird, yet when Jolly and Munk looked up, they saw, not one of the Ghost Trader's parrots, but only an albatross, who returned their stare with button eyes. The ghosts were almost invisible in the bright sunshine, mere shadows through which the light fell without breaking.

While Soledad took over the steering from Buenaventure, the two polliwogs clambered down into the cargo hold. The stink was almost unbearable. The pigs were standing closely crowded together on a thick carpet of straw. There were several troughs, a few of them with dirty water. Most were empty, however. The feed had to be poured out of the sacks into them.

Jolly held her nose. "This is so sickening."

"Oh, well." Munk waved it off and scratched one of the animals on the back. "We had a few pigs on the farm. It won't be enough to feed them twice a day. Their hearts will stop if they get too hot."

"And that means?"

"Really they need to wallow in mud. But for the voyage it would probably be enough to pour water over them now and then."

"All fifty?"

He nodded. "It's going to mean quite a lot of carrying."

"Walker will be thrilled if we flood his lower deck."

"Then we'd best start it right after feeding, while he and Buenaventure are asleep."

It was, in fact, an arduous grind to shake the feed out of the sacks into the trough and then, in addition, bring bucket after bucket out of the sea on a rope, balance it down the ladder, and pour the water over the pigs. Soledad was by no means pleased by the quantities of water the two were taking below deck, but Munk assured her that the largest part of it would evaporate within the shortest time among the overheated pig bodies. He was right about that, but gradually it made the stink even more unbearable, and now it seemed to rise up between the planks and over the entire ship.

They'd almost doused all the pigs when there was some sort of disturbance in the back corner of the cargo hold.

Suddenly a dark figure arose in the midst of the animals.

Jolly was startled, but she grew calm again as soon as she realized that under the crust of filth was a boy. "What sort of a pig are you, then?"

Munk's expression became even more unfriendly. "Isn't that—"

"Griffin?" Jolly pushed between the pigs to the boy. "Damn it, what are *you* doing here?"

Griffin smiled. His numerous braids were stiff from all the filth that covered him. "I was on the brigantine when the mast from the other ship crashed on the deck. I jumped overboard and swam behind your rowboat. Then I climbed aboard on the other side and hid down here." He thumped a pig on its bristly body. "Charming society, really. We have too many preconceptions about the poor beasts. They can be very considerate, and their conversation—"

"You ought to have shown yourself right away," said Jolly reproachfully. She wasn't sure what she felt about Griffin's sudden appearance. Satisfaction at his discomfort. And distaste. A trace of anger—but also . . . a certain relief that he'd survived the attack on Port Nassau safely. She'd already wondered if he'd managed to escape the flames.

"Show myself? And have my neck wrung by the giant up

there?" He waved his hand. "I had a little . . . incident with Buenaventure, if one might call it that."

"You cheated him at cards," said Munk ill-humoredly.

"We saw it all," Jolly agreed.

"You were in the harbor when . . . oh, man, that was really bad. I thought I was as good as dead. Did you see what he did to us? I never saw anyone hit like that." Griffin pressed his way through the pigs. "Do you think he'll throw me overboard?"

Jolly shook her head with a sigh. "Not as long as we pay for your passage."

Munk threw her a warning look.

"You'd do that?" Griffin asked, dubious. "Do you have that much gold?"

Munk's expression grew darker. "All the treasure in this world."

Jolly laughed humorlessly. "We've found a way to pay Walker *without* paying him."

"Sounds good," said Griffin. "So I can stay with you?"

"I don't know," said Munk. "Jolly said you were a good swimmer."

"Munk!"

Griffin frowned.

Munk grinned. "I saw gulls. It's certainly not far to the next island."

"*Of course* you're staying," Jolly inserted angrily. "And the first thing you can do is help us."

"Carrying water, hm?"

"We could appoint him swineherd," Munk suggested. "Then he could work off the price of the voyage."

Griffin turned down one corner of his mouth. "The company down here isn't any worse than up on deck with you, anyway."

"You!"

A pulsing vein appeared in Walker's forehead when he caught sight of Griffin. Jolly stepped protectively in front of the pirate boy, while Munk, wearing an amused smile, followed the drama from a safe distance. Jolly suspected that he was still secretly hoping that Buenaventure would throw Griffin over the railing on the spot. The antagonism between the two boys was mutual, and that annoyed Jolly. Griffin and Munk didn't even know each other, and yet there'd been a palpable tension between them from the first moment.

"You nasty little dung beetle!" cried Walker as he stormed from the cabin onto the deck. "You louse! You good-for-nothing horse thief! You miserable son of a—"

"Come on, Walker," said Jolly. "Calm down."

"I'll be hanged if I will."

"Then think about something else—about the treasure, for instance."

Walker stopped. "He swiped five ducats from my pocket, this rat! When Buenaventure sees him here, he'll—"

At that very moment the silhouette of the gigantic pit bull man appeared in the cabin door. For a long moment he stood there as if he'd taken root. Then they all heard an ominous crack as he clenched his fists.

"Oh my," whispered Griffin. He wouldn't allow Jolly to protect him, however, but shoved her aside and walked bravely toward Buenaventure and Walker. "Listen, can we perhaps settle this like gentlemen?"

Walker smiled grimly. "I'll have you hung from the mast by your pigtails."

Jolly knew that Griffin was an outstanding fencer, but she wasn't sure if he'd have a chance against the more experienced pirate captain. Entirely apart from Buenaventure, who would hack him into pieces with one blow.

The pit bull man stomped toward Griffin with ominous steps.

"Stop!"

Soledad's voice made them turn around. "That's enough!" she cried. "No one here is going for anyone's throat!"

"I didn't know you'd already taken possession of your father's inheritance, O Empress of All the Pirates," Walker said scornfully.

"Shut your mouth, Walker. And you stay where you are, Buenaventure."

"I'm the captain of this ship," Walker replied obstinately. "And I say he goes overboard."

"How many barrels of rum is his life worth, Walker?"

"Rum?" asked Walker, irritated.

Munk rolled his eyes.

Walker put his hands on his hips. "You can't keep doing all your business with hot air only. That isn't . . . fair."

"Your debts to my father were high enough to set a dozen bounty hunters on you. A dozen paid assassins, Walker. That means a dozen human lives. That should certainly balance the lives of a few pigs and this boy, don't you think?"

Walker exhaled sharply. "That is simply not a fair trade."

"You're a pirate, Walker. You've never made a fair trade in your whole life."

"Why not start today?"

Munk sat down on the deck cross-legged, pulled out his mussels, and grouped them in a pattern on the boards. While the others still argued and Jolly and Griffin looked from one to the other in amazement, Munk made a magic pearl arise in the midst of the mussels. It shimmered as it floated in the center of the pattern.

Jolly noticed it first. Then Griffin looked over, and finally Soledad and the two men.

"What the devil . . . ," Walker exclaimed.

Munk closed his eyes. Murmured something. Performed a complicated hand movement.

From the center of the glowing pearl, gold pieces rained onto the deck. Twenty, thirty doubloons pelted down one after the other, clinking and rolling around without leaving the circle of mussels.

Sweat poured down Munk's face as he wordlessly commanded the pearl to withdraw into one of the mussels. The gleaming sphere floated into a small, insignificant shell. Munk quickly snapped it shut, took a deep breath, and looked at Walker.

Jolly and Munk merely looked at each other, silent and anxious.

Griffin shook a dead fish from his boot toe and looked incredulously out to sea. "Is there someone here who can explain this to me?"

Meanwhile Soledad had succeeded in disengaging the horny legs of the spider crab from her hair. She angrily flung the repellent thing over the railing.

Walker interrupted his recitation of oaths. "That happened because of you, right? Of course—it would be *you!*"

"Nonsense!" cried Soledad. "How would they—"

"He's right." At first Jolly spoke softly, almost guiltily, but then with all the resolution she could muster. "Munk and I have experienced something like this before. But—"

"I knew it!" Walker swore again. "I sensed right away that you'd only make trouble for me."

"But," Jolly repeated emphatically, "it gets even worse."

Walker fell silent and looked at her darkly.

"The same thing happened before Munk's parents were murdered. I think this fish rain is something like a warning."

"Warning of what?"

Jolly looked searchingly around, but the sea was still lying there quietly. Suddenly, she had a thought: Whatever approached in the protection of the fish rain did not come *over* the sea.

"From underneath!" she exclaimed. "It comes from underneath!"

"What?" Walker snatched his saber from its scabbard;

"Do you think . . . that's enough . . . for him?" he asked in a faltering voice.

"Munk!" Jolly caught him before he collapsed with exhaustion. She held him fast and patted his forehead with her sleeve. He lifted his face, looked her silently in the eyes, and smiled.

"Oh, Munk!" she whispered, hugging him. "That was . . . fantastic!"

"Give them the gold . . . quick, before they change their minds."

She nodded, made sure that he could sit up on his own, then took the coins in both hands and carried them over to Walker. He was still staring at Munk, wide-eyed.

"He . . . can make gold?"

"Looks like it," she replied coolly and let the doubloons shower onto Walker's boots. "Enough gold for Griffin's passage, at least. And for us and for the pigs." She grinned wickedly. "Looks as if your debts to Scarab and Soledad are still open." Enjoying the moment, she stood on tiptoe and brought her mouth to his ear. "In your place I'd worry quite a lot about the bounty hunters."

Walker stood there openmouthed. Then he turned abruptly to Buenaventure. "Did you see that? The boy can actually make gold! We're rich!"

Buenaventure only growled; it was impossible to say if he agreed with Walker. Jolly had heard him speak with her own ears, but for some reason he appeared to be content to utter animal sounds most of the time.

Soledad chimed in from the bridge. "Take your gold, Walker, and leave Munk alone. I warn you—don't get any dumb ideas!"

The pirate gathered up the coins and tested each one by biting it. Then he looked at Jolly. "I still get the treasure all the same, don't I?"

She dispensed with a reply and hurried back to Munk. Griffin was crouched down next to him, holding the back of his head and dropping water onto his lips from a leather bag.

"Hey," he whispered, "I owe you one."

Jolly bent very close to Munk. "How long will it last?"

"The gold?" A fleeting smile played around the corners of Munk's mouth. "A week. Maybe ten days."

"And then?"

"Air," Munk got out with difficulty and coughed. "As Walker has already said: nothing but hot air."

"It will have to do." Jolly looked back over her shoulder at Walker and Buenaventure, who were whispering furtively together. "By that time we'll have long since arrived in Tortuga."

Gradually Munk's face regained its color. He was just making an attempt to get up when something slapped onto the deck beside them.

They all whirled around.

On the deck, not far from the mussels, lay a dead fish.

Walker brushed it off. "Some bird dropped that. No reason for—"

He broke off, for at that moment it began to rain.

But what was falling from the sky was not water.

The Deep-Sea Tribes

Within a few moments the deck was overflowing with fish corpses. Everyone on board was flailing their arms around to avoid the smelly wet bodies, which rained down on them with considerable force. Walker was hit in the head by a barracuda. Jolly was just able to avoid the flabby tentacles of an octopus. Soledad was especially unfortunate: A dead spider crab got entangled in her red hair and hung from the back of her head like a particularly tasteless head ornament.

The gruesome rain ended as abruptly as it had begun. Suddenly no more corpses fell from the sky. It was as if the *Carfax* had reached the other side of a storm from one minute to the next—or the eye of the storm, and the worst was still ahead of them.

Walker gave loud vent to his disgust and surprise, while

however, he probably didn't know himself whom he intended to threaten with it. "What by all kobalins is going on here?"

"Kobalins, that's right," whispered Munk, who'd realized at once what Jolly meant. "When the Acherus appeared, there were also kobalins in the water."

Griffin laid a hand on his arm reassuringly. "I've fought with kobalins. There's nothing else to do if one . . . *falls* overboard now and then." But his grin was halfhearted and didn't hide that he was just as uneasy as all the others.

"Wait!" cried Soledad from the bridge. "Do you feel that?"

All became quiet. Buenaventure's nose was pointed to the air, scenting, with only his jowls fluttering slightly with every breath. Walker's eyes wandered frantically over the deck, while Munk kept his eyes closed, as if concentrating on another spell. But the mussels had already been returned to his belt purse.

Shudders ran through the *Carfax*'s hull. They had nothing in common with the usual swaying and vibrating of a ship on the waves. It was a fine, almost delicate trembling, which crept from the deck up into the feet and legs of the crew.

"Footsteps," said Walker tonelessly. "Those are footsteps!"

But none of them moved. And the ghosts, who were going about their work unimpressed, floated weightlessly without even touching the deck.

"It's coming from the underside," said Buenaventure—the first complete sentence Jolly had heard from his dog mouth. His voice was deep and growling, with an almost unnoticeable speech defect, which in someone else would have been taken for an accent. But in Buenaventure's case, it was because his jaws really were not created for speaking: He couldn't say a sharp *S*; from him, it sounded strangely soft, almost humming.

Walker cast a glance at Munk. "You're right, boy. It is kobalins. But since when does it rain dead fish when they turn up somewhere?"

"There must be something else with them." Jolly's voice sounded so subdued that she was afraid no one else could understand the words.

"Acherus," murmured Munk.

"What?" asked Walker. "What did you just say?"

"My parents . . . they were killed by an Acherus."

Soledad tied the wheel with a rope and leaped down the steps to the main deck. She had drawn two of her throwing knives. "What's that supposed to be, an—"

"Acherus," said Munk once more.

"A huge beast," said Jolly, bringing an end to the discussion. This was no time for useless explanations about the Maelstrom and all the other things the Ghost Trader had said.

"I have a really lousy feeling about this business," said Walker.

The pit bull man growled in agreement.

"A weapon." Griffin looked around. "I need a weapon!"

Walker pointed to a chest that was bolted to the deck right next to the entry to the cabins. "Look in there!"

Griffin hurried over, flipped open the lid, grabbed a saber and tested its weight in his hand, then chose another. "Jolly? Munk?"

Munk exchanged looks with Jolly, then shrugged. "A pistol wouldn't be bad." He walked over to Griffin, found what he was looking for, and immediately began to stuff powder and balls into the barrel. "I never learned swordplay, but I'm a pretty passable shot. I think, anyway."

Jolly likewise seized a saber, while Buenaventure pulled from his belt a knife that was twice as wide and much longer than usual; it was toothed on both sides, like a saw. Jolly shuddered at the look of it.

"Something about this isn't right," said Munk when they'd all taken places in a tight circle, back to back.

Soledad, standing beside him, gave him a questioning look.

"If it really was an Acherus," he said, "he would have attacked long ago. Jolly and I fought with one, and he could hardly wait to tear our heads off." He shifted the loaded pistol nervously from left to right and back. "An Acherus wouldn't wait so long to attack."

Jolly thought that the creatures of the Maelstrom might differ from one another, like people, and that they were certainly not as predictable as Munk obviously assumed. Besides, the Ghost Trader had spoken of *the* Acherus, not of *an* Acherus. Nevertheless, she would almost rather that Munk be right—if it was an Acherus, they would at least know what they had to deal with. But the thing underneath them might be a thousand times bigger. And a thousand times more murderous.

"Maybe he's waiting for reinforcements," said Walker.

Jolly shook her head. "A creature like that doesn't need reinforcements. Besides, the deep-sea tribes are on his side. These tremors, they're—"

"Kobalin steps." Walker nodded. "They're swarming underwater on the hull and now sticking to us like ticks. But that doesn't mean they're actually attacking. Sometimes they just hang on for a few miles, before they're suddenly gone as if they'd vanished from the earth. Most kobalins would never dare to attack anything that's bigger than they are—especially not a ship."

"But there have been attacks on trading ships," Jolly countered.

Walker shrugged. "I've heard those stories too. Nevertheless, there could have been pirates behind them to make it look as if the attackers were kobalins."

Soledad wiped sweat from her forehead with the back of her hand. "My father would have known of that."

"Your father wasn't all-knowing, sweetheart."

Soledad was about to flare up, but Munk calmed her with a hand and gently shook his head. *Let it go,* his look said. *There's time enough for that later.*

Jolly found it admirable that Munk remained so in

command of himself in a situation like this. They both knew what a creature of the Maelstrom was capable of. Jolly could scarcely feel her legs with fear, even if she tried to keep it from showing.

The waiting was almost intolerable.

Jolly looked up at the solitary albatross looking down at her from the edge of the crow's nest. She imagined what it saw: six figures who'd formed into a tight circle, faces and weapons turned outward, in fixed, tense expectation, and around them a deck empty of human life, across which busy misty beings wafted like a miraculous cloud of pipe smoke.

No sign of attackers. No indication of danger.

And yet . . .

"Jolly," said Munk suddenly. "The Trader did give you command over the ghosts. They could help us now."

"I already thought of that." She grimaced. "Unfortunately, he forgot to tell me what I have to do."

"Good to know." Walker looked as if he'd bitten into a rotten banana.

"Just tell them to stand around us in a circle and fight anything that comes near us."

Jolly nodded halfheartedly and sought the right words, when Munk added, "You don't have to speak the order. Just think it."

"But on the island, you used some words . . . in a foreign language. . . ."

"The Ghost Trader explained it to me. But there's no time for that now."

You said it, thought Jolly. "Then you say the words."

"These ghosts obey you, not me."

"But I don't know the damned spell!"

Munk sighed. "It's not that simple. The words have to come from you yourself; you have to catch your thought and your concentration into syllables that come deep out of your insides—"

Walker rolled his eyes. "Could you two just keep your mouths shut? This is blather like the stuff in church."

Jolly gave him a poisonous glare. "As if you had ever in your life seen the inside of a church."

"I plundered one once."

"There!" cried Soledad. "It's stopped!"

No one breathed. Everyone listened.

The pirate princess was right. The scrabbling and scraping on the hull of the *Carfax* had stopped. Only the hissing of the waves was to be heard, the foaming against the bow of the ship, the creaking of the planks and the shrouds.

"Are they gone?" whispered Griffin.

Walker made two quick bounds to the railing, looked into the water, and made a commanding gesture with his hand. "Quiet!"

Again they were silent. Listening. And waiting.

Soledad was the first to relax. "No kobalin holds still for that long."

Buenaventure nodded, but Walker directed them all to their places with a gesture.

Munk stared at his pistol as if he'd suddenly forgotten

how it had come to be in his hand. "I'm coming over to the railing."

"No!" Walker's voice allowed no contradiction. "There's nothing to see here. Kobalins always stay below the surface of the water. If they attack, they do it through the hull. But we'd notice if we already had a leak." He grinned crookedly. "Besides, the uproar from our friends in the cargo hold would warn us."

The stories claimed something else. Every attack of the deep-sea tribes on a ship—when they ever dared one—began with the leaders climbing over the railing. Only afterward did the other kobalins start to break through the hull. The most important rule in a kobalin attack was therefore always, above all, to keep an eye on the deck. As long as none of the especially large and ugly kobalins turned up, the hull was safe.

Walker must know that. But then why did he try to keep Munk back from the railing? Jolly couldn't make any sense out of it.

It must be that Walker had seen something—and wanted to keep panic from breaking out!

An ice-cold hand moved down her back. Her knees, almost completely numb, nevertheless began to tremble.

She left the formation and dashed over to the railing.

"Toad!" bellowed Walker. "Don't do it!"

She no longer heard him. Her fingers clenched the wood as if she wanted to tear it out of its fastenings.

The water of the Caribbean Sea, so they say, is the clearest of any of the seven seas. But at this moment Jolly wished for the gloomiest broth in the world.

She could look some twenty, twenty-five feet down, and what she saw almost turned her stomach.

Kobalins were moving through the water. The sea was full of them, directly under the surface as well as in the darker, colder depths. Jolly didn't doubt that there were also more kobalins swimming where she couldn't see them. Thousands of them.

It was an army. Hundreds of armies.

The deep-sea tribes were gathering and moving in a southwesterly direction—on the same course the *Carfax* was taking.

"Why don't they attack?" Griffin asked.

Jolly was still numbed. She hadn't noticed that he'd moved over beside her. Now Griffin was standing on her left, Munk on her right. The others were also bending over the railing.

"It'd be better if none of you had seen that," murmured Walker. "It'd be enough if only one person never closed an eye for the next few days."

Jolly had too much else in her head to marvel now at Walker's consideration. Possibly she'd judged him unfairly, though. Not *entirely* unfairly. But at least a little.

The stream of the kobalin armies did not cease. As far and as deep as Jolly could see, the undersea hosts were moving. A muster of the deep-sea tribes such as there had never been before.

The Ghost Trader had been right: Things were in motion whose dimensions they were all still unable to evaluate.

"They aren't attacking because they have different orders," Jolly answered Griffin's question. "Before, when the dead fish fell from the sky, one of their leaders must have been passing the *Carfax*. The kobalins aren't creatures of the Maelstrom, and so the rain stopped. But the one who leads them comes from the Mare Tenebrosum. Just like the Acherus."

Walker, Soledad, and Griffin exchanged uncomprehending looks; only Munk agreed with a thoughtful nod.

And still the swarms of kobalins moved along beneath the *Carfax*, as if the ship weren't there.

"They must have scented the pigs," said Munk. "So a few of them broke ranks. Their leaders must have called them back before they could do anything to the hull."

"There must be ten thousand of them," said Soledad in a hoarse voice.

Walker stared spellbound at the water. "Maybe even more. I've never seen anything like this."

All were fascinated by the inconceivable spectacle under their feet. Fear lay in the air like an evil smell, and still none of them could tear their eyes away. Only after half an eternity, it seemed to Jolly, did the kobalin swarms begin thinning out and finally disappeared completely. Soon afterward the depths of the sea were again azure blue and clear.

Walker grabbed Jolly roughly by the shoulder and pulled her away from the railing. "Looks as though you owe us a few explanations. What's this Maelstrom you spoke of? And that other thing—Mare . . ."

"Mare Tenebrosum." She avoided his eyes, but only for a

moment. Then she looked at him defiantly. "Munk and I don't know much more about it than you do. The Ghost Trader spoke of it, of an endless ocean in another world . . . and of a maelstrom that is probably something like a gate into it. Sometimes creatures come out of the Mare Tenebrosum over to us, creatures like the Acherus. Somehow the Ghost Trader wants to keep things from getting worse, from this gate opening and—" She broke off and angrily shook Walker's hand off her shoulder. All the rage she'd kept bottled up since the death of Munk's parents broke from her in an instant and poured out onto the one who just happened to be standing next to her—Walker.

Not that it was falling on an innocent, she thought angrily.

"The Maelstrom is after Munk and me because we two are the last polliwogs," she went on furiously. "No idea why he wants to kill us for that. But I've lost my crew, Munk has lost his parents, we've been in flight for days, Kendrick's men have chased me through Port Nassau, and then we're almost roasted alive, too. Do you really think if either of us knew anything that would help us along, we'd keep it to ourselves?"

Walker looked at her, flabbergasted. "I've heard a lot of crazy sailors' yarns in my life, but this really beats all."

Jolly uttered an exclamation of fury, turned away, and went back to the railing. "This is just a waste of time."

Walker smiled. "You didn't let me finish."

"I'm sure I've missed some nasty witticism."

His smile turned into a broad grin. "I was going to say that until a few minutes ago I'd have thought anyone was crazy who told me that a boy could conjure gold doubloons out of a few mussels. But I saw with my own eyes what your friend did before. And if that's the truth, then perhaps all the other stuff that you've just laid out for us is too."

Jolly looked at him appraisingly. "And that means?"

Walker exchanged a look with the pit bull man. "That Buenaventure and I will help you. We'll take you to Tortuga. And also farther, if necessary."

Munk raised a suspicious eyebrow. "Why this sudden change of mind?"

Soledad stepped in front of Walker. "Because of you, Munk. Our selfless captain scents greater riches. He's selected you to be his personal doubloon mint." She gave the pirate a reproachful look. "Isn't that so?"

"Well, yes . . ." Walker sighed and lifted both palms as if to ward her off. "I admit, yes, I haven't always been a great friend to mankind. But who could resist the charm of a princess and her two young friends?" His white teeth flashed, and he bowed in Soledad's direction.

She shook her head. "I have nothing to do with this business . . . with strange seas and creatures and a gateway to another world. *This here* is my sea, and I'm content if I succeed in establishing my claim to it. The rest can go to hell, for all I care."

"There won't be much left of the Caribbean Sea and the pirate kingdom if the Maelstrom opens wide enough." Jolly suddenly heard herself talking as if it were the Ghost Trader himself who spoke through her. But they were her own words, and if she possessed any power to convince, it was only because she was now beginning to believe in all these things herself. First the Acherus, then the armies of the deep-sea tribes. The world was in turmoil, and in the center of these changes, somewhere in the breadth of the oceans, a gigantic maelstrom was turning.

Soledad thought over Jolly's words. "The Ghost Trader knows more about this, you say? And he'll meet you on Tortuga?"

"That's what he said, anyway."

"Then I'll stay with you until then. I'll hear what he has to say, and whether the situation really is so serious."

Griffin had been quiet for a long time, listening, but now he spoke too. "Do you really have any doubt after what we just saw?" With a kick he sent a dead fish slithering across the deck to Soledad. If he'd hoped that the princess would jump to one side in horror, he was disappointed: She skillfully scooped up the carcass with the toe of her boot.

"Anyway, I've never seen anything like that before," Griffin went on, "and what Jolly has just told us is at least an explanation." He grinned. "Not especially believable, but an explanation. And I'd rather fight against whatever is responsible for this here than wait in some harbor somewhere for ten thousand kobalins to suddenly come on land to find out if they like the taste of human flesh unsalted as well."

Jolly sent Griffin a grateful smile, but at the same time she noticed that Munk didn't look altogether happy about the pirate youth's decision. Still, he'd kept Griffin from going overboard.

Soledad still hesitated, but then she nodded slowly. "Might be you're right, boy." She turned around and made her way back to her place at the wheel. As she passed, she gave Jolly a quick wink. "Come with me for a minute? I want to talk with you."

Walker's face darkened. "Secrets?"

"*Women's* secrets," said Soledad with a slight smile. "You wouldn't understand a word anyway."

"I can be very intuitive," Walker said indignantly. "And sensitive."

"Of course. Jolly, are you coming?"

Jolly followed her up the steps to the bridge and watched as the pirate princess untied the rope with which she'd fixed the wheel.

"You've got yourself into a nice mess," said Soledad in a low voice so that the men on the main deck couldn't understand her.

"On account of the Maelstrom? I can't help it. I wanted—"

"I don't mean that."

Jolly still didn't understand.

"I mean your two admirers down there." Soledad pointed with a nod to Munk and Griffin, who'd just had brooms pressed into their hands by Walker to clean the deck of the fish carcasses.

"My . . . admirers?" Jolly burst into ringing laughter. "Oh, come on, what's this all about?"

"You're either not as mature as you pretend to be—or blind."

"Bilge!"

"Do you really not notice how the two of them look at you? And how they look at *each other*?"

"They don't like each other. So?"

"That glint in their eyes is not hostility, Jolly. And not hate, either. It's jealousy."

Jolly laughed nervously, but she avoided Soledad's probing gaze. "Griffin is a pest and a liar most of the time. And Munk is a know-nothing boy who plays with mussels."

"I didn't say that *you* are in love with either of them, but the other way around. Although I'm not so sure. . . ."

"Oh, don't worry about that!"

Soledad smiled slyly. "I only want to advise you to watch out. You appear to have plans, if you were serious in your talk just now. Your two friends won't make this business any easier. No enemy is worse than the one in your own ranks."

"You think one of the two of them could betray us? Out of jealousy?" She shook her head again. "Because of *me*?"

"Men do dumb things when they aren't thinking with their heads."

Jolly waved that off. "You'd better watch out for Walker, instead. I've seen how he stares at you."

Soledad grinned. "One man alone is as reliable as a nun's check. As long as Buenaventure doesn't act like a male dog, I can manage Walker. One gets used to such things." Her eyes sparkled. "You're a pretty girl, Jolly. . . . I know you don't want to hear that. But it's the truth. And someday you'll be a very beautiful woman. It doesn't hurt if you learn to see the amusement in such situations. And, who knows, perhaps the good captain will be quite useful to us."

"Just like Griffin and Munk."

Soledad sighed. "You don't have to admit that I'm right. Just keep your eyes open. And don't do anything that can set them against each other. A powder keg is harmless compared to that, believe me."

Soledad turned to her steering. As far as she was concerned, the conversation was over.

Jolly leaned on the railing of the bridge with both hands and looked down at the main deck. Munk and Griffin were struggling with the dead fish, swearing. They swept the bodies into heaps to throw them overboard. In spite of the nauseating job, they worked together like good friends.

But had Soledad possibly been right? Was the accord between them deceptive?

Like a powder keg, she'd said. *Don't do anything that can set them against each other.*

Tortuga

Walker was right in one respect, anyway, and the encounter with the kobalins had proven it: The pigs had to leave the ship.

The unknown being that led the hosts of the deep-sea tribes and caused the fish rain over them couldn't have noticed that Jolly and Munk were on the *Carfax*—what would have happened if he had, Jolly preferred not to imagine. But they dared not take the risk that the juicy prey below deck might attract the kobalins a second time.

Naturally, Jolly steadfastly refused to drive the Jean-Pauls overboard. Munk and Griffin supported her, while Soledad stayed out of the conflict. Walker raised a tremendous fuss until it occurred to him that they'd pass an island on their way to Tortuga where a handful of missionaries had established a small cloister. With Jolly's consent, he set a course to the island. That he speculated on thus gaining a small supplementary income, he prudently kept to himself.

They reached the island on the third day of their voyage without a very great detour. They met no more kobalins on the way. The voyage was proceeding swiftly with a good wind, and Walker told them he hoped to reach Tortuga the next day.

With the help of the extremely pleased and grateful monks, they managed to get the Jean-Pauls unloaded. Every single one of the gigantic fattened hogs had to be driven out of the cargo hold, loaded into the ship's boat, and rowed to land. The work was a sweaty, wearisome drudgery, which held them up for a full day, despite Walker's predictions. Jolly was happy and satisfied when they handed the last pig over to the monks. In spite of all the dirt and the swine manure, she was sure they'd made the right decision.

It remained for her and the boys to clean the cargo hold and scrub the deck. Walker supervised them like a slave driver. His eye watchfully on his workers, mindful of every spot of filth, he leaned back tranquilly and lit a meerschaum pipe.

"How about you helping us?" Griffin asked grimly.

"I'm the captain," Walker replied with a shrug, "not you. A small but significant difference."

"It is not! Clean your stupid tub yourself!" Griffin flung his brush with force into a full bucket. Dirty water splashed onto Walker's boots.

The pirate merely grinned. "Do I detect the spirit of mutiny? That carries twenty lashes, administered by my trusty and justice-loving steersman."

Buenaventure drew his jaws into something that might have been a pit bull grin.

Griffin snorted scornfully, but he scrubbed on. "It's pure spite! The ghosts could do it just as well."

Jolly had already come to this conclusion, but she'd found that despite what Munk said, she had no success with commanding the ghosts. She simply did not know how to bring the wraiths under her control.

Walker had followed her vain attempts with malicious glee and of course refused to give the ghosts the order to clean in his position as captain. He offered the three of them the threadbare lie that the crew was urgently needed for other tasks. Unfortunately, he had no other choice but to involve his passengers in the necessary work on board. This was only the law of the sea, he said with obvious enjoyment; and unfortunately, he was right about that: Even pirates held to certain rules.

"If he grins once more, I'm going to throw him overboard single-handed," Munk whispered and scrubbed even harder.

Griffin pointed to Munk's belt purse. "Can't you turn him into something? How about a pig?"

"Too hard."

"Then at least make his hair fall out. Or make him lose all his teeth."

"Also too hard."

"God in Heaven, you can make gold! So something like that should be a simple matter for you."

"The Ghost Trader said that there are few spells more difficult than the ones that change creatures—no matter if the change is big or small. Dead objects, yes. Sometimes even the elements. But a human being . . ." Morosely he wrung out his cloth. "Anyway, I can't."

Jolly glanced at Soledad, who was standing on the bowsprit of the *Carfax* and gazing absently into the distance. Naturally Walker had exempted the princess from the order to crawl around the deck on her knees and scratch off the swine dung. Jolly doubted that Soledad would have let herself be ordered by Walker to do anything anyway.

"I think I still see a hoof print . . . yes, right in front of you, Munk." Walker contentedly blew a smoke ring. "And, Jolly, please keep after it a little more, eh?"

Buenaventure made a sound like a dog rejoicing over the return of his master and mistress; this time there was no doubt that the pit bull man was laughing.

Jolly thought she was going to chew the edge of her wooden bucket with rage.

But she didn't.

She kept on scrubbing.

The island of Tortuga took its name from the highly individual shape of its silhouette on the horizon: The first French settlers had dubbed it *la Tortue,* the turtle.

Merely a few miles separated Tortuga from the shores of

Haiti, one of the largest land masses in the Caribbean. Tortuga was almost invisible in comparison. Had not the first Caribbean pirates decided to settle there in the previous century, the oval hump with its tropical forests would probably have been shown on only the most precise maps.

Buenaventure steered the *Carfax* around the inhospitable north coast of the island, past cliffs and rocky promontories, rounded a barrier reef in the south, and entered the fortified harbor. With its two narrow entrances, it was easy to defend. Unlike New Providence, there was no sandy beach here, but a paved harbor street just beyond the edge of the water. Behind it rose houses with tiled roofs. On each side of the city stretched a wild, rank jungle of mahogany, oaks, ironwood, and bougainvillea.

It was already dusk when the *Carfax* found a suitable anchorage. They could get away from there swiftly if they needed to make a dash for it. With the onset of darkness, the ghosts were hardly visible as they reefed the sails. Walker had warned beforehand of the sensation the ghostly sailors on the *Carfax* would cause, but his concern turned out to be baseless: Most ships in the harbor were deserted, and the few watches left on deck had other things on their minds than paying attention to the new arrivals.

The comrades left the ship in the care of the ghosts and went ashore on the gangplank. Jolly looked longingly at the waves that splashed against the harbor wall below them. She battled the urge to run down to the water and leap from wave to wave; it was like a craze that seized her after long sojourns on land or aboard ship. The waves seemed to call her name, the wind pulled at her. Even the smell of the saltwater seemed to her spicy and inviting at such moments. But she withstood the desire. She couldn't attract any attention now.

When she asked Munk if he felt the same way, he shook his head in amazement. "No," he said, "not at all."

On land, they separated. Soledad and Buenaventure wanted to listen for news of the Ghost Trader in the taverns. It seemed almost impossible that he'd reached the island before them, but it couldn't be completely ruled out—anyway, they'd lost at least a day with the unloading of the pigs.

Jolly, Munk, Griffin, and Walker, meanwhile, sought out the old flag maker of whom the Ghost Trader had spoken. Silverhand was well known on Tortuga; in fact, there was probably hardly any freebooter flag hoisted in the entire Caribbean that hadn't come from his workshop. He embellished the famed skull not only with crossed bones but, to order, with sabers, pistols, even beer pitchers; another popular motif was skeletons, some armed with sabers, others with wine goblet in hand.

"Welcome," Silverhand greeted them, shaking Walker's hand cordially. He regarded Jolly and the two boys with slight suspicion, although Munk's admiring fascination with the many flags on the wall quickly placated him. "Just look around, boy," he said in a voice that sounded like the hinges of a rusty treasure chest. "I make two copies of every flag, one for the valued customer, the other for my collection. Every scurvy villain who prowls these waters and orders a

Jolly Roger from me is immortalized in this room—almost every one of them finally got themselves strung up by the Spaniards or the French. Some flags vanished forever when their ships went to the bottom; others burned, along with the crew. But they live on in Silverhand's workshop and recall their captains . . . and the gold they left behind."

He let out a snarling laugh. It struck Jolly that his hands were just as bony as the skeletons on his flags. But the most conspicuous features of old Silverhand were his scars. Jolly had already met a number of men who proudly carried the souvenirs of many a battle. Silverhand's scars, however, were not from saber blows or pistol balls. Walker had told them the old man's story as they'd made their way through the narrow streets: After he'd been at sea for many years, as sailor and as mate, even as cook, he finally landed on the tub of a particularly evil, degenerate freebooter. For some long-forgotten offense, that captain had the slight little sailor keelhauled—one of the most terrible punishments to be imposed aboard a ship. The victim is drawn across the hull beneath the ship on a rope. Any who don't drown remain marked for life: Depending on the condition of the ship, the rough wood inflicts the most horrible wounds on the poor devil. The tub Silverhand had signed onto was in pitiful condition, the hull covered with mussels. The sharp edges and points cut Silverhand's skin to ribbons, until it was hanging from his bones like a knitted garment.

Today his body looked as if all the pirates in the Caribbean Sea had sharpened their knives on him. The raised stripes ran every which way; his mouth was crooked in his face, and one eye was missing. His fingers were all that were left whole, so that he could earn his keep with meager pay in a flag maker's workshop. Soon he'd taken over the business, and now for more than twenty years he'd provided the corsair ships of the Caribbean with those symbols that instilled fear in law-abiding men.

"What can I do for you?" asked Silverhand, leaning his broken body against a pile of bolts of black fabric. Jolly estimated that he was at least eighty, ancient for this part of the world, where most men died young, on the gallows or in cannon fire.

"Show him the spider," said Walker to Munk. Munk pulled the little box out of his belt pouch, snapped open the cover, and handed it to the flag maker.

"A vicious beast, I'll wager," the old man said after he'd taken a long look at the spider. "So you aren't here because you're interested in my flags."

"I think they're fantastic," said Munk sincerely.

Silverhand grinned with his crooked mouth. "You're a good boy. Tell me, why are you showing me your spider?"

"It's really—"

"My spider," Jolly broke in. "I belong to Captain Bannon's crew. My name is Jolly."

"Bannon?" Silverhand scratched the back of his bald head, which was just as scarred as every other part of his body. "Bad business, that. I heard the *Maddy* was sunk. Bad, bad business."

Jolly told him what had happened.

"Spiders. Well, well." Silverhand brushed a hand over the upper bolt of fabric as if he'd just discovered it was there. "Beautiful creatures, in my opinion. But dangerous. As deadly as the plague."

"I wondered if you'd perhaps ever seen one like this in your voyages."

"Is that why you've come? Because I've been around more than anyone else?"

Jolly nodded. "That's what someone told us, anyway." She looked around and noted that Walker was listening attentively to her every word as he regarded her with a look of amazement.

Strangely, it was Silverhand who gave her the explanation for it. "You have much of Bannon about you, my child. The way you talk, the determination in your look. How long were you with him?"

"As long as I can remember."

"Then you must be the little polliwog he caught for himself."

Again she nodded, although it made her uneasy.

"A lot of fellows were damned envious of him. He was lucky, he was. Polliwogs, those were the most valuable treasure a person could think of. I wasn't at sea anymore at the time, but everyone was talking about it. Here and in the taverns and aboard ship. Some stopped at nothing to get one for themselves. Murdered to get their hands on the little wights."

Jolly's uneasiness grew. She hadn't forgotten what Munk's

father had intimated: that possibly Bannon hadn't bought her in the slave market but killed her parents and carried her off.

"The spider," she said with a trembling voice, pointing to the open box in Silverhand's bony fingers. "Perhaps you'd take another look at it."

But the old man's uninjured eye remained fixed on her, as if all the others had suddenly left the workshop. He measured her with looks, appraised her, burrowed in her thoughts as if in a drawer.

"Silverhand!" It was Walker's voice that finally broke the spell. "We don't want to take any more of your time than necessary. Do you know spiders like that or not?"

Reluctantly, the old man took his eye off Jolly and stared into the box again. "Hmm," he said lingeringly. "It's certainly a rare specimen. I'd like to wager it comes from the mainland. I've never seen one with a pattern like that in the islands, anyway."

"Are you sure?" Walker asked.

"Not sure. But I'd be pretty surprised to be wrong." He gave the little box back to Munk, who immediately put it away.

Jolly was disappointed at Silverhand's vague information. Why the devil had the Ghost Trader sent her here?

"Do you know where on the mainland it could have come from?" Munk asked, noticing Jolly's disappointment.

"No, no idea."

Walker intervened again. "Are you absolutely sure?" He

pulled out one of Munk's doubloons and flipped it over to the old man with his thumb and forefinger. Silverhand caught it up and swiftly made it disappear, but he only shook his head a second time. "I'm sorry. I'd tell you if I knew."

Walker took a deep breath, thumped Jolly on the shoulder, and nodded to the old man. "Thanks for your help, Silverhand. We'll be seeing you." Then he led Jolly and the two boys to the door.

They were on the threshold of the workshop when Silverhand's scratchy voice called them back.

"There is perhaps one possibility," he said.

Jolly whirled around. "What sort of a possibility?"

"The oracle."

Walker's eyes narrowed. "God in Heaven, man. We don't need any soothsayers, but—"

Jolly interrupted him impatiently. "Where do we find this oracle?"

Silverhand gave her a narrow, almost lipless smile. "Down in the harbor, the ship with the fanciest figurehead. It's a mermaid, but bigger and more beautiful than all the others. Just go join the other people; around this time there'll be a crowd there."

"Who's aboard this ship?" Walker asked mistrustfully.

"Aboard?" Silverhand giggled. "Not a living soul. That tub's a wreck that will never sail anywhere. But it talks. The damned figurehead talks."

Walker shook his head. "Silverhand, what's the idea?"

"It's the truth, believe me! Old Silverhand doesn't need to lie to you." His eye plunged into Jolly's mind like a knife blade. "The figurehead is the oracle. And if she wants to . . . only if she wants to . . . she will answer your question."

The Voice in the Wood

"I'm going to burn that whole infernal wreck!" the pirate approaching them as they reached the harbor was bellowing at the top of his lungs. Two other men were holding him by the arms, as if they were trying to lead him away, while he struggled to tear himself loose and turn back. "Nothing's going to be left . . . not a goddamned board. That . . . that thing's ruined me. Ruined, hear me? Telling me my ship is going down on the next voyage! Who's going to hire on with me now? That monster! Devil's work, I tell you! Devil's work and witches' haunt!"

His two companions tried to calm him, but the pirate wasn't listening.

"I'll do her in. I don't care if she's wood or flesh and blood! I'll burn her, that's what they do with witches! No one's going to play around with me like that! Not with me!"

The two men pulled their excited comrade into a side street. "Come on, Bill, a little drink will get you thinking about something else."

Jolly and the others had stopped and now watched the three vanish into a tavern. "Ruined me!" they heard once more through an open window, and then the man's voice was swallowed in the noise of the taproom.

"Did he say witch?" asked Griffin, frowning.

Munk hooked a thumb into his belt. "Do you think he meant the oracle?"

"Oracle! Bilge!" said Walker with a snort. "Silverhand isn't quite right in the head, everyone knows that."

A number of pirates were gathered at the harbor in the light of freshly kindled torches; among them were a few strumpets and maids, small children with dirty faces, and a handful of ship's boys of Jolly's age, who had taken up positions on boxes and barrels. The flames illuminated their faces and made them stand out golden against the dark blue of the evening sky.

Walker stopped a man. "What're all these people doing here?"

"The oracle is speaking to the people."

"Where do we find this . . . oracle?"

"See that old tub over there, the wreck, with only the bow still above water? The figurehead . . . she answers all the questions you ask her."

"Does she have a name?"

"Oracle."

"Ah . . . I thought so. Thanks, friend. I'll drink to your health later."

The pirate, on whose head sat a moth-eaten cocked hat, examined him with newly awakened interest. "I know you. You're Walker, aren't you?"

Jolly surreptitiously pinched the captain on the arm.

"Walker? Is he here on Tortuga, then?" He shook his head. "Sorry, friend, you've made a mistake."

The man's face took on a suspicious look and he leaned forward, as if he intended to sniff Walker to find out the truth. "I saw the *Carfax* lying in the harbor."

"Oh?" Walker gave him a fleeting nod, then left him standing. "So long, friend. Thanks for the information."

Out of the corner of her eye, Jolly observed uneasily that the man was looking after them as they approached the crowd. They quickly pushed in among the men and women to escape his mistrustful gaze.

"Do you think they're looking for us here?" Jolly whispered into Walker's ear.

"Your Maelstrom?"

"Kendrick."

Walker massaged his temples thoughtfully. "If he actually managed to escape from New Providence, Tortuga is a close-lying destination. Most here accept him as emperor. Of course, the *Carfax* is the faster ship. On the other hand, we've—"

"Lost a day," she said gruffly. "Yes, I know."

"Not including the time your swine friends' additional

weight cost us during the first three days." He was too uneasy to make any serious reproaches to Jolly. "Yes," he said after a short pause. "Kendrick could be here."

"And have put a bounty on me and Soledad?"

"Very possibly."

Jolly gnawed on her lower lip and wished she could make herself tiny in the midst of the pirate horde. The wild fellows smelled evil, of spirits and beer, of smoke and sweat. Nevertheless, she was suddenly grateful for the closeness, for it concealed her from the eyes of the man Walker had spoken to. When she looked around, searching for him, she couldn't see him anymore.

"Is there a problem?" asked Griffin, whom she'd lost sight of for a moment in all the confusion. Munk was right behind him.

"Everything's all right," she responded wanly.

"Now, what about the oracle?" asked Munk. "Are you going yourself or shall I?" The little box with the spider lay in his hand, the cover closed.

"I'll do it." Jolly took the little box.

"That isn't a good idea," said Walker warningly. "If they really are looking for us—"

He broke off, shaking his head as Jolly, ignoring his words, pushed her way through the crowd.

The noise was louder up front, but the many heads blocked her view of what was going on there. Jolly made herself as thin as she could, once even crawling between the legs of a gigantic freebooter. Munk tried to follow her, but she was much more nimble than he and reached the first row long before he did. Someone cursed when she pushed in front of him, but he didn't push her aside when he saw that she was smaller and he could see over her.

The figurehead rose over the quay, illuminated by several torches people had planted around her.

The face of the mermaid was, like her flawless body, carved of dark wood. Pupilless eyes looked out over the heads of the people, majestic despite the pitiful condition of the rest of the ship. Her features were rigid as stone. Only the flickering torchlight provided an illusion of life.

The figure was twice the height of a man and stood almost erect, because the galleon's stern was sunk into the harbor basin. Only a part of the forward deck, the bowsprit, and the figurehead itself rose out of the night-dark water. The rigging had rotted and fallen long since. The wooden statue was about five yards from land, so that it was out of reach of any hands.

A dozen men and women yelled over each other, each struggling to get his or her question to the fore. Two strumpets were scratching and hitting at each other, because each claimed to be the next in line.

"Does it go on like this all day?" Jolly asked one of the old sea bears who was observing the scene with relaxed amusement.

"All day? Oh, no." He drew on a little pipe that had seen better days. "The oracle only speaks at dusk, from sundown till dark. After that it's quiet again till the next evening."

"Oh," Jolly sa
sunk into the se
in the sky.

"Too late!" cried s
today!"

"There's no poem yet,"
the poem!"

Jolly turned to the old sai
poem?"

"Every night the oracle recites a p
a tradition."

Jolly was surprised, but she thought p
custom among oracles. After all, she'd never
before.

"Is it a good poet?" She was just talking to con
appointment. Now she'd have to wait till the next
ask her question about the spider.

"Good? By Neptune's algae punch!" The old man ro
his eyes heavenward. "Rarely heard a worse poet. Utterly ter
rible, Heaven and Hell! But there's a few here who remember everything and make songs for the taverns out of them."

She politely returned his laugh but was interrupted when a grating voice sounded from the figurehead's immobile head.

"Silentium! Quiet! I ask your consideration for those who understand something of poesy!"

Jolly started. So that was the voice of the oracle. It sounded more masculine than feminine.

fell silent.

ped forward between the onlookers to stand
"Pretty crazy, huh?"

nodded and listened.

acle cleared its throat audibly, but then it raised its
ice:

ce lived a most gallant corsair,
was his saber, black his hair;
ed to feast on frutti del mar—
a ship was lacking.

He strangled children and agéd dames,
whose heads he hacked from their very frames;
he plundered all of Kingston Town—
only the ship was lacking.

Rum tastes good for breakfast (he said),
Why not for dessert, too? (he said),
Rum in the morning, rum before bed,
but none of it helped: For the ship was lacking.

Booty in hand, he went to buy one,
newly launched, a lively, spry one.
Then he went to drink a quick one.
But the morning after: The ship was gone!

And thus, he learnéd one thing clear:
Sometimes ships just disappear,
Weigh anchor themselves, isn't it queer?
And what doesn't disturb them? The captain's lacking.

And the corsair? He stayed on land,
and was happy when, along the strand,
the wrecks of two or three ships he found.
He built himself a house of them.

Jolly blinked dazedly in the torchlight. No one said a word.

"Uh," said Munk, looking as if he had a toothache. "That was . . ."

"Not good?" Jolly suggested.

At that moment the crowd burst into loud shouting. The pirates all tried to out-cheer each other. Fellows who couldn't tell a poem from a swear word praised the great poetic art of the oracle in their gravelly voices. Others prophesied a golden future for him as a master of fine-sounding pirate poetry.

Jolly looked at Munk. "They aren't serious, are they?"

Munk shook his head in perplexity. "I guess pirates just don't understand art."

Griffin stuck his face out of the crowd, glowing with enthusiasm. "Hey, that was great, wasn't it?"

Jolly and Munk exchanged another look. "Totally great," they chorused. Munk make a gesture of sticking his finger down his throat, and suddenly Jolly was laughing so hard that she could hardly get her breath.

"What's the matter?" asked Griffin, confused.

Jolly just laughed harder, Munk joined in, and even the old sea bear grinned before he stuck his pipe between his lips again and walked away. After a few steps, he merged with the darkness.

Jolly gasped for air and was finally able to breathe again, but she still wasn't calm.

"So, can someone perhaps tell me—" Griffin was beginning, when a hand landed on his shoulder and shoved him to one side.

Buenaventure stood behind him as if he'd just risen out of the pavement.

"Got to get out of here!" said the pit bull man. "Kendrick's bounty hunters are right behind us."

The rest of their laughter stuck in Jolly's and Munk's throats as they realized how serious he was.

"They're looking for us," said Buenaventure. "Everywhere!"

Walker appeared beside him. "What're you waiting for?"

Just then Soledad joined them, her sweat-soaked hair sticking to her face in strands, a harried expression in her eyes.

"Run!" she yelled.

Jolly grabbed Munk by the hand and together they started running.

At the end of the narrow dead-end street lay the entrance to a tavern.

A handwritten sign with poor spelling announced that because of "certin avents" the previous day, the bar would be closed today for straightening up.

Since the street had no other exit and Walker was against going back and looking for another hiding place, Buenaventure raised his hand and pounded loudly on the wooden door.

"Can't you read?" roared a voice from inside. "Of course not, naturally you can't, uneducated riffraff! I should have thought of that, you mindless wine bags."

"Come on in, bring courtesy in," murmured Soledad.

The door opened a crack. A baldheaded man with one swollen eye stared out at them. Buenaventure had stepped to the rear, but obviously the sight of Walker was enough for the landlord.

"Closed!" he said hostilely and was about to shut the door again.

"Ho, ho," cried Walker and quickly shoved his foot into the crack. "A good landlord never turns away guests."

"Guests can go jump in the lake. It'd be good if this whole accursed island drowned in the sea. I don't want anything more to do with your lot."

"Think it over again," said Walker amiably, beckoning the pit bull man to step forward, "because otherwise my friend here is going to pee down his leg—in a manner of speaking."

The landlord looked up at Buenaventure unimpressed. "Dogs not allowed here. They smell bad, do their business in the corners, and beg for food under the table."

"There are voices on the other side of the crossing," said Griffin. "We should hurry."

Buenaventure shrugged, placed both his huge hands

against the door, and shoved it in, along with the landlord.

"Uncouth people," scolded the landlord, gesticulating excitedly. "And you have females with you too, probably the strumpets of all the fellows together and—"

Soledad planted herself in front of him, angrily placed her hands on her hips, and brought her face very close to his. "If you value your life, landlord, and even more, your teeth, then shut your trap right now!"

Astonishingly, this impressed the landlord much more than the threatening appearance of the gigantic dog man. He looked disbelievingly at the princess for a long moment, then he grumbled something unintelligible and made his way to the bar.

"So sit down, in God's name," he cried. "Take the candle over there and light as many as you want with it. What do you want to drink?"

Walker bolted the door on the inside. "I see you're a man with a big heart and superior mind. We know how to value the honor of stopping in the house of a gentleman."

"Yes, yes, yes." The landlord dismissed him angrily and took his place behind the bar.

They ordered beer and rum and water, besides all the food the kitchen had to offer—there were just two items, potato stew and chicken soup.

"No fish?" asked Walker disappointedly.

"No fish." The landlord vanished into the kitchen.

The taproom was in awful condition. Half the furniture had been smashed in the fight the night before. Jolly saw flecks of dried blood here and there on the churned-up straw on the floor.

A half hour later, with food and drink long served, a heavy knocking came at the door.

Walker, Buenaventure, and Soledad immediately went for their weapons. Jolly and the boys jumped up from their places. Griffin grabbed the saber he'd brought from the *Carfax*, Jolly drew her dagger.

"I can't see you," said a voice on the other side of the door, "and yet I know you're there."

Walker's lips were as narrow as a chalk stripe. "Isn't that — "

A smile flitted over Jolly's face. "Yes," she said. "It's the Ghost Trader."

"How did you find us?"

The Trader gave Jolly an indulgent smile. "There are ways and means," he began soothingly, "which are beyond your imagination—"

"Sure. And *really*?"

His smile grew broader. "I listened to the men who're looking for you. They're combing every quarter, and this is the one where you were seen last. As I know Walker, he'd lead you to a tavern. . . ."

The pirate wiped the beer foam from his upper lip and raised an eyebrow in disapproval.

". . . and he's sly enough not to choose one where you and Buenaventure would attract notice right away, so it had to be one that was closed. I found this one here and had only to listen at the door to be certain." He looked around them with a frown. "Just as certainly, the bounty hunters at your heels can come to the same conclusion. And there appear to be a great many of them."

Soledad nodded. "Buenaventure and I heard it in a dive in the harbor. Kendrick has placed a pretty little sum on my head—and on yours, Jolly."

Walker scratched his head. "Then this would probably be a good time to say good-bye."

The princess grinned at him. "Kendrick knows you and Buenaventure brought us away from Port Nassau. Now you're on his list too."

"Marvelous," said the captain darkly.

Buenaventure made a growling noise, but only Walker could know what it meant.

"How did you get here?" Jolly asked the Ghost Trader. He ran his hand over the dark plumage of the two parrots sitting on his shoulder.

"As fast as the wind."

"Yes, yes," she said with an exaggerated yawn, and she imitated his deep voice: "For there are means and ways, which are beyond our—"

The Ghost Trader interrupted her. "In this case, there are, in fact."

She pressed her lips together and examined the Ghost Trader closely. In the shadows of his hood his face had become serious again. She wondered if there weren't even more lines than a few days before.

"The sea eagles have brought bad news back to New Providence." He drank up his rum in one draft but didn't order a new glass. "There is greater danger threatening than I feared." He paused. His one eye rested on Jolly for a while, then wandered farther to Munk. Jolly thought she saw sorrow but also determination in it.

"It is time to arm," said the Ghost Trader. "The hunt has begun, the polliwogs are awaited."

"The Maelstrom?" asked Griffin.

The Ghost Trader seemed to notice the pirate boy consciously for the first time. Then he looked at Jolly. "Have you told them everything?"

Jolly shivered under his searching look, but she nodded. Then she reported to him about the host of deep-sea tribes and the invisible being that had led them.

The Ghost Trader clenched his right hand into a fist. "That only confirms what our allies in the east reported to me."

"*Our* allies?" asked Walker skeptically.

"The allies of all free men!" said the Trader sharply. "And of those who wish to remain so."

Walker snorted disparagingly, but he was silent. Jolly had the feeling that he had much greater respect for the Ghost Trader than he wanted to admit. Even Buenaventure uttered no sound. The landlord had first offered him a bone, in all seriousness. For a long moment Buenaventure had looked as if he'd have rather eaten the entire man instead of a bone. But then he'd only asked for another beer.

"Who are these allies?" Munk asked the Ghost Trader.

"I cannot tell you. Not here, where the walls have ears." He cast a meaningful look over at the landlord behind the bar, who was polishing the same glass for the third time. "But you'll learn to know them if we come safely away from this island."

"Do you doubt that we'll manage to do it, then?" asked Jolly.

Walker's eyes widened. "The *Carfax*! Kendrick will try to sink it." He leaped up so quickly that his chair tipped over backward. "Damn it all, we have to get to the harbor!"

"Calm yourself," said the Trader, "and sit down again. The ghosts are taking the best care of your ship. If Kendrick tries to board, he'll receive an unpleasant surprise."

"You've been aboard, then?" Jolly asked.

"Before, yes. And I ordered the ghosts to kill anyone who tries to set foot on the deck without permission."

Jolly shuddered.

"Could Silverhand help you with the spider?" asked the Trader.

"No. He only said it probably came from the mainland."

Sighing, the Trader shook his head.

"He sent us to this oracle in the harbor," said Jolly.

The Ghost Trader waved a dismissive hand. "The last living oracle I saw . . . oh, long, long ago. In Delphi. Whatever that thing down in the harbor may say, it is not an oracle."

"Delfin?" Walker perked up. "I knew this beer joint on Jamaica that was called that."

"*That* I most certainly did not mean," replied the Trader

with a reproving look. Insulted, the pirate pursed his mouth and looked back into his pitcher of beer.

"As always. Bannon must wait," said the Trader.

"No!" Jolly flared at him angrily. "It's on account of him I've gotten involved in this whole madness in the first place."

"Some heroes have gone on their journeys for the least thing and instead returned home with the crown of the world."

"I don't want any crown," she said snippily, "only Bannon."

"Now wait a minute," interposed Griffin. "You were the one who told us all about the Maelstrom. And about how important it is to do something against him. Did that all mean nothing, then?"

Munk also turned to her. "Griffin's right, Jolly. If polliwogs are necessary to bring this business to an end, then we both have to try it."

Jolly looked at the Ghost Trader again. "Munk can help you. He's a much better polliwog than I am. He can give orders to the ghosts, and then this business with the mussels. . . ."

"You can do that too, if you only give yourself a chance. And perhaps even more."

"Me? Bilge. I don't understand anything about magic. And ghosts give me goose pimples. I can walk on the water, that's all."

"Where I intend to take you, you'll learn to handle magic." The shadows around the Ghost Trader's eye were suddenly as deep as well shafts. Jolly grew dizzy. "In Aelenium you will understand everything."

"In—"

He kept her from saying the word with a wave of the hand and again threw a warning look over toward the landlord. "Quiet! There's been too much said already."

"Anyway, I'm not going anywhere where I can't find Bannon."

"Bannon is dead," said Walker abruptly. "Everyone knows that."

"He is not!"

"The ship must have sunk, Jolly. Otherwise someone would have found it. Believe me, no one could have survived."

"And what about me?"

"You're a polliwog."

She felt the tears come into her eyes, and that angered her so much that she fell into a grim silence.

Griffin slipped his hand over hers and stroked it gently with his index finger. She wanted to push the finger away angrily, instead whack him one—whack anyone in sight!—but then she thought that it really didn't feel so bad, and she even felt a little comforted.

Out of the corner of her eye she saw Munk turn away.

God, she thought, *whatever am I doing here?* Even though, really, everything was clear—she had to find Bannon, someone had to conquer the Maelstrom—she was more confused than she'd ever been in her life.

The Ghost Trader took up the discussion again. "The important thing now is to take the two polliwogs to that place where they are awaited. Walker, will you help us with the *Carfax*?"

The pirate looked anything but happy. "There was talk before of a certain treasure. . . ."

The Ghost Trader's face turned gray with anger, but he said nothing.

"Very good," said Walker hastily, "perhaps it will be enough if the boy does a few of his doubloon spells."

"Doubloon spells?" The Ghost Trader's eyes turned to Munk in surprise.

Munk shrank a little in his chair and shrugged.

"Ah," said the Ghost Trader suddenly, "of course—the doubloon spell!"

Walker nodded enthusiastically. "And you say Jolly will also learn something like that?"

Jolly had stopped listening, but the Trader nodded. "Of course."

Walker thought about it. "Hmm, then couldn't I . . . I mean, I was certainly a good student, who—"

"Can you walk on the water?" the Trader asked him.

"No."

"Then forget it."

Walker sulked for a moment, then he straightened and exhaled sharply. "Anyway, the *Carfax* stands at your disposal. Right, Buenaventure?"

The pit bull man signaled his agreement with a wave and emptied an entire pitcher of beer in one draft.

The Ghost Trader stood up. He threw a handful of coins on the table. "Then it's decided. We must get away from this island as quickly as possible."

They departed, leaving the relieved landlord behind, alone.

Outside in the street, the smell of fire met them. There was the sound of excited voices in the distance.

Walker grew pale. "That's coming from the harbor! The *Carfax*!"

The Wisdom of the Worms

The mermaid was on fire.

It looked as though someone had laid a mantle of flame around her. Man-high flames flickered around her wooden body. Her head had vanished in a green-yellow flare, with only her coal black face shining through the glow now and then. The empty eyes looked accusing, almost reproachful.

The voice of the oracle was silent.

Men and women were running excitedly along the quay. Several had formed a bucket brigade to try to keep the flames from jumping to nearby ships. The wreck itself could no longer be saved.

Jolly and the others ran the last stretch, fearing that Kendrick's bounty hunters had succeeded in setting the *Carfax* on fire. But when they turned out of a side street onto the quay, they saw Walker's ship lying unharmed in the darkness. If in fact anyone had tried to attack the *Carfax*, the ghosts would have repelled the attack. But everything looked quiet there at the moment.

When Jolly came to a halt in the confusion around the burning figurehead and peered through the smoke and fire with tearing eyes, she saw Bill, the angry pirate they'd watched earlier, being held on the ground and tied up by several men.

"Was he the one?" she asked one of the pirates.

The man nodded grimly. "Threw an oil lamp at the head, the dirty, rotten swine!"

"She's to blame!" howled Bill, trying in vain to defend himself against those holding him. "She's—" A blow from a fist silenced him.

"String him up!" bawled a woman.

"Burn him!" cried another.

Several pirates clustered together and looked as if they intended to carry out the demands. But just then a troop of uniformed Frenchmen appeared from the fort above the city and led the arsonist away. For a moment it looked as if some pirates meant to challenge the soldiers to give up the miscreant, but then reason triumphed. The French administration on Tortuga tolerated the activities of the pirates as long as they paid their duties; it would have been foolish to put such a lucrative collaboration at risk for the sake of a burning shipwreck.

"To the *Carfax*!" said the Ghost Trader. "This is a good chance to disappear without attracting attention!"

Everyone except Jolly started to leave. Depressed, she stood there staring into the fire, past the bucket brigades. Again, one less opportunity to find out what had happened to Bannon.

The flickering prow of the wreck rose over the water like a pyramid of fire. The surge of the heat against Jolly was painful. The air around her wavered.

She ran to the edge of the water. Someone almost ran over her, spilling half a bucket of water, and bellowed at her to get out of the way or help. Jolly paid no attention. Instead, she looked down into the harbor basin where the fiery, shimmering waters vanished under a ring of black smoke.

There was something in the water down there.

Something that was moving.

It was a bit longer than her arm, light-colored and hairless like a newborn, and it was curling and stretching in the water as if it were trying desperately to stay on the surface. But the smoke and fire clouded Jolly's vision, and she wasn't sure if her eyes were deceiving her. Perhaps that floating thing was just a piece of debris.

And yet, it *was* alive. Something that was threatening to drown if she didn't help it.

Jolly looked quickly over her shoulder, saw that her comrades stood waiting, then jumped from the quay down onto the water.

The crash onto the waves was hard and hurt her knees, but it didn't throw her off her feet. She immediately started running, earnestly hoping that the men onshore were too busy to notice her.

With rapid steps she approached the thing in the water. The heat down here was even worse, trapped between the burning wreck and the harbor wall. Sparks floated through the night in golden swarms and landed on the neighboring ships, but they went out without spreading more fire. Crew members stood behind the railings and threw buckets of water down onto the hulls. One man saw Jolly and shouted something to his comrades.

She paid no attention and ran on.

One thing she saw now for sure: The creature in the water was no child.

It wasn't even a human. In fact, it looked like . . . yes, a worm!

But this worm was almost two feet long and as thick as a man's thigh.

"Help me!" cried the worm, although Jolly saw no mouth on it. "Hurry up and help me, you silly thing! I'm drowning!"

She knew that voice.

Jolly seized the worm in both hands and lifted him out of the water. Then she ran on, out into the darkness of the harbor basin, away from the fire and the bellowing men, away from the heat, the smoke, and the hundreds of eyes that followed her.

"What are you?" she asked the slippery thing in her hands. "*Who* are you?"

"Dumb questions!" answered the worm, and now all the fear had vanished from his voice. "Who should I be, you ninny! I am the oracle. . . . I am the Hexhermetic Shipworm."

THE WISDOM OF THE WORMS

No one was charmed by the creature that Jolly had brought aboard the *Carfax*. Least of all Walker, who reminded her that shipworms nourish themselves on the *wood of ships*. And what was it made of, this whole damned ship, on which their lives depended out there on the sea?

"I can feed him," said Jolly. She thought she'd seen some planks in the cargo hold, wooden beams and boards that were stored there for repairs. Certainly Walker could part with a little piece of one of them.

"If he takes one bite out of my ship, he goes overboard."

"Boor!" retorted the worm.

"What did he say?"

"He's thanking you," Jolly hurriedly reassured him.

"Thanking, bah!" murmured the worm. "The ruffian isn't worth the wood to make his coffin."

Walker was already on his way to the bridge. "And no poems!" he called over his shoulder before he joined the Ghost Trader and Buenaventure, who were standing up there at the wheel and discussing the course. "One false rhyme on my ship and . . ." He drew his finger across his neck.

Jolly held the worm in front of her with both hands and stared into his face—at least where she supposed his face to be.

There were no eyes to be seen, only a broad shield of shell, at whose edge there was a mouth opening. He had six plump, stumpy legs, and his body twitched nervously when he was in a bad mood.

"How about a 'Thank you, Jolly, for saving my life'?" she

flared at him angrily. "And kindly stop insulting my friends." Internally, she was surprised at herself: Was Walker her friend?

The discussion of this problem had to wait, for the worm launched into a tirade of curses and rude language.

"Walker's right," said Griffin, regarding the strange creature. "We should throw him overboard."

"Oh?" retorted Jolly venomously. "I can remember when the same thing was supposed to happen to someone else. Weren't you quite happy when Munk prevented it?"

The corners of Griffin's mouth twitched, but he said nothing more.

Munk came to his aid. "That was different, Jolly. That . . . thing there is no human. It's ungrateful and shameless, and it knows more curses than Walker and Buenaventure together. Besides, it looks as if it stinks."

"I do *not* stink!" the worm said excitedly. "You little—"

"Quiet!" Jolly had to think, and she couldn't do it when everyone was talking at once. The only one who wasn't getting into it was Soledad. The princess was standing a few steps away and looking through the forest of ship masts back at the quay. The wreck was still burning. The smoke floating over the harbor might be helpful in their flight. The ghosts had been busy making the ship ready to run out. The powerful chain winch creaked as one of the wraiths hoisted the anchor.

The worm cleared his throat. "I would like to insist that I do not—"

"Take him below for now," Munk interrupted. "Walker

keeps looking over here, and the Ghost Trader doesn't look exactly happy either."

"That fellow pawed me over from stem to stern when Jolly brought me aboard," the Hexhermetic Shipworm fumed. "What's he got against me?"

"What's he got against me?" mimicked Griffin in a squeaky voice. "I've heard that lime helps against shipworms. And salt." A devilish grin flitted across his face. "We could try pickling him. Maybe he'd be quiet then."

"Eeeeeeh!" the worm squealed in horror, and he shrank in Jolly's hands to something that looked more like a ball than a worm.

Jolly stroked him soothingly on his shield. "Don't worry. The Trader was only afraid that you could be a creature of the Mael—belong to our enemies," she amended quickly.

"Maelstrom?" asked the worm, stretching out to his full length again. "Were you just about to say Maelstrom?"

Jolly exchanged an uncertain look with Munk and Griffin. Both boys looked just as nonplussed as she was.

"Yes," she said finally. The Trader had decided the worm was absolutely safe, so she assumed that she could trust him.

"Ma-Ma-Maelstrom," stammered the worm and then uttered a nerve-shattering noise that sounded like a vocal bosun's whistle.

"Now what's the matter with him?" Griffin rolled his eyes.

Munk went to the cargo hatch and opened it. "Down there with him for now. We can talk more below."

Jolly nodded and stepped onto the first step of the ladder. She turned around once more to the princess. "Anything suspicious?"

"Two ships over there are setting sails. That could be coincidence—or not."

"Damn!" Griffin followed Soledad's line of sight, but Munk pulled him toward the hatch.

"Walker and Buenaventure know what to do."

Jolly went ahead, and the two boys followed her. The smell of the pigs still lurked in every crack of the empty cargo hold. She doubted if she could ever look at a pig again without its turning her stomach.

"Over there," she said, pointing to the pile of wooden planks. "Walker can afford to do without a piece of that, I guess."

"What's that mean, a piece?" The worm flipped out of her hands and wriggled across the floor on its short legs, much more agilely than she'd have thought possible.

"Hey," cried Griffin, "watch out!"

"He's going to eat a hole in the hull," Munk prophesied darkly.

Jolly had noticed before that when things became serious, the two boys were always of one opinion—and that seldom coincided with her own. Anyway, that spoke against Soledad's dark presentiment.

She made a leap after the worm and managed to grab him by one of his bustling little legs. He squealed and scolded like a drunken ship's cook.

"I must protest most keenly! One does not treat a Hexhermetic Shipworm in this fashion!"

Jolly held him high. This time she clasped him firmly, and he soon stopped trying to defend himself. "You're hungry, aren't you?"

"My stomach is growling."

"Then kindly listen to me: You will eat only what I give you, understand? No holes in the ship's wall. No eaten-away masts. Is that clear?"

The mouth opening twisted into something that might be an offended pout. The shipworm sulked. "Yes, yes," he said crossly.

"Umm, Jolly?" Munk raised his hand as if he wanted permission to speak. "Ask him how much a day he eats."

"Ask him yourself."

"I am not *deaf*!" thundered the worm anew. "And I speak your language, boy."

"Then give me an answer," Munk said.

"One plank a day might be enough to keep me from starving to death."

"A *whole* plank?" Griffin groaned.

Jolly could imagine Walker's face when he learned of that. "You don't really need so much, do you?"

"Do you want to be responsible for my dying of hunger?"

"Perhaps," said Griffin, earning a mean look from Jolly.

Naturally she was just as upset as the two boys over the shipworm's brazenness. But something told her there was more to him than just an amazing stream of impertinences.

She was about to rebuke him again when he slipped out of her hands and scrabbled over to the woodpile so fast that even Munk and Griffin were flabbergasted.

With an indescribable sound, the worm ate his way along one plank in a flash: He clapped his mouth over one end and then simply ran forward, while his jaws reduced the wood to a cloud of sawdust and splinters.

He'd already devoured half the plank when Jolly caught him by the back legs. His jaws ground and chewed on, but now they were catching only on air. After some moments he gave up. Instead, he deluged the three of them with a now-familiar flood of maledictions and invective.

"So," said Jolly, "now you're going to answer a few questions for us." Turning to Griffin, she called, "Better close the cargo hatch. Walker doesn't have to know anything about this."

"Are you going to torture me?" the Hexhermetic Shipworm cried.

"Torture?" Jolly stared at him, dumbfounded.

Munk reacted faster. "Of course," he said in a menacing voice. "You should know that I am a grand master of mussel magic, and if it pleases me, I can turn you from a Hexhermetic Shipworm into a grunting green caterpillar with the wave of a hand."

"You . . . you'd do that?"

Munk pulled a handful of mussels from his belt pouch. "I already see," he proclaimed ominously, "that what you need is proof of my skills."

"Oh no, oh no."

"Sure?"

"Jolly!" cried the worm accusingly. "Why didn't you let me drown? A quick death would have been better than the company of such rude fellows." As he spoke, his voice got higher and thinner.

Jolly bit back a grin. "They're boys, you know? They're stronger than I am. If they want, they can do what they like with you."

"And they would love to," said Griffin.

The shipworm, after a short hesitation, shook his rear feet free, cast a longing look at the remains of the plank, and then sighed. "Oh, all right. I bow to raw force."

"What do you know about the Maelstrom?" Jolly asked.

The worm wiggled himself upright on the pile of boards and gulped. "Well, he's . . . big."

"Have you seen him, then?"

"Not directly. But I've heard about him."

"Who from?"

"Never heard of the wisdom of the worms? We have at our disposal a knowledge that exceeds your powers of imagination by far, you pale, ugly bipeds."

Griffin rolled his eyes. "Another one."

"So?" Munk asked. "Who told you about the Maelstrom?"

"Other worms. Brothers and sisters who lived on the wood of ships that were caught in the suction of the Maelstrom. Most were drowned with man and mouse, but a few ships broke up beforehand, and one or another piece of flotsam made its way back to civilization. The inhabitants spread the information about the Maelstrom everywhere. There are shipworms on every ship and every island—although most of them naturally are smaller and do not have the advantage of my keen intellect."

"Where exactly is the Maelstrom?" The Ghost Trader could have answered this question, but as long as he made a secret out of it, maybe the worm could help them along.

"Out in the Atlantic, beyond the outer islands."

"Can you possibly be somewhat more exact?" asked Griffin impatiently.

"Northeast of the Virgin Islands. It's said he arises from the bottom of the ocean, in a place that had a name from the time when there was still other life under there besides a few blind fish. 'Crustal Breach,' people called it then."

Jolly recalled one of the countless charts that Captain Bannon had kept in his cabin. He'd often studied them with her, initiating Jolly into the meanings of the strange signs, lines, and nautical terms, as he maneuvered the ship surely through the Caribbean with the help of all these particulars. The Virgin Islands lay at the edge of the Caribbean island world, forming the northernmost tip of the Lesser Antilles. On the other side of them there was nothing but thousands of miles of open sea, an endless horizon, an empty waste of water above uncharted shoals. There were regions into which a ship never cruised—as if they'd been created for the powers of the Mare Tenebrosum.

"What else do you know about the Maelstrom?"

The shipworm wriggled backward and forward uneasily. "Well," he began, "what do you actually know about him?

Especially your oh-so-powerful master magician?"

It took Munk a moment to realize that it was he who was meant and not the Ghost Trader. He looked as though he wasn't entirely comfortable about it. "That's no concern of yours," he said quickly. And, as if in corroboration, he shoved his hand into his mussel sack.

The worm drummed his feet on the wood, the way humans sometimes drum their fingers on a tabletop with impatience. "There are things going on, everywhere in the islands," he said, and for the first time he sounded thoughtful. "There are extraordinary creatures around, and the kobalins are gathering in swarms, completely contrary to their usual habit. Before, the deep-sea tribes fought among themselves, but now they unite into mighty armies on the march, which all move in a certain direction."

"To the northeast?" asked Griffin.

"Of course."

"We saw them," said Munk.

"Then I wonder why the one-eyed fool gave the order to sail the ship in the same direction." The shipworm gnashed his chewing mechanism as if he'd just discovered a few delicate shavings within it. "We'll all be swallowed up if we come too close to the Maelstrom."

"He's right," said Griffin to Jolly and Munk. "I heard the Ghost Trader order the course to the northeast."

"Aelenium," said Jolly, lost in thought. "That was the word he mentioned. Our destination, I think."

"In any case, that's no island I ever heard of," said Griffin.

"Perhaps it has another name," said Munk.

The shipworm had reacted when Jolly spoke the name, but now he was the picture of unconcern. She'd noticed, however. "You know what it is, this Aelenium. Don't you?"

"Oh, yes?" The shell on the shipworm's head turned greedily in the direction of the partially eaten plank. "If I weren't so hungry, then . . . perhaps . . ."

Jolly bent threateningly over him. "You *know* it."

"Possibly."

"We could pull his legs off one at a time until he—"

"Griffin!"

"My stomach just growled again," said the worm, unimpressed. Obviously he'd realized that Jolly would prevent any application of force. "And when my stomach growls, I can't think. And I remember nothing. Especially things that are so many miles away . . . and that one or another here possibly has a certain interest in."

"You're a monster," said Jolly.

"Can I eat now?"

"Only if you promise to tell us all you know about Aelenium afterward."

"Yes, yes."

Jolly pointed to the half plank. "And only the rest of that one, understand?"

The Hexhermetic Shipworm threw himself onto his food. In no time there was only a heap of fine sawdust left of the plank and two or three splinters, which he greedily gathered up with his mouth opening. "One shouldn't waste anything," he said as he chewed. "Never let anything go to waste."

"We're picking up speed," said Munk, letting his eyes roam over the creaking sides of the *Carfax*.

Griffin nodded. "It's about time, too."

Jolly placed her hands on her hips and stared expectantly at the smacking worm.

"Aelenium," she reminded him.

The worm gave a heartrending sigh, then bent his six stumpy legs in front of him and launched into a verse:

Aelenium, the beautiful,
I find no words,
she is—

"Enough!" Jolly placed her index finger against the head shell threateningly. "No poems, Walker said, and that also goes for us down here."

"No rhymes," confirmed Griffin.

"No verse," said Munk.

"No feeling for poesy!" cried the worm indignantly, but he thought better of getting into another argument. "Aelenium is not an island," he said after a short pause. "Aelenium is a city."

"A city in the middle of the sea?"

"Certainly."

"That's nonsense," Griffin declared with a dismissive wave. "He just wants to eat the ship out from under our behinds, that's all."

"I do not . . . or maybe I do. But nevertheless, I'm speaking the truth!"

Munk frowned. "Aelenium is a *floating* city?"

"Of course."

Jolly's eyes narrowed. "So it's something like a ship?"

"No, different. Stranger. Aelenium lies at anchor, on a chain that is many miles long and reaches down to the bottom of the sea. Besides, it is—to my regret—not built of wood."

"What, then?"

The worm trembled suddenly. A movement ran through its body like a wave—and gave vent in a noisy belch.

At the same moment, the ship shook. Jolly and the boys were thrown off their feet. She succeeded in grabbing onto a supporting beam, but then her hands slipped down and splinters bored into her palms. She let out a scream of pain, saw blood between her fingers, and instinctively let go.

Griffin, who was already back on his feet, caught her. Not especially gallantly, not even intentionally, as she supposed—but his hands shot out and caught her before she could hit the back of her head on the planking. *He really is* devilishly *fast,* Jolly thought.

"Thanks," she gasped, wiped the drops of blood on her trousers, and looked for Munk. He'd fallen quite a distance from them against the side and was holding his head and cursing softly.

"Everything all right?" she asked with concern.

He nodded and made a pained face. "My head hurts. But it will pass."

"Sure?"

"Yes." Now he was more careful and didn't nod again.

All three looked at the Hexhermetic Shipworm.

He'd rolled off the pile of wood, but he was standing on his short legs again—and he belched again.

This time the *Carfax* was not shaken.

"That was a cannon shot!" Griffin exclaimed. "A ball must have landed right beside the hull!"

Behind them the hatch to the cargo hold was flung open. Soledad leaped down the upper steps, looked around in the half dark, and finally discovered them around the pile of boards.

"Come on up!" she cried. "We're under attack! Kendrick's bounty hunters have found us!"

Sea Battle

Two ships had taken up pursuit of the *Carfax* in the moonlight.

One was a schooner with two masts, narrow hull, and great spreads of sail, which allowed it to gather speed swiftly. The shallow construction made it easy to turn and especially suited for maneuvers in shoaled waters.

"Few cannon," said Walker as Jolly and the boys came to stand beside him on the bridge. "The scurvy fellow is racy but not especially dangerous."

"Oh, yes," said the Ghost Trader gloomily. "He'll try to cut us off so that the other ship will catch us. These aren't competing bounty hunters—they're working together."

Walker was silent while he considered this possibility.

Jolly looked over at their second pursuer, a sloop like the *Carfax* that lay as deep in the water as a fully loaded trading ship—with the difference that the sloop was loaded with guns, certainly far more than they had at their own disposal. If the schooner were to succeed in passing and holding them up, they'd be sitting ducks for the overwhelming firepower of the second ship.

The bounty hunters must have been waiting for the *Carfax* to leave the harbor. With a confrontation on land, too many other pirates would have mixed in, greedy for the gold that Kendrick had set on Jolly's and Soledad's heads. Here in the open waters, on the other hand, no one would interfere with their business.

Walker snarled orders from the bridge. Buenaventure clamped his paws onto the wheel, and Soledad stood like stone at the railing, a throwing knife in her hand, as if she expected to deal with the boarding crew of the bounty hunters at any moment.

As usual at the beginning of a battle, sand was strewn on the deck so that the crew wouldn't slip and so waste precious time. In view of the ghostly crew of the *Carfax*, that was really unnecessary; the weightless ghost sailors moved without ever touching the deck. Many of them now gathered around the cannons and made them ready for the fight.

The wind freshened the farther Tortuga fell behind them. The bow struck the foaming sea and a deep throbbing and pounding came from the innards of the ship. The schooner was still on a level with them and sailing hard into the wind. The crew of the bounty hunter fired off their guns several more times, but all the balls landed in the churning waves far from the *Carfax*. Each time, the ship shuddered, but there were no hits that might have caused damage. Walker decided not to waste powder and iron until both ships were in a better fighting position. After a while, the schooner also gave up firing at the *Carfax*, trying merely to cut her off and not to sink her. That task was left to the sloop at her rear.

"They're dumb to waste the first broadside that way," said Jolly to Munk, without taking her eyes off the enemy ship. "The first loading is always the most carefully packed and targeted—at the beginning of a fight, the crew still have enough time for it. In the heat of the fight it has to go faster, and the shots are more uncertain."

"Do you know these ships?" the Ghost Trader asked Walker.

"The schooner is the *Natividad* under Captain McBain. He's not a bad fellow, if you don't have passengers aboard with a price on their heads." Walker sent Jolly and Soledad a dark look.

"Think of the gold," Jolly said.

"Believe me, I think of nothing else."

"You should, however," countered the Ghost Trader. "For instance, how you and your hairy friend there are going to get us out of this alive."

"I could always just hand the two of them over."

There was a whizzing noise, and something struck the railing beside Walker's hand with a dull thump—Soledad's throwing knife. The blade was hardly an inch from his pinkie finger.

"Just try it," she called over, "and the next one will stick in your forehead."

The captain beamed. "Your charm is, as always, breathtaking, lovely princess."

"So many have said that—and after that, nothing more at all."

Walker laughed softly and turned to Buenaventure. "Not any closer to the wind," he commanded. To the cannoneers on deck, almost invisible in the moonlight, he called, "All stand by for firing!"

Torches flamed up in the darkness.

Munk bent toward Jolly. "You said it was wrong to shoot right now."

"Right now—but maybe not in one or two minutes. If the schooner stays on course, that will bring her nearer to us. Walker wants to be sure we're ready at the best possible moment."

"Bannon taught you a lot about fighting at sea," said the captain approvingly. "Not bad for a little toad."

Griffin bit his lower lip. "They're going to fire any minute."

"What about the sloop?" asked Munk.

"Still too far behind us," Jolly said. "The *Natividad* made the mistake of challenging us too early. Instead of placing us under fire, she should have used her speed to catch up to us and cut us off."

Walker agreed with her. "McBain always was an impatient fellow. He was trying it on his own, and that's to our advantage."

"Do you know the captain of the second ship?" asked the Ghost Trader.

"I know the ship, the *Palomino.* She last belonged to a pirate from the Lesser Antilles, but the word is that he lost her in a dice game to someone else. He may be called Konstantin."

"Constantine," corrected Soledad, who'd hurried up to the bridge in three quick leaps. She pulled the throwing knife out of the railing. "He was once a good friend of my father's. Then he became one of those who betrayed him. It was through him that Kendrick got the opportunity to kill my father."

"Ah," cried Walker. "That gives the whole thing a piquant note, doesn't it? Now the affair becomes personal."

Was Soledad hoping to cross swords with her father's betrayer? Her eyes glowed with pure battle lust. The Ghost Trader was examining her with concern. What would he do? He wouldn't allow anything—or anyone—to thwart his mission.

Jolly's eyes roamed over the tense faces of her companions, and suddenly she felt sad. Deeply, incomprehensibly sad. Not all of them might survive till the end of this voyage.

The *Natividad* fired again.

Something snarled away over them. But before they all realized they'd missed death by a hair, Walker roared, "Confound it! They must have heavier guns on board than I thought."

"Fire," said the Ghost Trader calmly. "Right now."

"Yes, you're right." Walker whirled around and bellowed orders over the deck.

Seconds later the cannons of the *Carfax* spit death and destruction over the *Natividad.*

Whomever the ghosts had been gunners for in their first lives, they knew how to serve a cannon. And how to hit a target precisely with the first shot.

The thunder of the guns shook the *Carfax* down to the keel. For a moment the rigging trembled, as if the ship had run aground. Yellowish powder smoke wafted back over the deck and was snatched overboard by the headwind. Munk, who'd never experienced a sea battle before, squeezed his eyes shut as the acrid smoke floated over him. But Walker inhaled deeply, as if he enjoyed the smell, and Jolly gripped the balustrade more firmly, as if to support herself against the wind and the smoke of the guns.

The storm of iron swept away over the deck of the *Natividad,* shredded parts of the rigging, and made the remnants of ropes and sails rain down on the crew of the bounty hunter. Two balls tore holes in the hull of the schooner above the waterline; from the interior came the screams of the wounded and dying. Splinters sprayed in all directions like daggers. The balls had hit the cannon deck of the *Natividad* and destroyed several guns at one blow.

One figure stood grimly up on the bridge, undisturbed by the destruction aboard the ship, and roared orders: Captain McBain. He didn't consider giving up on the basis of a single hit. His angry shouting resounded over the gap between the two ships and sent a shudder down Jolly's back.

The ghosts immediately began to load the cannons again,

but the remaining guns of the *Natividad* were also ready to fire.

"Now it's their turn," Griffin whispered. For the first time Jolly saw real concern on his face. Somehow that didn't go with the life-loving, high-spirited boy she knew.

There was no point in taking cover. Cannonballs could break through any railing, any plank wall. The companions could just as well stand up here and await their enemy's attack; none of the grown-ups thought of sending Jolly and the boys below. They treated them as equal crew members. Now it was almost the way it had been on the *Skinny Maddy,* when Bannon and his crew had plunged into an apparently hopeless situation—and yet in the end came out of the battle as victors.

Cannon thunder wiped away Jolly's memories. Smoke came from the gun ports of the *Natividad,* befogging the entire ship.

"Watch it!" roared Walker, and they all ducked.

Iron fanned out over the deck of the *Carfax,* wood shattered, and part of the rigging tore apart. Jolly saw a ghost struck by a direct hit of a cannonball, shatter into bits of fog, and immediately put itself back together again. It became clear how superior the *Carfax*'s crew was to that of the bounty hunters. New courage spread through the companions, even more when Walker called, "No mast damaged! No holes in the hull!" In a rapture of triumph he hit Buenaventure on the shoulder. "Now we'll get 'em."

The next broadside from the *Carfax* exploded over the sea, and the smoke that enveloped the *Natividad* this time was no longer that of her own guns. One ball must have hit the powder magazine, for a fire broke out under the deck of the schooner. When the smoke around the bridge cleared, Jolly saw with a shudder that Captain McBain had vanished—and with him a large portion of the stern cabin.

Walker rejoiced even louder; Buenaventure let out enthusiastic barks; and even Soledad became so high-spirited that she threw her arms around the captain's neck—if only for a moment. Almost immediately she bounced back, astonished at herself, and brushed off her clothing. Walker grinned and whispered something to the pit bull man that made him burst into yelping laughter.

The dark mien of the Ghost Trader remained unaltered. "They're turning away," he said softly. Jolly wondered why the wind didn't push his hood back. It was as if the power of the elements couldn't affect him, as if the wind made an arc around him.

Where were both parrots, anyway? Hugh and Moe had been invisible since the beginning of the battle.

Walker waved over at the *Natividad* and watched with satisfaction as the damaged schooner fell behind.

"What's happening with the *Palomino*?" asked Griffin, and answered himself after a look back over the stern: "She's still following us."

"She's slower than we are," said Walker.

"Possibly," said the Ghost Trader, "but not very probably."

The captain looked at him in surprise. "What do you mean?"

With his long arm, the Ghost Trader gestured toward the mainmast. The tip was bent forward, along with the crow's nest and the topsail. A painful crunching and breaking sounded, and then the top four feet of the mast plunged to the deck. A tangle of snapped ropes and torn canvas crashed onto the planking and buried several barrels of drinking water beneath them. Ghosts shredded apart like smoke, reassembled themselves somewhere else, and immediately wafted over to begin the work of repairs.

"Goddammit!" Walker exclaimed.

Soledad sprang to the balustrade and looked out onto the main deck. "One of their balls must have grazed the mast."

Walker reacted at once. Without wasting any more time, he discussed with Buenaventure how to proceed. Finally he turned to his passengers. "I think it will work. Even if there turns out to be no carpenter among the ghosts, we'll hardly slow our journey and will at least maintain the distance."

"And the *Palomino*?" asked Jolly.

"She'll follow us, that much is certain. And strike as soon as we get any slower."

"We can't run away from them all day long," said Munk. He looked as if he were mulling something over in his mind. Jolly noticed that his right hand lay on the pouch with the mussels.

Walker raised a disapproving eyebrow. "It's only an hour so far, boy. We can only wait to see what time brings—perhaps an advantage we haven't taken into account yet."

"Or the end," said the Ghost Trader.

Jolly ran to the aft railing and looked toward the bounty hunter's ship. The *Palomino* was following them at a distance of just about a mile, maybe less. A hard race stretched before them.

Now everything depended on whose side the wind and the sea favored. Both, as she knew from Bannon, were fickle allies.

By the next afternoon the *Palomino* was still behind them, the distance unchanging. She followed them like a shadow, and her silhouette on the horizon depressed the spirits of all of them. As long as the enemy ship stayed behind them, her guns offered no threat. If, however, she should succeed in catching up to them and showed them a broadside, they were done for. Each of them was clear about that, even Munk, who'd learned more in the last hours about sailing ships and duels on the high sea than he could have imagined in his dreams.

Jolly climbed up to the bridge, where Buenaventure held his position at the wheel alone. "What course are we taking?" she asked.

The pit bull man looked once more at the distant horizon in the west, then at Jolly. Each time she looked into his round, brown dog eyes, she was overcome with remarkable sadness, despite the menace and strength that radiated from the gigantic steersman. A tiny piece of the tip of his tongue showed red between his teeth.

"To the east," he said in his growling voice. "And to the north."

"I know that. I thought perhaps you could tell me something more exact."

Buenaventure's jowls drew up into a pit bull smile. "He didn't tell you anything, did he?"

"No. Nothing at all." Jolly followed his eyes to the Ghost Trader, who stood in the bow, one hand on the railing, the other on the silver ring under his robe. The two black parrots were sitting on his shoulders again as if they were stuffed, except that the wind was ruffling their feathers.

"He doesn't talk with anyone anymore. Not even with Munk. I think he's really very worried." *Not about me or Munk or any of the others,* she thought. *Only about Aelenium. Everything boils down to that.*

The Hexhermetic Shipworm had refused to tell them any more about the floating city. He was sulking. Walker had imprisoned him in an old metal birdcage, which he'd brought out of the captain's cabin in a blazing fury. Jolly had to blame herself for the fact that the captain really had every reason to be angry: When he'd climbed down into the cargo hold during the night to check what reserve wood, masts, and planks they were carrying, he'd discovered that the shipworm had not been idle during the sea battle—he'd polished off a good half of all the wood reserves.

Jolly had thought Walker would never stop yelling. Especially when the worm offered to repay the loss with a poem.

Jolly had no pity for the worm. He was greedy, dishonorable, and altogether unbearable. In addition, she reproached herself for leaving him unsupervised. It bordered on a miracle that Walker hadn't thrown him overboard right away.

Now, anyway, the Hexhermetic Shipworm sat in his prison at the foot of the mainmast, offended and silent. The birdcage was shaped like an onion dome, and Walker had locked it with a padlock. During the first few hours, the worm had sworn without interruption, until Griffin threatened to slice him into pieces with a cutlass. Since then he'd only occasionally grumbled about robbing freedom, misbehaving, and growling stomachs, but most of the time he was silent.

Buenaventure snatched Jolly from her thoughts. "If nothing gets in the way, we should be under way for eight or nine days. After Haiti, we keep the Mona Passage lying to the starboard; then we have to sail right out into the Atlantic. So says your friend with the one eye, anyway. But I don't know if that will work out." He noticed her gaze, and the dark skin of his forehead wrinkled. "Why are you staring at me?"

"I—I didn't know that . . ." She was completely astounded at his unexpected torrent of words, but she broke off, shaking her head. "I'm sorry."

"I can talk like anyone else," he said, "if that's what you meant."

"But you don't do it. Or only rarely."

"Only when there's something to say." He went back to watching the sails and the sea. In the south, many miles away, the coast of Haiti moved past, hardly more than a dark stripe across the horizon. The sun burned in the deep blue sky, and the wind blew strong and drove them briskly forward. The air smelled fresh and salty.

The distance between the *Carfax* and the *Palomino* had hardly changed. Sometimes the enemy ship came a little closer, then fell back again. If the weather didn't turn, the nerve-wracking pursuit could go on like this for days.

"What did the Trader tell you?" Jolly asked. "I mean, about our destination."

"Only that it's a place in the Atlantic beyond the Caribbean Sea. And that it's called Aelenium. Never heard of such an island, but to be honest, it doesn't interest me that much. I'm happy if everyone leaves me alone and I can steer the ship in peace. Walker does the business and determines the destination. Usually, anyway."

Jolly sighed. "Then I'd better not disturb you any longer."

He let her get to the steps before he spoke again. "You can stay, if you like."

Jolly turned around.

Buenaventure's jowls curled into what might have been a grin. "Can I ask you something?"

"Sure," she said.

"What does it feel like to walk on water?"

She walked over in front of the wheel and leaned with her back against the balustrade. "I don't know what it's like if you *can't* do it." She thought for a moment. "I can't stand to be on land for long. At least not far away from the sea. Once

Bannon undertook an expedition into the Yucatan jungle, because someone told him that old Morgan had hidden a treasure in a temple there. I couldn't go with him. I mean, I tried, but on the third day Bannon sent me back to the ship with two of the men. I couldn't get air anymore, my feet felt as if they were as heavy as cannonballs, and finally I could hardly even move my legs. Just as little as you know what it feels like to walk on water, I don't know how you can walk on land for a long time."

Buenaventure thought about that for a while. "We don't even think about it. We walk on solid ground just because we can. It's natural." After a pause, he added, "I think I know what you mean."

She gave him a smile. "For us polliwogs, it's just the same. We walk on water because we can. And just the way other people don't think about walking along a street, it's nothing out of the ordinary for us to jump from wave to wave. Well, except for the difference that on a street you don't have to worry about kobalins and sharks."

The pit bull man flicked the tips of his folded-over ears. "Then it was probably a dumb question on my part."

"Oh, no." Impulsively she stepped to his side of the wheel and hugged him. She reached just about up to his hips. "I wanted to thank you, besides."

He'd almost let go of the wheel in surprise. "What for?"

"For helping us."

"You're going to pay us, after all."

She let go of him and smiled. "Not for everything," she said. "Certainly not for everything."

Buenaventure, the pit bull man, the veteran of the dog-fighting pits of Antigua, returned her smile, and from then on they were friends.

Fire and Smoke

On the fifth day of their flight, Walker gathered them all in the captain's cabin. Only Buenaventure stayed behind on the bridge at the wheel. Possibly the pit bull man knew what Walker had to say to them anyway. Sometimes it was as if there was an invisible bond between the two; one knew what the other was thinking, and both acted like two inseparable halves of one man.

"That's enough," said Walker energetically, supporting himself with both hands on his captain's desk and the spread-out charts. "We have to get free of the *Palomino*. I'm fed up with this scurvy lot."

Through the narrow panes behind his back they could see their adversary's ship on the horizon. It was sailing in their wake, unchanging. Walker's hope that the bounty hunter would be forced to give up early because of his larger and hungrier crew had turned out to be premature. Captain Constantine had provisioned himself for a long chase.

Only now did Jolly have some conception of how high the price the pirate emperor had set on her head must be. She felt quite sick at the thought.

"We must sail to the islands in the south," said Walker, tapping his finger on one of the charts. "This silly cat-and-mouse game is getting too boring."

"You intend to force a confrontation?" asked the Ghost Trader.

"If I can determine the battlefield—yes."

"Do you have an idea, then?"

"There's a group of small rocky islands, hardly more than a few points and combs rising out of the sea. It isn't far from here; we could be there by evening. Maybe we'll succeed in getting rid of them there."

Soledad joined in. "You intend to try to lead Constantine onto a reef?"

Walker shrugged. "I don't know if he's familiar with the region—in any case, I've been there often. A few Spaniards have bitterly regretted that they followed me there."

The Ghost Trader wasn't convinced yet. "How much time will we lose?"

"Half a day, perhaps a whole one. Not more."

The shadows under the Ghost Trader's hood seemed to grow darker, as if his face was sinking to an indeterminate depth. "I'm not sure that that's a good proposal. They can't touch us once we reach Aelenium."

"*If* we reach Aelenium. And what about Constantine then? Will your friends sink him? Otherwise, he'll turn back to Tortuga or Haiti and tell all the world of your little secret."

Soledad supported the captain. "We have to shake him."

"He's one of those you want to see dead, Princess." The Trader examined her. "But there are things that are more important."

"I don't have to *see* him," she replied coldly. "It's enough if I *know* that he's dead."

"Toughness will not help you if the Maelstrom becomes all-powerful first."

Soledad held his look for a long time, but then she turned away.

"I'm the captain of this ship," said Walker with emphasis. "And I make the decisions." Perhaps that was why he'd assembled them in the cabin, to let the environment underline his authority as commander of the *Carfax*.

The Ghost Trader nodded slowly, his parrots imitating the movement. "Do what you think right, Captain. But never forget what's at stake."

That's exactly the question, Jolly thought. *What the devil really is at stake?*

Griffin pointed to a slender container standing on a wooden shelf between leather-bound books. "What is that?" he asked, although he had to know that it was an urn.

"My mother," said Walker. "God bless her, the amazing woman."

Jolly raised an eyebrow. He noticed it and smiled.

"The bravest, wildest, most merciless, and bloodthirstiest pirate on both sides of all latitudes."

"Was this her ship?" Jolly asked.

"You bet. She designed it and had it built. She was the first woman captain in the Caribbean and the goddamned best."

"A woman pirate captain?" Jolly was thunderstruck. She'd often dreamed of becoming one herself, but she didn't know that there'd ever actually been one.

"A freebooter body and soul," declared Walker, full of pride and also a little wistfully. "More men went to their deaths for her than I can count . . . and I can still count to a thousand." He grinned broadly. "On a good day."

A woman pirate. Captain of a ship. With command over a whole pirate crew.

That alone would make it worth it to see this thing through to the end, Jolly thought.

She cast a last look at the urn, and it was as if a voice were speaking to her: *You can be like me, Jolly,* said the dead pirate woman in her head. *You can be like me, if you really want to.*

And finally she became conscious of what the Ghost Trader meant when he said it was the future that was at stake. No longer an empty phrase, no vague, indeterminate goal without value and shape.

The future reverberated in her.

Perhaps it would in fact be worth it to fight for it.

Munk was sitting cross-legged in the bow of the *Carfax* when the first jagged rocks appeared on the horizon. He'd spread his mussels in front of him on the deck. Again and again he laid them out in a new pattern, gathered them up impatiently, sorted them out again, exchanging individual ones or staring broodingly down at them and massaging his temples.

After the high in Walker's cabin, Jolly was seized by another, utterly contrary feeling that she had suppressed for much too long. Oppressive, piercing despair overpowered her.

She could no longer endure the inactivity and brooding mood aboard. It wasn't only Bannon's loss that ate into her mind, not only the grief over him and her friends on the *Skinny Maddy*. It was the loss of her earlier life, the playful outlaw existence among the pirates, that was giving her trouble. At this moment she just wanted to be somewhere else, not here, not under the watchful eye of the Ghost Trader; even his silences evoked calamitous premonitions and fears.

In her former life on the *Maddy*, she'd often climbed up to the crow's nest, even taken watch out of turn, in order to be alone, to think, to remove herself from the others for a while; from the deck, the crew, even from the sea. She remembered that again now, when the confinement aboard the *Carfax* was becoming so uncomfortable that she thought she was going to suffocate.

She swung herself up into the shrouds and climbed up the network of ropes to the tip of the mizzenmast, the farthest aft of the *Carfax*'s three masts. Under her flyweight, the taut ropes hardly sagged. The hemp cut into her palms, but she enjoyed the pricking and scratching because she remembered it from before. When she closed her eyes now, at half height over the deck, she could imagine that everything was the way it used to be, with Bannon and the others; for a moment she felt light and carefree; the wind blew past her nose and was almost like a medicine that got her on her feet and brought her to herself.

The mizzenmast had no lookout platform, but it didn't matter. She sat down on one of the two highest yards, held on firmly with one hand, and let her legs dangle.

Many fathoms below her lay the deck of the *Carfax,* and now it appeared to her very small and insignificant in the middle of the blue ocean waste. The Trader was as tiny as an insect and at one stroke lost all his menace. At this height, even the ghosts were visible only as pale phantoms, vague blurs over the red cedarwood of the deck planks.

If she stretched a little to one side, she could see the remains of the rigging of the mainmast and look past the foremast at Munk, bent forward over the mussels, which he moved over the deck with skillful hands, like a shell-game dealer. He was also very far away now—but he'd be that way if she were standing right next to him too. In the last few days he'd withdrawn deeper and deeper into himself, speaking and eating less and less. The change he'd shown after his parents' deaths was taking place faster and faster, and she grew quite dizzy at the thought of where the change might lead. Vanished was the Munk who'd scrubbed the deck with her, vanished also was the curious boy of a few days ago who'd experienced his first sea battle with amazement. Munk had taken a road that led him through deep shadows, and she wasn't sure whether the daylight would really appear at the end.

But she didn't want to think about it now. Her eyes followed the flight of the gulls who accompanied the sailing ship on its course. For a moment Jolly was overcome by the confusing feeling that she could do the same thing, simply push off from the yard and waft over the sea. *Who knows,* she thought with bitter amusement, *perhaps polliwogs can walk on much more than water alone?* How would she ever find out if she could fly if she didn't try it?

She had to force herself to repress the thought, even if she wasn't entirely successful. To think about something else, she looked over at the *Palomino.*

The bounty hunter was sailing in their wake, small as a toy or one of the tiny ship models Bannon used to place on his sea charts sometimes to plan the course of a battle or an ambush.

Yes, she thought, it did actually help to withdraw up here. A new perspective, a new point of view. And the feeling of unbounded, absolute freedom: For the moment she wanted to believe in it, wanted to be like the gulls, like the foam on the waves, like the wind over the endlessness of the sea.

And then suddenly Griffin was beside her.

She hadn't noticed that he'd followed her up the mast. Nimbly he pulled himself from the upper end of the shroud to the opposite yard of the mizzenmast. They were now sitting beside each other, their faces forward, separated only by the broad wooden trunk of the mast.

"Am I disturbing you?" he asked.

She was tempted to say yes, but then it occurred to her that he wasn't disturbing her at all, that she was even grateful for his nearness. The feeling was almost weirder than the urge to leap off into the air a few minutes before.

"No, I was only . . ." She stopped, but he finished the sentence for her.

"Looking for a little space?"

She smiled. "Perhaps. Yes."

Griffin nodded as if he understood exactly what she meant. *And yes,* she thought, *he really does understand.*

He noticed that she was looking at him, examining his profile, and pointed quickly down at Munk.

"He's been doing that business with the mussels for days now," he said, lowering his voice. "Does he really think that's going to help us somehow?"

Jolly sighed softly. "Anyway, he's doing something. The two of us can only sit around up here and wait."

"Too true."

"Maybe he really will think of something. Once I actually saw him call up a gust of wind. If he really exerts himself . . . I don't know how something like that works and if it's even possible . . . but if he really exerts himself, maybe he can make us go faster." She shook her head. "Or make something else happen. I have no idea."

"Turn us into frogs?"

She smiled in amusement. "Would you like that? To be a frog?"

"Only if I could find me a princess and kiss her."

Jolly looked down at Soledad, who was making practice throws with her knife at a target on the mast. Soledad paid no attention to the wailing of the shipworm, who was sitting only a scant six feet under the target and flinching at every knife throw.

"She is very beautiful, isn't she?"

"Yes." Griffin smiled. "But *she* isn't the princess I meant."

Jolly looked at him. She had a sharp remark on the tip of her tongue, but then she realized he was serious, and her sarcasm fizzled unuttered. "You're making fun of me," she said, although she knew better.

"Has he kissed you?"

"Munk?" She laughed nervously. "Of course not."

"But he'd like to."

"Where do you get that?"

"Because I've spoken with him."

"About me?"

Griffin nodded. "About how it would be to kiss you."

She was unprepared for his frankness. Instantly there was a lump in her throat. "You are completely crazy. Don't you . . . I mean, don't you have anything better to do?"

"Count flying fish? Or shark fins?" He laughed, and the multitude of blond braids on his head whirled around like the arms of a water plant. But then he was serious again. "Of course, that was before Munk preferred to talk with his mussels instead of with the two of us."

She wanted to change the subject, but his honesty, and

even more, his strange look, which she couldn't deal with at all, made her uneasy. He disconcerted her, and that made her embarrassed.

Jolly had *never* been embarrassed. Until today.

"May I?" he asked straight out.

She became panicky. "May you what?"

"You already know—kiss you?"

"God—no!"

"Too bad."

She looked quickly down at the deck to make certain that none of the others were listening. Wasn't Soledad stealing a look up at them now and then?

"You are impossible," said Jolly to Griffin.

"I'm a man."

Now she had to laugh. "You're a cheeky rascal, Griffin, a swindler, and a loudmouth—but a man, *that* you most certainly are not." She pointed at their pursuer on the horizon. "And the way things look, chances aren't too good that you'll ever be one."

"Another reason to clear the matter up now."

"You talk as if it were about fighting some sort of a duel." His grin was making her livid. But she also had a strange, warm feeling in her belly, and that confused her so much that her knees were trembling. Or was it the other way around?

"Maybe, only maybe, I might let you kiss me if we were stranded together on a lonely island—and all the wild pigs and the tree spiders were already eaten." She looked at him once more, as angrily as possible. Then she let herself fall backward, reached out in a horrifying moment of complete emptiness around her, then grabbed the yard with both hands, whirled around like an acrobat and landed with hands and feet in the shrouds. While Griffin stared after her open-mouthed, she climbed quickly down to the deck and joined Soledad.

"Show me how to do that?" she asked in a quavering voice as she pointed at the knife.

Soledad looked at her in amazement. "Didn't Bannon teach you that?"

"I . . . but I want you to show me again."

"You're all flustered. What happened?"

Jolly looked Soledad in the eye and realized that the princess knew exactly what had just happened.

"Nothing. I—"

"Aaaaaaarrrrggggghh!!!" wailed the Hexhermetic Shipworm. *"Fire! The ship is burning! Save me! . . . Save meeee!"*

Everyone whirled around.

Forward, in the bow, flames shot up and made the sky over the jib flicker. But it wasn't the ship that was burning.

It was Munk.

Jolly plunged forward, Soledad right behind her. Griffin did gymnastics down the shrouds and ran to one of the ropes on which a bucket dangled outside on the ship's wall.

Munk sat cross-legged in the midst of the flames and held his hands over a magic pearl, controlling it as it floated in the center of the mussel circle. He seemed not to feel the heat. The fire flamed out of his skin, out of his hair, even out of his eyes—but it did not consume him.

Munk was burning—and didn't even notice it.

He lifted his head in surprise when the others stormed up to him.

"What—," he began, when the full load of water from Griffin's bucket hit him in the face. He started, lost control of the floating pearl, and shouted a warning.

The pearl swept out of the charmed circle that had been holding it, twisted upward in tight spirals, jerked from starboard to port like a ball of lightning gone wild, made a circle around Buenaventure, then with a hissing sound whisked over the railing and out into the emptiness over the ocean.

It was barely a hundred yards away and hardly visible any longer when it exploded. A fireball bloomed high over the sea, stood for a few seconds in the violet evening sky like a second sun, and then collapsed until it was again the size of the pearl, and finally went out.

The flames around Munk's body were extinguished. Wet through, he sat there, swore softly—and immediately began to try out a new pattern for his mussels.

"Munk!" Jolly crouched down beside him. "Munk—what was that?"

He lifted his face. She was horrified as his feverish gaze skimmed over her. His eyes twitched, his lids fluttered nervously like butterfly wings.

"I can't do it," he murmured over and over. "I simply can't do it."

Jolly shook her head and was about to reach for the mussels when he hit her arm.

"Damn it, Munk—that hurt!"

"Don't touch!" he gasped out vehemently.

She pulled her hand back, but she didn't take her eyes off his fevered face. Suddenly black material rustled beside her. When she looked up, the figure of the Ghost Trader rose over her.

"Leave him," he said firmly. "Munk mustn't be disturbed now."

Jolly leaped up and planted herself angrily in front of the Trader. "He's sick!"

"No. Only exhausted."

"Then he needs to take a rest."

"Too many hopes rest on him. He must not give up now."

"But he's trembling. His eyes . . . did you see his eyes?"

"I say to you, he does not need rest. Not now. What he urgently needs more than anything else is success."

Munk's voice interrupted them. "I was so close. So close . . ."

Griffin set the wooden bucket down on the deck with an audible noise. "I'm beginning to believe you've lost your mind."

"By all the sea devils!" Walker's voice broke the silence. Even Munk looked up to the bridge.

Walker was standing up there with the telescope and looking back over the stern. "They're doing what I would have done long ago in their situation!" he called without looking around to the others. "They're lightening."

"What does that mean?" asked Munk.

"They're throwing ballast overboard," Jolly explained in a trembling voice.

"What ballast?"

"The cannons!" cried Walker. "They're rolling some of their guns overboard." He let the telescope sink. "Now they'll have us. They'll catch up."

It was a labyrinth.

A labyrinth of rock needles, shapeless gray domes, knife-sharp combs of stone, and a few single, densely forested island spines.

The *Carfax* reached the first rocks of the bizarre island group just at the moment they all believed the *Palomino* would be level with them any minute. Even with its remaining cannon, the bounty hunter had overtaken the *Carfax*. Captain Constantine had loaded the sloop with enough weapons to win a war single-handed. From the open gun ports projected muzzle after muzzle. Smoke rose between them. The torches were already burning, the cannoneers were waiting for their captain's order to fire.

Just when it looked as if there was no escape left, Walker maneuvered the *Carfax* through a lane into the interior of the island labyrinth. Constantine had to turn in order not to run aground—there was no space in the narrow passage between the rocks for two ships side by side.

"How much time will that give us?" asked the Ghost Trader.

"Not much." Walker acted neither relieved nor proud of his skillful maneuver. "We can't cross between the rocks forever. The winds here are treacherous and the tides—" he broke off and shook his head. "And if we drop anchor, they'll have us that much faster."

"And so?" asked the Trader.

"We can only hope that Constantine is mad enough to follow us right away. That's our only chance. If I really do know my way around here better than he does, I can probably lure him onto a reef or a sandbar."

"In the dark?" asked Jolly skeptically. Bannon had also relied on maneuvers of that kind, but he'd always refused to take too-narrow passages by night. The risks were numerous and hardly possible to estimate.

Walker nodded grimly. "Unfortunately, we don't have a choice."

Meanwhile it had grown dark. The moon appeared to be almost full. It shone like a silver coin among thousands of diamonds on black velvet. The beauty of the firmament formed a confusing contrast to the fear that gripped them all. Even Buenaventure panted louder than usual. Jolly wondered how, after so many hours without sleep, he was still able to carry out Walker's orders so exactly. And yet she was certain that the pit bull man, of all her companions, knew best what his limits were. He might be a veteran of many fights, like his friend Walker, but in his dog eyes there dwelled a wisdom that could compete with the Ghost

Trader's. As long as he was steering the ship, she had no fear of running onto a reef or crashing against one of the icy gray cliffs.

The moonlight drew all color out of the jagged island landscape. Even the few forested islands hardly differed from the bare rock slopes by night. There must be a dozen islands here, crowded very close to each other, the peaks of a craggy, undersea mountain. The narrow, multiple twisting passages reminded Jolly of the tangle of streets in harbor cities, and here just as there, the enemy might be lurking in one of the side passages. They'd left the *Palomino* behind for the moment, but at the same time they'd lost sight of their opponent. Had Constantine also dared to press on into the confusion of the islands? Was he waiting for them behind the next dome, the next cliff?

Creaking and with sails whispering, the *Carfax* pushed between steep rock walls and points, through waters that appeared traitorously calm but under whose surface lurked currents and shallows. The few sounds were thrown back from the rocks, sometimes as echo, sometimes as something that sounded as if a living being had mimicked the sound and crowed back in the night.

Griffin had climbed to one of the yards on the foremast and was sitting there with legs dangling high over the water, looking over the night island landscape.

"There!" he called suddenly. "There they are!"

"Heave to!" bellowed Walker.

Buenaventure let the wheel rotate, ghosts scampered

over the masts. The *Carfax* began to turn across the narrow passage. Thus they could receive the *Palomino* with a broadside as soon as she sailed across the next crossing into their target zone, whether from the left or from the right.

The masts of the bounty hunter slid over the edges of some cliffs, then the entire sloop became visible. She didn't turn into the cleft in which the *Carfax* awaited her but sailed sideways across it and blocked the exit.

"Fire!" screamed Walker.

And "Fire!" also bellowed the captain of the enemy ship.

Seconds later the air was full of iron. Powder smoke burned in Jolly's throat and shortened visibility on board to a few yards. Cannonballs broke through the wall of smoke, shredded the billows apart, and struck rope and sail. Wood burst in a deafening detonation. Everyone aboard lost his balance, some fell to the deck, others grabbed onto the sides or the railing. Loudest of all screamed the Hexhermetic Shipworm in his onion-dome cage, although he was the only one who was still in the same place he'd been before.

Jolly looked upward.

The yard on which Griffin had been sitting was empty.

"Oh, no!" Her heart did somersaults as she ran over to the railing.

Walker shouted orders continuously, ghosts hurried everywhere. Soledad and the Trader had vanished behind the smoke somewhere, but Jolly had seen them. And Munk . . . yes, Munk arranged his mussels.

"I'm going to look for Griffin!" she bellowed and climbed over the railing.

"Jolly! No!" Walker's voice made her hesitate for a moment. "There are coral banks everywhere here. It's swarming with—"

Sharks, she added in her mind and pushed off. She had no time left to explain to the captain that the sharks would do nothing to her. Griffin, on the other hand, was defenseless and at their mercy in the water.

Her feet struck against the churning sea, fighting for a hold. A boiling wave crest rose up right between her legs, and Jolly lost her balance. As long as she was standing upright, the sharks wouldn't notice her; but when she was lying down, they could see her silhouette from below.

She was on her feet in a flash. Because of the huge clouds of powder smoke, her vision extended no more than ten feet. She saw the hole the ball had torn in the *Carfax*'s hull, but it was too high to seriously endanger the ship at the moment. She couldn't tell from here how things stood with the *Palomino;* the bounty hunter's ship remained invisible behind the walls of yellow and gray smoke.

"Griffin!"

She called his name into the acrid mist, but there was no answer. The yard had been high enough that Griffin could have broken his neck when he hit the water, but she didn't want to think about that at all.

It was pitilessly dark, now that the smoke swallowed the

moonlight. The oil lanterns aboard the ship sent out a weak light, but it hardly reached down to the water; sulfur yellow, the lanterns hung like fuzzy stars in the darkness over the railing.

Jolly knew one thing for sure: If Walker decided to end the battle, he would extinguish the lanterns so that the *Palomino* would lose their trail in the darkness. By then, at the latest, Jolly had to be back on board or she would wander around blindly in the dark for an eternity.

"Griffin, damn it!"

He was the best swimmer she knew. But if he'd lost consciousness on impact with the water . . . or worse yet, if a cannonball had hit him up there . . .

May I? he'd asked her. *You already know—kiss you.*

That idiot. If he'd simply done it, then she would probably have . . . oh, no, of course she'd have defended herself.

Or would she?

"Griffin, where are you?"

Her foot caught on something in the water. She stumbled, fell forward, and just caught herself on all fours. At the same time a wave rose beneath her, shot up, and struck her in the face with the force of a punching fist.

She didn't see black—the smoke and the night had long provided for that. No, lights flamed in her forehead so brilliantly that she shut her eyes, lost her sense of up and down, and for a moment lay unconscious.

That's what she figured, anyway, for when she opened her

eyes again, she was floating on the waves like a piece of wood. Her head bumped against something soft with every roll of the water and there was a pain at the roots of her hair—something was pulling on it.

Her face felt swollen.

Her head ached.

Something shot past her, a dark triangle that cut through the waves like a saber.

With an oath she tried to stand up and avoid the shark's attack. But it didn't attack her, was perhaps cautious because of the noise on the surface, avoiding the commotion produced by the intruders into its waters.

Jolly came swaying to her feet. With that she was out of the shark's field of vision. Searchingly, she looked about her.

Everywhere smoke, everywhere darkness.

And no *Carfax*.

The ship was gone.

"Goddammit!" she cried into the mist—and then she saw what had tripped her before.

Beside her floated Griffin, clinging fast to a splintered piece of wood in whose sharp points her hair had been caught a moment before. His braids danced on the waves that broke against his head and his shoulders.

He was facedown in the water.

He wasn't moving.

Jolly bent forward, pulled his head out of the water, tugged at him, called his name desperately.

"Don't do this to me," she stammered helplessly. "You aren't to die, hear me? You simply can't die now!"

A movement beside her swept her mind empty instantly. It was no longer only a single shark around her.

There were several, six or seven.

And the circle they formed around Griffin and Jolly was closing in every second.

The Decision

The *Carfax* had completed a turn and was now ready to sail back on her original course through the island labyrinth, away from the other end of the rock passage, away from the *Palomino.*

"We'll have to leave Jolly and Griffin behind," said the Ghost Trader tonelessly in the deathlike stillness as the companions stood next to each other at the railing, staring into the tumult of smoke and black waves. The water seemed to boil, as if all the hidden currents had suddenly decided to rise to the surface.

"No!" Munk's cry made the others recoil. "We'll look for them both and take them aboard."

"If they don't turn up again by themselves . . ." Walker left the rest unsaid. His face was wet with perspiration. He was responsible for them all, and the strain of command was showing.

"Jolly is somewhere out there!" Munk's face still glowed feverishly, but the anger in his voice left no doubt that he was in control of his mind. "Jolly is a polliwog! She doesn't just drown."

"In this sea? Who knows." But Walker wasn't getting into an argument with Munk, turning instead to the Ghost Trader. "You say we should leave them behind?"

The Ghost Trader's face was hardly discernible under the hood. It was as if Walker spoke into a black chasm. "It is not an easy decision. But we must bring at least one polliwog alive to Aelenium, cost what it will. Otherwise"—he lowered his voice—"otherwise everything else was in vain. The whole mission, our voyage so far . . ." He turned to Munk. "Even the deaths of your parents."

"You've lied to me from the beginning!" Munk took a step back from the Trader, but he stood firm against the threatening gaze of the shadowed eye. "You've always known where all this would lead. The mussels you brought me . . . the visits to the island. . . all only to prepare me and sometime get me to Aelenium."

"What's false about that?"

"You've decided about my whole life, without me or Dad or Mum being aware of it. But now . . . now I decide what I do. And I will not go to Aelenium before Jolly is back on board." He hesitated imperceptibly. "And Griffin."

Soledad shouted Jolly's name into the mists once more, but again she received no answer. She'd already tried at least twenty times, without success.

The second salvo from the *Carfax*'s cannons had brought the *Palomino* a little off course and carried her behind the cliffs. The ghosts had been faster than their opponent in making the guns ready to fire, and so they were able to get off a second broadside at the bounty hunter first. Constantine was probably at that very moment maneuvering to bring the *Palomino* back into her old position. Only from there could he place his opponent under fire.

It was clear to every one of them that this was their only chance to gain a new lead. They didn't know how badly the two salvos had damaged the enemy ship—the smoke still lingered between the cliffs and blocked the view—but it could only be a question of time before the fight continued.

If they really intended to risk a retreat, it must be now.

With or without Jolly and Griffin.

"We have no choice," said the Ghost Trader. "Nothing is as important as our mission to get a polliwog to Aelenium. It's the only way can we stop the Maelstrom."

"*Your* mission," said Munk scornfully. "Not ours."

"You still don't want to believe it. If the Maelstrom unfolds his full power and opens the gate to the Mare Tenebrosum, we are all lost. The Caribbean. The entire world. And you, Munk, are the key to our salvation. Only you can control the Maelstrom. But for that I must get you to Aelenium."

"Me—or Jolly."

The Ghost Trader nodded. "I would rather have brought you both there. Two polliwogs can do twice as much as one. But

I'd rather lose our chance for half than give up the whole. If we do not leave now, we gain nothing at all. Perhaps we would find Jolly and take her on board. But what then? The *Palomino* shoots us to pieces, you and Jolly die—and the Maelstrom triumphs." The Trader walked up to Munk and took him by the shoulder. "This isn't only a possibility, boy—it's an incontestable fact. Either we give up Jolly and Griffin now—or the world will soon perish."

Soledad had listened in silence and did not join in the talk now. But her expression revealed her thoughts. She wanted to save the two of them, wanted to do everything for them so that they wouldn't be left to an uncertain fate out there. But she also recognized the fatal truth in the Ghost Trader's words.

"Munk," she said quietly, "it's your decision."

Munk hesitated for a moment; then, moving wearily, he began to climb over the railing. "I'll go and look for them."

"No!" The voice of the Ghost Trader sounded different from just a few seconds before, roaring like a storm wind and shot through with icy cold. "Soledad is wrong. It is not your decision." His hands drew a symbol in the air, and at that moment three ghosts came down from the rigging and pulled Munk gently but firmly back onto the deck.

Munk cursed and resisted, but the grasp of the wraiths was unrelenting.

"I am sorry," said the Ghost Trader softly, and all except Munk recognized the sincerity and sorrow in his voice. "But it can be no other way. Do not believe that it is easy for me."

"Let me go!" bellowed Munk, as the ghosts pulled him away from the railing and held him in the middle of the deck. He had tears in his eyes now, and his tired features showed only anger and desperation. "You can't do that! Soledad! Walker! You can't simply leave Jolly behind."

The princess lowered her eyes and said nothing.

Walker turned back to the bridge, but his steps seemed heavy, as if the air in front of him had turned into something firm. Everyone saw how very reluctant he was to give the next order.

"Full speed ahead!" he said, then—hesitantly—he repeated it once again more loudly.

Buenaventure didn't move. "The girl," he growled. "What's going to happen to the girl?"

Munk was screaming and cursing down below on the main deck. The Hexhermetic Shipworm, on the other hand, was silent and had lowered the head with the triangular shell; he almost seemed to be grieving for Jolly and Griffin as much as the others were.

"Walker," said Buenaventure. "We can—"

"You heard him."

The pit bull man hesitated, and for a long moment it looked as if he'd refuse the order. But then he let out a high-pitched howl, full of pain and despair, placed his paws on the wheel, and did what had to be done.

"Thank you," said the Ghost Trader, and he turned and went forward to the bow, entirely alone. No one followed him, no one wanted to be near him.

"Jolly!" Munk roared again, but the mists swallowed his voice.

The *Carfax* began moving and quickly left the scene of the battle behind her.

Jolly mustered all her strength and dragged Griffin's torso out of the water. He was heavy, not only because he was a boy and a bit bigger than she was, but more because he was hanging limp over the debris like a corpse. To make matters worse, his clothing had soaked up a lot of water.

The *Carfax* had vanished. Impossible to say whether it was hidden behind the next cloud of mist or whether it . . . no, the others certainly wouldn't leave her in the lurch.

But would the Ghost Trader gamble on the lives of two polliwogs if he had the chance of at least saving one? He'd never left any doubt about how important it was to get them to Aelenium. At least one of them.

She gasped for air and felt she was going to have to give up. But then, just as unexpectedly, she got herself under control again. Somehow she had to pull Griffin out of the water.

The sharks came closer. Their circle was now only a few feet away from the two castaways.

Jolly dropped to her knees, pulled Griffin's left arm around her shoulders, and using all her strength, heaved herself onto her feet. She uttered a scream under the strain, so loud that in spite of the cannon smoke, it echoed from the rock clumps. She stumbled, fell back on her knees. Tried again. And succeeded.

This time she managed to pull Griffin up. With her left hand she firmly clasped his arm, which still lay around her shoulders; she threaded her right hand under his belt in the back and held him upright as well as she could.

She'd gotten a helpless person to safety once before, a seaman on the *Skinny Maddy*, but that had been on land, and the man had had firm ground under his feet, in spite of his weakness. But Griffin was no polliwog, and the water offered his feet no resistance. Jolly had to bear his full weight and still be careful that his legs didn't sink deep enough to attract the attention of the sharks again.

Somehow she managed to drag him forward. The shark fins vanished, except for one in the water, and even the last predator kept its attention on its prey for only a few heart-shaking moments longer and then gave up.

Onward! Jolly thought grimly. *Don't think! Just keep moving forward!*

Eventually she would have to stumble onto a bank. The passage hadn't been very wide, and although Jolly had lost her orientation in the haze, the rocks couldn't be far away.

Forward! Get moving!

"Jo-Jolly . . ."

"Griffin!" She almost let go of him in her relief. She turned her head in order to look into his face, but she couldn't. Had he opened his eyes?

Griffin made retching noises, and then he shot a surge of water over her shoulder.

"We're going to make it!" she got out in a groan.

Once more he tried to say her name. Then she felt him go limp again.

"Griffin! Come on—you have to help me! Hold on tight!"

He didn't move again.

And yet—he was alive!

The relief gave her new strength. Desperately she fought against the high waves, against the smoke in her lungs, against the blindness in the midst of darkness. The wind had freshened and now began to disperse the mists. The moon showed itself again and mixed its icy light with the billows of smoke to a depressing twilight. Anyway, Jolly could now see something again.

The rocks, there ahead!

Several mounds rose out of the water ahead of them. Right behind them was an incline of rubble, covered with strange silhouettes. Only on coming closer did Jolly see that they were tree stumps.

With iron will, she passed the outer rocks and dragged Griffin onto land with a cry of triumph. She wasn't sure whether anyone could hear the cry except herself; perhaps it existed only in her head. She felt empty and exhausted.

Little pebbles crunched under her feet, then under both their bodies when they collapsed, partly side by side, partly on top of each other.

Again she blacked out, and again she didn't know later how long she'd been unconscious. Perhaps for only a few minutes, perhaps for an hour. Possibly even longer.

When she opened her eyes again, the smoke was gone.

Just like Griffin.

Panicked, she felt about her, but she could grasp only bare stone, loose rubble, and—a hand. Fingers closed around hers, then a face appeared over her. Griffin's blond braids dangled down and almost touched her cheeks.

His smile looked exhausted—but it was a smile.

"Looks as if polliwogs can see into the future," he said. His face was very close above hers, but at the moment she didn't find it uncomfortable. He was alive.

"Into the future?" she repeated, as if she'd heard him wrong.

"You know what you said to me?"

"I've said a lot in recent days, I think." She tried to sit up, and he eased back a little to make room. But only a little, only as much as absolutely necessary.

"You said I could kiss you when the two of us were stranded on a lonely island."

"Oh, there were . . . restrictions," she said with an uncertain smile. She ought to have been thinking about a thousand things, about the *Carfax,* her companions, about the outcome of the sea battle with the *Palomino,* and about what was going to become of them, alone on the shore of this clump of rock.

His smile grew a trace wider, almost the old Griffin again. But then stood up and stretched out his hand to her.

"Can you stand up?"

His abrupt withdrawal made her even more uneasy than his closeness a moment before. "I wasn't the one who almost drowned," she said, but she took his hand and let him pull her up.

Before she saw it coming, he caught her in both arms.

"Griffin," she said, shaking her head. "This isn't the moment to—"

He gave her a kiss on the forehead and let her go. "Thank you for saving my life. It was you who pulled me onto land, wasn't it?"

She nodded. "What's the last thing you remember?"

"The cannon thunder. And that I . . . that I . . . I was sitting up on the yard, wasn't I? And I fell down, I think."

Once again she nodded. "I came after you to look for you. Everything was full of smoke, and when I finally found you, the *Carfax* was gone . . . both ships."

She looked out into the rock passage. Debris was floating on the waves in the moonlight. The surf cast a few pieces of wood onto the shore, pulled them out again, threw them back. Nowhere was there a ship to be seen. Also there was no noise in the distance, no voices, no cannon fire.

They were, in fact, alone.

"What if she went down?" Griffin was following her eyes. The pieces of flotsam and the empty water between the islands called up the same fear in both of them. And yet an inner voice told her that her first thought had been right: The Ghost Trader had left them behind.

Was she disappointed about that? Or angry? She'd need a while to find the answer to that.

Wasn't it what she'd wanted all along? Munk should bear

the responsibility alone. Magic, conjuring—that was nothing for her. She walked on the water. She was a pirate.

Just like Griffin.

"It's not over yet," he said. "Not at all."

She didn't answer. Instead she turned around. "Let's go," she said as she began to climb the pebbled slope. "Maybe there's life here somewhere."

Maybe humans, she thought.

Or a creature like the Acherus.

She shuddered.

Aelenium

Three days later a dense wall of fog darkened the sunrise on the horizon ahead of the *Carfax*. The flaming red of the sky, shot through with golden streaks and veins of light, first blurred, then disappeared completely in the billowing grayness.

"There it is," said the Ghost Trader with barely concealed relief. "Our destination lies behind that fog."

"Aelenium?" asked Soledad, who was standing beside him at the railing.

The one-eyed man nodded under his hood. The two parrots on his shoulders uttered shrill cries that sounded almost like human laughter.

"Maybe we can lose the *Palomino* in the fog," Walker called down from the bridge.

The Ghost Trader didn't turn around. It was as if he spoke

an invocation to the rolling mist, which soon obscured their view entirely.

"We will that," he whispered. "We will that."

The bounty hunter's ship was still behind them, battered and much slower than before—just like the *Carfax*. Two cripples who, limping and groaning, were putting up a stubborn race.

The onion-dome cage dangled on a chain over the railing. The Hexhermetic Shipworm had demanded to be moved there so that he could see something and not, as he put it, "have to stare at your stinking feet and a few rotten barrels all day long."

The fog reached for them with ragged fingers and, within a very short time, enveloped them. To Soledad, it seemed as if it had come to meet them, but the Ghost Trader knew better: "The fog lies in a wide ring around Aelenium. It keeps most people from daring to approach."

"And those who try it anyway?"

The Trader himself was now only a dark blob in the middle of the gray mist. "Some turn back, others remain."

With a shiver, Soledad thought of shipwrecks on the bottom, many fathoms deep or miles under the sea.

"Is the *Palomino* following us?" she called up to Walker to distract herself. The captain, too, was only a silhouette in the fog.

"I didn't see them turn around," he replied. "But I'd be surprised if Constantine gave up after so many days." He spoke softly with Buenaventure, then turned to the others again. "Be quiet. If they can't hear us, maybe they'll lose our trail."

For quite a while nothing was heard except the creaking of the boards and the rigging, accompanied by the splash of the waves against the hull.

After minutes, an eternity, there was an earsplitting grinding and cracking, followed by a grisly bursting.

Soledad waited for an impact that would knock her off her feet—but it didn't come.

For a moment she was convinced that the *Carfax* had run aground. Then she heard noises far behind them. The tiny droplets of fog carried the sounds forward like millions upon millions of tiny mouths sending them a message.

Cries wafted over to them.

Wild screaming, wretched, provoking pity. Cries from many throats, each individually so dejected and final that there was no doubt as to what was happening to those poor souls.

They were death cries.

Somewhere behind them, deep in the dense fog, the crew of the *Palomino* was dying. And their ship died with them.

"Good God," Soledad whispered. She was completely rigid, no part of her moved. Even her lips felt as if they'd turned to ice.

The Ghost Trader's hand clutched the railing, a corpselike shadow around it.

"Those weren't the powers of Aelenium," he said tonelessly. "They are not so pitiless."

And then, as if at a secret signal, their eyes traveled to the bow.

There sat Munk, cross-legged. He'd laid the mussels out around him in a circle. Inside, glowing fiery like the pupil of a sea monster, floated a pearl. Munk made a motion of his hand, much more skillfully than before; immediately the pearl ducked into an open mussel and was swallowed as the shell snapped shut.

"Was that *him*?" Soledad realized that she'd spoken aloud only when the Ghost Trader nodded. Only once, very briefly.

"By the gods," slipped out of him so softly that only Soledad could hear. She believed she recognized something like fear in his voice for the first time. Her knees trembled; thoughts whirled in her head.

"Munk?" she inquired.

The boy raised his head and looked at her. His smile in the fog was triumphant and icy.

She was about to make herself go over to him when a powerful draft whipped away the fog over their heads; tiny eddies appeared in the white clouds and almost swept them off their feet. Something large floated over the deck of the *Carfax*, above the shattered mainmast. It vanished into the fog again just as quickly. Yet soft, rushing sounds still came through to Soledad's ears, the lifting and falling of powerful wings.

"What was that?"

"Don't worry," said the Ghost Trader reassuringly. He'd regained his composure. "That was one of the first harbingers of Aelenium. We're about to reach the other side. The fog will thin any minute."

Munk calmly packed up his mussels. There was perspiration on his forehead and soaking his clothing, but he didn't bother about it. Only his fingers trembled slightly, and he was breathing a little faster.

Soledad wasn't at that moment sure what made her more afraid: Munk's magic thrusting of the *Palomino* into a watery grave or the powerful creature that hovered, invisible, around the masts.

She forced herself to take her eyes off the boy. Later there would be time enough to concern herself with him. With what he had done—and *how* he had done it. And what he might still possibly bring about, for good as well as bad.

Out beyond the bow she saw the red-yellow glimmer, which was now dawning through the mist: the morning sky over Aelenium. A brilliant panorama like a veil of gold dust on a sea of scarlet. With every wave that broke against the *Carfax*'s bow, the water took on more and more of the color of the sky, until the fog finally drifted away entirely and left them in a fire of red and copper.

"Aelenium," whispered the Ghost Trader beside Soledad at the railing.

She could do nothing but stare ahead with eyes wide, lips parted. She didn't see how the others on board were reacting, what Walker said or thought or what the Hexhermetic Shipworm was doing in his cage.

She could only . . . look.

The fog ring enclosed a circular field of water two or three miles in diameter, perhaps larger. The sunrise glowed and sparkled on a forest of roofs and towers, a many-colored hodgepodge of low houses, fortresslike crenellated walls, and palaces in the character and multiplicity of bizarrely frosted cakes. There were bridges between pointed gables and look-out platforms, some roofed, others open, and as finely worked as if they were made of porcelain. There were rows of porticos and spiny citadels; free-floating staircases that stretched like spiderwebs between facades, towers, and sky-lights; waterfalls that bubbled out of openings in the facades and disappeared into invisible canals and reservoirs in the confusion of buildings. Hardly any of all this appeared to have an obvious, practical purpose, as if the architects of Aelenium had let their feelings for beauty and elegance have free reign, without giving any thought to the habitability of the floating city.

In the center of the haphazard jumble of interconnected structures rose the white cone of a mountain, very steep and regular on all sides. Its tip was cut off straight, as if by a knife blade, which made it look like the crater of a volcano. Whether there was an opening yawning up there or whether the artificial top was finished off with a platform was impossible to discern out at sea. Water flowed along its flanks in deep cuts and formed a golden pattern as it reflected the morning sun.

Stretching into the sea all around Aelenium were broad jetties, which grew progressively narrower toward their ends.

It took Soledad a moment to grasp that these jetties were actually the points of a gigantic star.

Aelenium was sitting on a sea star.

A sea star that floated flat on the water, as big as an island, built up to its outer edges.

Actually . . . *built up*?

As they came closer, Soledad realized that the star city hadn't been artificially built as she'd at first assumed. All points, prickles, roofs, and walls consisted of coral, as if over millions of years, layer upon layer had collected on the upper side of the sea star and created a masterpiece that, at first sight, one could very easily have taken for the work of an overzealous builder.

Did it look exactly the same on the underside? Was there a bizarre mirror image underneath the upper side of the city? Empty, sea-flooded spaces and endless tunnels; pointed towers on which colonies of mussels grew and crabs sought plankton; unoccupied rooms through which a predator glided now and then, in majestic darkness and silence?

We'll find out, she thought suddenly, for she was just realizing that she would actually be a guest in this wondrous structure. They were allies, perhaps even friends. They had nothing to fear.

And yet there was a bitter taste beneath all her astonishment and wonder, a deep anxiety. Panic, almost.

What kind of a place was this? Where did it come from?

Aelenium might have grown out of thousands and more thousands of tons of coral, but that couldn't just have happened by accident. The stairs, jetties, and friezes had been built up for a purpose, with the leisureliness of the eons. For the purpose of being inhabited.

But by whom?

She saw still more, high over the coral cathedrals and sea-foam minarets: gigantic ray creatures with purple-veined wings, between which sat men, tiny riders in comparison to the mighty creatures. Three of them now broke out of the wall of mist, in a fluffy explosion of tatters of fog. Soledad recognized the sound of the rushing wings again. It was the same as before, when something had circled around the tip of the mast.

There were riders not only in the sky but also on the water: Men on bony seahorses with long, pointed snouts and eyes as big as plates, horned bodies, and gracefully navigating tails, which enabled the animals to bear their masters in wide arcs through the waters of Aelenium.

The princess saw all this and at the same time knew that it was only a fraction of the wonders that awaited her and the others in the coral city.

One of the giant rays sank down to them until it hovered only some twelve feet over the deck of the *Carfax,* with leisurely wing beats and gently waving tail point. A man with long black hair bent between the wings and greeted the Ghost Trader with a wave of the hand that looked both ritual and exotic.

"Welcome back, old friend!" cried the ray rider. "And

welcome to your friends and companions. They shall dwell under our domes and eat our food." It sounded like a polite formality, not like an invitation that came from the heart.

Soledad exchanged a look with the Ghost Trader before he replied to this greeting: "Have my thanks, D'Artois, captain of the Ray Guard! I am glad to be back again. And I bring you what I promised."

Where have you led us? Soledad asked him with her eyes, but he only smiled mysteriously, the way he frequently did. There was nothing for her to do but keep silent and wonder and try to calm her heartbeat and hold her weak knees still.

Suddenly Munk was standing beside her, staring expressionlessly at the coral structures of the star city.

"Jolly should have seen this," he whispered. "She should be with us now, nowhere else." His head jerked around. He first looked Soledad in the eyes, then glanced over at the Ghost Trader. "We've betrayed her."

Then he fell silent again and looked toward Aelenium.

Walker, following the ray rider's directions and with Buenaventure's help, slowly maneuvered the ship to one of the sea star's points, which extended out into the sea a good two hundred feet from the actual center of the city.

"Betrayed," Munk murmured again.

Soledad fought the impulse to move away from him, only a little bit away, out of his immediate proximity. Perhaps that would have stopped her shivering.

Munk stood motionless beside her, a boy who'd just drowned a whole ship's crew in the sea with a wave of his hands. Without hesitation. Without scruple.

The *Carfax* slowed, the ghosts reefed the sails, then finally the anchor dropped.

Aelenium received its savior.

End of Volume I

About the Author

Kai Meyer is the author of many highly acclaimed and popular books for adults and young adults in his native Germany. The first book in his Dark Reflections Trilogy, *The Water Mirror*, was a *School Library Journal* Best Book, a Book Sense Pick, and a *Locus Magazine* Recommended Read. It also received starred reviews in *School Library Journal* and *Publishers Weekly*, and has been translated into sixteen languages. Kai Meyer lives in Germany.

About the Translator

Elizabeth D. Crawford is the distinguished translator of the Batchelder Award–winning novels *The Robber and Me* by Josef Holub and *Crutches* by Peter Hartling. She lives in Orange, Connecticut.